"Boyd and Hollingsworth combine forces to create a heroine so vivid I swear I've met her before. Evocative, tense, H_2O will get under your skin and keep you reading 'til the last page."

— Tosca Lee, NY Times bestselling author of *Forbidden*

"H_2O opens with gripping emotion, and sustains its appeal until the breathtaking conclusion. Even if you've never read speculative fiction before, you'll love this story's otherworldly depiction of the Love that will not let go. Don't miss this!"

— Janelle Clare Schneider, author of *A Distant Love*

"Be prepared for a wild imaginative ride as you open the pages of H_2O. As the protagonist, Kate, begins to experience strange visions connected to water, the reader is immersed in an evocative and spiritually awakening experience unlike any other. Hold your breath and take the plunge!"

— C. S. Lakin, author of **The Gates of Heaven** fantasy series

"H_2O transforms a life-giving element into an intense, fascinating read!"

— R. J. Larson, author of *Prophet: Books of the Infinite*

"Gracefully capturing the human condition like the fine detail of an artisan's brush, H_2O grips your emotion and intertwines a sense of being refreshed and alive. This brilliantly told story, I truly believe, has the power to heal and make life whole again. Who would have thought water was so powerful?"

— Angus Nelson, speaker and author of *Love's Compass: When We've Lost Our Way*

"Using colorful and imaginative language, Boyd and Hollingsworth artfully weave an ancient gospel truth into a modern narrative."

— Bruce Martin, author of *Desperate for Hope*

"Take one of the most stunningly creative story concepts ever imagined, add a compelling, passionate heroine named Kate Pepper, then spin her life out of control at the mere touch of the most common substance on the planet—*water*. These are the makings of a fascinating tale and an irresistible spiritual journey. H_2O manages to be hip and contemporary while also remaining timeless. The story drew me in and pulled me along—and didn't let go until the final page. I recommend it!"

— Jim Denney, author of the **Timebenders** series and
   Answers to Satisfy the Soul

Living Ink Books
An Imprint of AMG Publishers, Inc.
Chattanooga, Tennessee

H2O

the Novel

2

THE ETERNAL ELEMENTS

AUSTIN BOYD
BRANNON HOLLINGSWORTH

H$_2$O, The Novel

Volume 1 in The Eternal Elements series

Copyright © 2011 by Austin W. Boyd and Brannon Hollingsworth

Published by Living Ink Books, an imprint of
AMG Publishers, Inc.
6815 Shallowford Rd.
Chattanooga, Tennessee 37421

This is a work of fiction. Names, characters, places, and incidents either are the product of the author's imagination or are used fictitiously. Any resemblance to actual persons, either living or dead, events, or locales, is entirely coincidental.

Print Edition	ISBN 13: 978-0-89957-806-4	ISBN 10: 0-89957-806-3
ePUB Edition	ISBN 13: 978-1-61715-246-7	ISBN 10: 1-61715-246-3
Mobi Edition	ISBN 13: 978-1-61715-247-4	ISBN 10: 1-61715-247-1
ePDF Edition	ISBN 13: 978-1-61715-248-1	ISBN 10: 1-61715-248-X

First Printing—October 2011

THE ETERNAL ELEMENTS is a trademark of AMG Publishers.

Representation by the Leslie H. Stobbe Literary Agency.

Cover designed by Daryle Beam at Bright Boy Design,
Chattanooga, TN.

Interior design and typesetting by Reider Publishing Services,
West Hollywood, California.

Edited and proofread by Susanne Lakin, Christy Graeber, and Rick Steele.

Printed in the United States of America
15 14 13 12 11 10 –V– 7 6 5 4 3 2 1

DEDICATION

To the author of life, water, and forgiveness.

CHAPTER ONE

WATER SPILLED over the blade of my knife like liquid silk. Flushed by the stream, raw fish swirled down the kitchen drain on a mysterious journey, headed back to Puget Sound and home. Fluid poetry gushed from the tap, beauty rinsing away grime. I held my hand under its caress, entranced. Water was too special, too eternal, to be so common.

"Aren't you finished yet?" Xavier asked, shaking his head as he peered into the kitchen sink of my Seattle condominium, just an arm's distance from the fish I prepared. "I can't believe people eat this stuff."

I dangled a fresh slice of buttery-rich raw tuna before him and winked. He jerked back as though contact with beady-eyed water creatures might taint him. Perhaps he feared that one brush against piscine slime would transform him into a rough guy on the wharf or a wrinkled old man sitting by a pond with a cane pole.

"Skip the drama, Xavier," I said with a laugh, biting into the sweet flesh. I brushed bangs out of my eyes with the back of my hand and waved another slice of tuna in his direction. He ignored me.

"My guests will be here in half an hour," he said, retreating toward the den. "The main dish still has scales on it."

"You can't see tuna scales, X. So, quit worrying. I'll be ready." I picked up a quarter section of tuna waiting to be skinned and drew in a long whiff, pretending to take a bite out of the whole fish. Xavier just shook his head.

"They're donating for your cause, but they're here to eat my sashimi—and they'll love it." I popped a second slice of tuna in my mouth and savored it as I went back to slicing fish. "Go pour some more wine or something." I sighed, wishing he'd go out for a walk and leave me alone.

When I looked up from the knife a few moments later, he stood halfway across the room, his eyes narrowed. I knew the look. "I'll bet that stuff is what makes you fat," he said, the last ugly word drawn out for emphasis. The thin arches of his eyebrows rose like black scalpels above eyes that probed for any hint of something soft. Sky-blue irises, devoid of love, scoured my nakedness on the hunt for the plump evidence of joy—as if eating around him could ever be called joy. In his mind, I was failing him, stuck at a hundred and two pounds in a tight size two.

I looked back down to the dead fish, my only friend, and pushed the knife hard against its firm, cool flesh. I knew my failings. But not as well as he did, apparently. I love to cook. I love to eat. And even if I am a size two, the joy of food has left its mark—however slight—on my middle.

"I lost another pound," I offered, almost under my breath. I didn't have to see him to feel those black scalpels above his eyes stripping away what little dignity I had left. The truth was easy to see. My tummy was soft. And it always would be. "I'm sure it's not water weight." My voice cracked in the midst of the lie.

"What-eeeever, Ms. Pepper." He frowned and turned away, not looking back.

"Shut up!" I slammed my left fist on the cutting board and stepped toward him, knife in hand. Xavier spun around and caught my glare. When I waved the long razor-sharp *Fujiwara* in his direction, he backed out of reach. Harping on my weight was one thing, but now he'd gone too far.

Every time I hear "whatever," I'm stuck back in Queens trying to drag a conversation out of my couch-potato father, Norman Pepper. It was the throwaway phrase for "don't bother me," uttered by an emotionally absent father, a man glued to his TV and recliner—the epitome of sloth. In my mind, *fat* is the logical root word in *father*. I hated the unforgivable softness of my midriff, but I despised his podgy addiction to laziness. That *W* word summed it all up for me, in one miserable excuse for a man I could never call "Dad."

I sliced an *X* through the air with my knife as I glared at Xavier. He turned with a shrug and walked toward the bay window. The cutlery shook in my hands, images of my father springing to mind, salt rubbed in raw mental wounds.

The shaking worsened as I watched Xavier move with a feigned slowness, spinning around to drop into a seat in the den, a glass of wine in one hand and a remote control in the other. His gaze was locked with mine. I felt my grip tighten on the knife. Surely, he wouldn't do this.

I watched him settle into the padded chair, like viewing a movie running at half speed. My lover raised the remote control like a digital rapier and pointed it toward me. He made a loud *click* with his tongue and pushed a button, presumably to command me, his human television. He drew out my father's disgusting epithet once more, for effect. "What-*ev-er*!"

"Stop it!" I screamed, pivoting to my left to impale the tuna. With a trembling arm, I rammed my knife through the fish and deep into the cutting board's hard maple. Xavier didn't blink; the hint of a smile played at the corners of his mouth. We faced off, wrapped in the temporary armor of a prickly silence.

I choked back a dozen words I'd regret, then turned away and let him win the standoff. I could hear him snicker his trademark "beat you!" when I started to retrieve the thousand-dollar slicing knife. I hesitated, hand to the hefty weapon, and glared at him. He shut up. I wiggled my precious *Fujiwara* out of the wood, and then returned to the sink, fish in hand.

I had to cut something.

❖ ❖ ❖

The artery under Xavier's left temple wriggled like a scared earthworm. Watching him pace in the den for the next half hour while I finished slicing tuna, I knew he was close to a meltdown. Almost as close as I'd come to losing it, enduring his verbal jabs about my weight while I slaved away to prepare a sushi dinner for his clients. But this dinner—and his customers—meant nothing to me.

My rude boyfriend is the unlikely hybrid of a giant redwood and Bruce Willis. He's a towering shaved-head stoic and a brilliant executive with a rock-hard body. Xavier has many faults. He's selfish, hypercritical, impatient, and punctual to a fault. His obsession with time defines him. Yet his strengths make him tolerable—he's gorgeous, well connected . . . and rich.

I despise ordinary.

❖ ❖ ❖

Never slice fish when you're angry.

That thought shot through my mind as a piercing sting mingled with the familiar dull thud of knife contacting wood. Mentally distracted, I watched an inch-long serving of the fleshy base of my palm tumble into the pile of sliced tuna.

Human sashimi, I thought. What the Japanese call "pierced body."

But it wasn't fish; it was part of me. The damage finally registered when blood started to flow.

I screamed.

Xavier reached me a couple of heartbeats later and pressed a white cotton cloth into my wound. The rice vinegar on the wet rag, used to wipe out my sushi molds, shot daggers of pain into the severed muscle. My body's red spilled across a pile of sliced yellowfin, mingling with the wet pinkness of raw tuna flesh in a Hannibal Lecter platter of seafood and human blood. Xavier took one look at the ruined morsels, his face white with a pitiful jumble of empathy and fear, then thrust his face into the sink.

He vomited. And the doorbell rang.

◆ ◆ ◆

"Kate! What happened?" Andrea asked she entered my kitchen. She never noticed Xavier's mess; he'd churned the last of it down the disposal. My blood drew her attention. I suspected that her-boss-slash-my-boyfriend welcomed the momentary distraction.

Saved him again.

"We need to get a dressing on that," my one and only girlfriend said, her hand shaking. She plucked the thin sliver of my left palm from the pile of sushi and dropped it into a glass of cold milk. "There's a doc-in-the-box on West Garfield. We'll take you there."

Her face said more, like she could read my mind. I imagined she could follow the invisible counter that clicked off the number of times Xavier had complained tonight when I ingested even a morsel, or exposed a hint of cellulite through skintight slacks. Size two slacks, no less. Maybe she understood, without saying, why I'd been distracted. My heart hurt worse than my hand.

"There's no time for doctors, Andrea. Our party starts in an hour." My words were for Xavier's benefit, in vain hope of some sympathy. I couldn't expect he'd cancel this dinner; it was too important. "I've cut my palm like this before. Really, I'm okay. It'll grow back." I forced a smile.

"You amaze me, Kate," she replied. "You carve your hand into sashimi, and all you can think about is feeding a bunch of snobby rich folks."

"They're our clients, Andrea." Xavier's color—and his voice—returned. "I'll take Kate to the doctor. You finish this up while we're gone."

"And what? Host your party, too?" she asked.

"That's what I pay you for."

Andrea shrugged, looked at me with a "you love this guy?" roll of the eyes, and grabbed a rag. "Okay, boss. Come wash her up. I'll get a dry cloth while you get some water on that." She motioned to the sink, and he complied.

Xavier hates blood. He never looked at my hand, but his warmth felt good when he took me gently by the wrist and shoulder, then started the water.

Before the liquid swept over my wound, I remembered slicing my hand in third grade while crawling over a ragged chain-link fence outside the elementary school playground. The sting of water when Mother washed me was a fresh memory. I braced for a repeat sting, but it never came. Somewhere between Xavier's warm touch and the silver stream of water before me, I lost all connection with reality.

For the briefest time—like a micro-dream when you fall asleep driving and then snap awake—a picture formed in my mind of a basin, perhaps a wooden bowl, filled with water. A cream-colored rough-woven garment, maybe a robe, lay beside it. Nothing else. I remember thinking, in that split second, that there was nothing like this in my kitchen. The mental picture flashed into view, and then it evaporated. On, then off, like a camera flash.

Was it for a heartbeat or for a minute? I had no idea. One moment I'd pulled closer to Xavier, and the next he stood there, holding me up, my knees reduced to rubber. When I regained my bearings, his hand pressed a dry cloth into my freshly washed crimson palm. My hand was wet; I could feel its dampness and see the water's sheen, but I had no memory of the washing. Seconds of my life had vanished.

"Kate? Did you hear me?"

Xavier's huge blue eyes, dotted with the tiny black spot of his pupils, shone like mirrors. My face reflected in his blue. The waxed line of scalpel eyebrows made perfect umbrellas over his eyes, deep set above high cheekbones. I let him hold me up while I tried to remember what just happened.

"Kate?" he implored. The tone of his voice was soothing, inviting. He blinked and it broke the spell. It felt good to be held.

"Yeah?" A sandpaper tongue stuck to the roof of my mouth. Wasn't it just a moment ago that he had taken me in his arms and thrust my hand under the tap? I couldn't remember the embrace of the cool wetness. Only the basin of water, and the cream-colored robe. I shook my head, desperate to reboot.

"I—I'm okay," I said. "I need to sit."

Xavier lowered me gently, and I settled on the cool tile of the kitchen floor, pressing the cotton mitt into my wound. I looked up at Andrea, her mouth agape where she stood near the sink.

My girlfriend reached toward me, her palm to my forehead. "What just happened?"

✦ ✦ ✦

A few minutes later, after a drink of water and Andrea's gentle touch with a cool wet towel, I could stand again. I glanced at the clock, time now my enemy. I took a fresh white cotton towel from Xavier and wrapped it around my palm, then motioned to my flesh in the glass of pink milk. "I need to stay, Andrea. Can you go to the doc by yourself? Ask about sewing that back on while I bandage up and get dinner ready." I secretly hoped Xavier would object. But he didn't. No surprise there.

"You fainted, Kate! Your hand's sliced up, and you just bled all over a catered meal. *You're* the one who needs to go." She stamped her foot like it made a difference. Xavier tried to butt in; I pushed him back with my good hand.

"Please, Andrea. Really. I'm better. I can finish the tuna. Hurry over there and call me if the doc says I need to come in. Otherwise, we'll let it grow back like the last time." I shoved my white cotton paw toward her. "Do this for me, okay? But hurry back. I need you here when the guests arrive."

"Go," Xavier barked. "Kate's right. Find out what the doc says while we get this dinner wrapped up."

"We?" she asked, eyebrows raised. I pinched her forearm, shaking my head.

Don't taunt this bull.

Andrea relented and headed for the door with her gory glass. "Mr. Compassion," she whispered to me, then spoke up as she headed for the door. "Be sure to get some antibiotic ointment on the wound, boss. If you don't, the flesh will knit into the gauze before she can change that bandage. And keep it dry."

"Just go, Andrea," Xavier replied, distracted by his iPhone and the *ding* of another e-mail. He left me standing at the sink.

Dry. Yes.

My good hand touched the faucet handle, recalling the first drip before I'd blanked out. I traced the chrome lines of the spigot, the curved silver of a gooseneck spout reflecting a distorted view of the room around me. Distorted like the strange moments when Xavier had held me at the sink.

Missing moments. Seconds of my life that had mysteriously vanished.

✦ ✦ ✦

Five days later

Xavier is tight. Tight with his money, and tight-lipped. I hate empty talk, so we fit well together. But it's special when he splurges on me, because I know he's really trying to make a point. He made that point on Thursday night.

The restaurant? Exquisite. When he told me a special dinner awaited, I knew something was up. No one goes to a restaurant like Canlis on a whim. It takes reservations far in advance and a wad of cash. But it's worth every penny. The private table for two near tall windows had a stunning view of Lake Union and the Cascades.

"Did you see this?" I asked. Napkins folded like swans craned their pale-blue necks over brilliant silver cutlery that adorned starched white tablecloths. A handwritten card atop the menu spoke to my heart. " 'Cooking is like love, Kate,' " I read from the dainty card. " 'It should be entered into with abandon, or not at all.' That's me!" I turned and took Xavier's hand. "Thank you. For this."

Xavier nodded and took a seat next to me. He shrugged. "You deserve it. You serve the finest sashimi in Seattle."

I massaged my left hand, remembering the sting of the slicing blade.

"You really put yourself into that dinner," he said with a grin. "Very fresh. And they loved it. Corporate got a very nice thank you from my guests, by the way. You outdid yourself." He reached out and laid a gentle hand on my bandaged paw.

"The things I do for you . . ." I said with a wink. "But this is a huge gift. Thank you."

"Has Andrea forgiven me?" he asked. "She's been a cold shoulder at the office."

"She'll come around. She's a little upset I didn't take her up on the palm transplant and the milk preservative." I smiled. Dear Andrea was crushed that she'd gone all the way to the medical clinic to learn that you're never supposed to put severed flesh in milk, and that the sliver was too small to sew back on. But at least she'd tried.

"Keeping it dry?" Xavier asked. He fidgeted with the obscene watch on his wrist, his monster timepiece worth more than months of my salary. His eyes darted around like they had on our first date, desperate to connect—yet failing. I caught his gaze at last and forced my best smile.

"This place is posh, X."

"Wait till you try the wine," he replied. His eyes went to the wine list. "Their collection won the Grand Award."

I reached out and tried to dislodge the list, to pull it down and get him to look at me. He lowered it and kept chatting, his eyes diverted to the fancy menu.

"You've got to try their special salad—romaine, bacon, Romano cheese, mint, and oregano. With a lemon, oil, and coddled-egg dressing."

"You sound like a cook," I said, leaning toward him, then scooting partway around the table to get closer. "I thought you hated the kitchen."

He smiled, looking up past me, his eyes still focused beyond the windows. "Maybe so, but I love to eat." He opened the menu for me and looked my way. At last. I didn't move, marveling at the depths of his blue eyes. He took my good hand, holding it for a long embrace, and I squeezed his fingers.

The warmth of Xavier's hands tingled my spine, a magic electric connection I'd felt the first time his skin met mine. He still had the touch, the gentleman who'd swept me off my feet when I moved from Silicon Valley to Seattle. That man appeared less often as we became more comfortable—and more familiar—with each other. I missed those early days, the marketing manager in hot pursuit of his company's newest employee. It was exciting to be noticed again, to be desired.

Mother used to comment about men all the time that "familiarity breeds contempt." Familiar as a worn slipper in our relationship, I craved the passion and spontaneity of our early days. Lately it seemed I competed with work for his time. I'd birthed his mistress; the promotion I'd helped him to win had spirited him away. A nagging voice reminded me that our relationship would never be the same—thanks to me.

An hour later I leaned back, comfortably full after we'd sampled soups, split a Canlis salad, then ordered a lamb shank for him. I grazed on occasional morsels of his main course. "Delicious dinner, X. But please, no dessert." I waved my hand over a tummy pressed too tightly into my dress. "No room."

Xavier's eyes narrowed to slits as they followed my movement. His gaze never wavered, his visual scalpel maintaining a steady focus.

Not tonight. Please!

A waiter approached to refresh my glass of water, a blessed distraction from the frigid stare that disrobed me. The evening—particularly Xavier's long gaze into my eyes, not my dress, and his unabashed holding of my good hand in public—had been perfect. Until now. I longed for the feel of his long fingers drawing mine into his warm palm.

"Thank you," I said, extending my glass to the young waiter, who tilted a crystal pitcher of ice water. When he poured, a few cold drops spilled on the back of my hand, rolling slowly down to my wrist.

I nearly dropped the goblet.

A wave of dizziness swept over me, disorientation like I'd not felt since I was seventeen—a desperate dizziness I'd worked hard to forget. I re-gripped the glass, but my leaden arm fell, upsetting more water and spilling icy wetness on my fingers. Another bout of confusion engulfed me. I fell forward.

For the briefest of moments, all I saw was gray. Clouds. Leaden gray storms swollen to the breaking point. Ready to rain crocodile tears. I reached out, stabbing for a handhold in the midst of a fog where there was no up, no down. I bumped hard into the table and the gray evaporated. I could hear the crash of glass and silver as my conscious sight returned, my eyes locked with Xavier's, his filled with surprise. Or fear.

Upended by the table, Xavier's fresh glass of Shiraz teetered and spilled onto his chest, inky red trashing a starched white shirt and expensive dinner jacket. At first, the poor waiter dove for a towel to wipe me dry and steady my arm. He spun about, all elbows and thumbs in a failed attempt to control the damage, thrusting a wet towel at my cursing boyfriend. The young man gushed apologies, convinced the spilled wine and water had been his fault.

But was it?

I let go of the glass and grabbed my own napkin, then put a hand to my forehead. I steadied myself against the table with the bandaged mitt, determined to focus on Xavier. Head cocked to one side, dabbing at a twenty-dollar glass of wine he wore from chest to waist, he snarled something vulgar under his breath and waved the waiter on.

Moments later he grabbed the arm of the approaching maitre d' and spoke sharply to her in a hushed voice. At the limit of his patience, he nearly made a scene. He released the head waitress, pushing her away, and then turned on me, eyes boring into my middle.

"Kate. What's wrong with you anyway? You keep flaking out." He reached for a fresh napkin while his scalpels sliced through my dress in the tense silence, then he blurted out, "Are you pregnant?"

He watched me for a moment, and then resumed furious wiping on his blood-red shirt. "God, I hope not. There's too much at stake." He looked up again, shaking his head. "Not pregnant. Not now."

A thousand choked-back words caught in my throat. I turned and reached for my sweater on the back of the chair. "We need to go," I hissed.

"Sure," he mumbled, throwing down the trashed napkin. He stood and moved to my side. The waiter babbled apologies, drawing the attention of other patrons. A woman to my right, with ears too keen for my liking, crooned, "She's expecting! Help her up!"

Xavier seemed to remember his manners again and offered me a hand with my chair. I pushed him away and stood, unsteady.

"I want to go home, X."

"No. My place. It's closer."

I shook my head—his apartment was the last place I wanted to be right now. I narrowed my eyes. "Take me home. Now."

After that last gaffe, the thought of his bachelor pad disgusted me—a hideous white-walled prison three blocks from the office. A place he called "modern," blanketed with the overbearing smell of gaudy leather. It suffocated me, and for some reason the starkness of his place always led to sex.

Pregnant? I wondered. *Surely not. Not again.*

"I can take better care of you downtown," he insisted.

I ignored him and headed for the door, carefully placing one foot in front of the other. I felt groggy, as if waking from an operation or a deep dream. Not all my synapses were firing, and it took some work to walk to the exit. I needed to be alone, to get outside in the fresh air. He could deal with the bill.

When I passed through the doors into the chill night, the young waiter who'd poured the water caught up with me, a sequined purse in hand. "You left this, ma'am. I'm sorry—" He steadied me while I walked down the steps to the car, then handed me off to a valet, another of Canlis's well-coordinated restaurant team.

The valet held my arm, and I slipped into the front seat of Xavier's Mercedes Roadster.

"Thank you for joining us. Come back again," he said before he closed the door.

By myself? Certainly.

With Xavier? It would be a long time . . . if ever.

◆ ◆ ◆

"Want a bath, Shogun?" I tapped at the glass of his aquarium, and my little Japanese fighting fish darted at a finger, ever on the attack.

As the tiny carnivore circled about, seeking a path through the glass to my flesh, I watched the lights of Xavier's sleek black Roadster fade away when he left my condo. He didn't hover, but he'd been known to stalk when spurned. It was a relief to see him drive off, wine stain and all. I could deal with this dizziness—if left alone.

"I'll start the shower, Shogun. Just shout if you want to join me," I joked, tapping the glass once more. My fish darted for the fingernail, ready to feast.

Pregnant?

Xavier's question haunted me. Unexplainably dizzy, then blanking out at the sink last Saturday. Disoriented and falling apart tonight at dinner. The same not-quite-nauseous, I-want-my-balance-back disorientation that plagued me for weeks a distant twelve years ago. Dizziness that started weeks after a romantic Valentine's date during my freshman year of college—the night of my first moment of weakness. Xavier's question brought it all back. History has a habit of repeating itself, and I'd taken precautions to make sure there were no more dangerous moments of weakness—and no pregnancy.

Or at least I thought I had. Stripping down in the bathroom, I pressed my right palm against the curse of my soft belly, a chill sweat forming on the back of my neck.

I commanded the voice-activated shower to turn on and protected the bandaged hand with a sheet of Saran Wrap. Tonight I'd let the stall fill with steam. I'd soak in the elegance of hot velvet spewing from multiple showerheads, forgetting the night's pain under the caress of a delicate water massage. My liquid silk.

Xavier had once returned to my condo when snubbed, and tonight could be a repeat. I locked the door to the bathroom, just in case; he had a key to my place. The bathroom remained my one retreat and the shower my ultimate indulgence, a place to luxuriate under the caress of streams of hot water. Steam engulfed me when

H₂O

I stepped into the refuge of the large tiled stall. I savored the vapor's hot embrace as it billowed, then plunged my hair under the shower.

The first skewers of spray stabbed me like a dozen knives.

Vertigo overwhelmed me in an instant, and my feet slipped, no longer under my control. Reeling, I fell forward to the floor under a stream of near-scalding water. Instinctively, I reached with my right hand in a futile grab for the shower door's handle. My left arm jutted out and took the brunt of the fall. A hot searing pain radiated up from the raw slice on my palm, and nausea tore through me. I shivered under a torrent of liquid heat.

My head swam with strange wet images in the tortuous moments of a pre-vomit nightmare. Mental pictures of water swirled in my head. Lakes, rivers, springs, and water jugs. Cool cups of water, and boiling pots. Through it all, I *saw* the word—I *heard* the word—"pregnant!" Fear gripped me with a nauseating paralysis.

Then I saw nothing.

Only blackness.

CHAPTER TWO

"NINETY-NINE percent effective when used properly. Detects pregnancy as early as one day after a missed period." I read the instructions a dozen times the next morning, desperate to learn the result, yet scared to peel open the package. I'd walked this path twelve years ago. I had no desire to walk it again.

I paged through my iPhone, opening calendar appointments from my seat on the toilet, mentally reliving each day for the past month as I sought some clue as to when I started my last cycle. Searching for some event that would trigger the memory, prove to me I hadn't missed something. But it was pointless. The calendar didn't lie. Tomorrow was "patch change day." I never missed that event, listed in bold red on my digital calendar. If the patch worked—as it had for years—I had another week to go until cramps.

I tore into the package, ripping through the blue wrapper, desperate to get this over with. Wet it, wait, read it. Three minutes crawled by as my eyes burned text into the damp strip. Letters began to emerge slowly from the background of the saturated material, and I could feel that telltale nausea grip me like it had when I'd been a scared teenager. I closed my eyes, wishing the magic color onto the stick.

I held my breath and opened my eyes, then looked up at the ceiling and walked my gaze down the wall to the floor, across tiles to the base of the toilet and up my calves to the test strip in my hand. My fingers ached from their tight grip on the tiny device.

"No change," I sighed aloud. "Not pregnant."

✦ ✦ ✦

An hour after the home test, I was on the road. I celebrated freedom, racing along dark predawn highways while I hugged the backbone of my second obsession—a Suzuki Hayabusa—the world's fastest motorcycle. I loathe mediocrity.

My father grounded me once for riding around Manhattan on the back of Spike LoFaso's chopper. I recalled those two months of lockdown misery with a perverse sense of justice every morning when my chrome-and-blue beauty growled to life. Xavier calls riding the Hayabusa my "guilty pleasure" aboard "a two-wheeled mortgage." Mother says that riding the bike is "improper, something a true lady would never do." I think it's quite proper. I'm the only woman in Seattle who can go from zero to sixty in only three seconds. I proved it again this morning.

Ironically, I can thank my slug of a father for this obsession with speed. He never got his internal speedometer off zero the whole time I lived at home; he stayed stuck to his easy chair like a human slipcover. He never budged, yet I intended to move very fast. The faster you move, approaching the speed of light, the slower you age. Beat that, Oil of Olay.

Five minutes after I gave the "Ice Rocket" its ritual morning highway workout, I pulled off my helmet in the special parking "jail" stall assigned at our corporate garage in downtown Seattle. That's what Andrea calls it—the jail. A special steel cage in the parking basement of our office building where no one could ever heist my ride. You never park a collector's bike like mine in an open lot.

"Kate!" a man yelled from far behind me. "How fast today?" Justus, Andrea's boyfriend of two years, waved and ran in my direction.

"A hundred and five on I-5," I yelled back. I shook my hair free. Shoulder-length cuts were great with bike helmets, and shorter was better. The salon princesses upstairs who trotted around with long tresses could keep them. I preferred short and sassy over hair-clogged drains and hours at the mirror with a hot straightener.

He came closer but his eyes never left my bike. "You're crazy, you know. The cops are gonna nail you one day."

"Maybe. Life's full of surprises." I smiled. Justus was perfect for Andrea. Wholesome goodness, a straight arrow. Probably never broke the speed limit or looked twice at another woman. There weren't many like him. "Why so early today, Mr. Fowler?" I asked, watching his lanky form amble into my space.

"I came for you. I mean, the Riddle briefing's at nine thirty, right? You asked tech support to arrive early. So here I am."

"Oh yeah. Thanks. Sorry to drag you in at this time of day."

"No prob. Gave me a chance to check out your mean machine. D'you ever take it to the desert when you lived down south?" he asked, buffing a fingerprint off the gas tank's deep-blue flake finish. That color, like the sky after a bitter northerly, was my special touch.

"Every couple of months. Went to Bonneville once, too," I said, motioning toward the gate. Time to lock up the Ice Rocket and get to work.

"And?" he asked, his jaw dragging behind him. I pushed him out of the jail, pulling the gate closed behind us. I had places to go, but to be honest, I enjoyed his attention.

"Lost my nerve at a hundred and fifty," I said. "A stunt man from Los Angeles took her up to a hundred eighty once. Beyond that—" I winked. "Suicide."

Justus stood speechless, not a common sight. "You gotta go?" he asked as I picked up my bag and helmet.

"No. No rush," I lied, mindful of the ticking clock but desperate to have someone to talk to. After last night, it felt good to be noticed.

Justus helped me with my helmet and messenger bag as we walked. While we waited for the elevator, he pointed at my left riding glove. "Andrea said you sliced your hand up pretty bad." His voice sounded somber. "You gonna be okay?"

The hand throbbed inside the tight leather confines, particularly after last night's fall in the shower and this morning's ride. "Oh, it's fine. Thanks." I unbuttoned my jacket while we waited, pulling the sleeve off gingerly.

"Let me help," he offered, extending a hand to assist me with a taut jacket. When the elevator opened he had his arm behind me, jacket in hand. His strong biceps radiated warmth where they touched bare shoulders. That contact sent shivers through me. I snatched the leather jacket from him, and then moved to the far side of the car. We rode nine floors in silence.

"I . . . I could use some help, Kate," he said at last when we neared my floor.

"Yeah?" My heart thumped, the thought of Andrea—my only girlfriend—meeting us as we stepped out. This was too intimate. The door opened to dark halls, the automatic lights still dimmed. We were alone, and my heart skipped again.

"It's Andrea," he said from behind me. I froze.

I turned, and he handed me my bag and helmet; I'd almost dashed away without them. "I really care about her, Kate. That's no surprise; you know that. But she's got me frazzled. I thought . . . well, hoped you could help."

"How?" My voice echoed in an empty hall. There were always ears lurking in this company, siphoning up juicy tidbits. I wished he'd asked me this in the basement. Justus looked down at his feet for a long time, then back up, and blurted it out.

"What do women want?"

That one caught me by surprise. I knew the answer, my version of it at least. I'd never expected someone would force me to verbalize that truth. Before I could grab the words, they dashed out of my mouth.

"Women want to be noticed."

A dozen thoughts ran into each other, memories of last night's dinner and Xavier's insult. My presentation today. Worries that Andrea would walk up. Or worse, that X lurked around the corner. Dreams of a bouquet of flowers waiting on my desk.

"Noticed? How?" he asked, head cocked to one side. The poor boy was clueless.

I flashed a quick smile, no desire to be Ann Landers for my girlfriend's hunk, and turned toward the ladies' room—my safe haven. This connection had to end. "Think on it, Justus. I've got to go, okay?" I saw his face fall before I spun around. He wanted more.

At the door to the restroom, I paused and looked back. Justus's eyes had a faraway look. "Tell Andrea I'll see her after the staff meeting," I said. "She wanted to know how dinner went last night."

"And?" He reminded me of a dry sponge, ready to absorb whatever I gave him.

"It was dinner, Justus. That's all. Bye."

✦ ✦ ✦

What am I running from?

I stood in front of my office locker, safe inside the executive washroom, and put a finger to my throat. My heart raced. I hated that.

I stared for a long moment at the washroom mirror, wishing my heart to slow, breathing deeply. A bruise on my cheek stared back at me from below a careful application of makeup. The throbbing hand screamed through tight leather. Another bruise on my bare shoulder showed above a black camisole. I hoped Justus hadn't noticed the damage; I looked like I'd weathered a minor fight last night. The shower had won the first round.

Something tempting, something dark and sensuous, tugged at me from deep inside. It made my heart quicken again, made me shiver. The truth? When I'd shed the jacket, and felt his bare arms against my skin, I'd wanted Justus to notice *me*. That thought made me feel dirty, yet quickened my pulse all the more.

Why did it have to be Justus?

I despised myself; my mind played the elevator scene over and over, fantasizing about what might have been. A fantasy I would never want, yet something that a part of me—the hidden part of me—wanted very badly.

◆　◆　◆

Focus, Kate. It's time for work.

Some bikers wear boots and never shed them. I'm probably one of the few that don stilettos once they leave the road. The leathers come off, top and bottom, and skirt and blouse are waiting in my special locker. That's another valued perk at Consolidated Aerodyne. I stock my wardrobe with two weeks of outfits, and some poor girl makes sure they're fresh and pressed every day. The mystery woman also keeps my shoes ready. This month it's a long rack of Italian Fendi stilettos.

Today, I would be in a black Cinderella moire stiletto sandal with a top strap. I'm tall enough, yet these shoes give me four more inches. Enough to go eye to eye with the men in this office. As I fastened the last strap, my mind wandered back to Justus again. His question made me uncomfortable, mostly because it made me confront myself.

"*What do women want?*" For any other man, that would have been a leading question. Knowing Justus, he simply wanted to understand Andrea. I'd brushed him off with a hasty escape into the restroom, and then let fantasies about his intentions play games with my head. But I knew the answer when he asked. I knew exactly what I wanted. What we all want, if we're honest. I ran my hand down the length of my skirt, gathering the silky material between my fingers.

Women dress to be noticed.

I want to be noticed by a man.

There's a part of me no one ever sees, the part I've shoved down deep until wounds expose the inner me. Wounds like last night's verbal gash. Mother used to say that I built a shell around myself to protect the vulnerable inside. Justus cracked my shell this morning, or at least made me confront it.

I don't simply want be noticed by a man.

I want to be cared for.

A tear formed at the corner of my eye and I touched it. Something I'd not felt in years. I rubbed the salty drop between my fingers as a dozen poems ran through my head all at once, sweet verses like Elizabeth Barrett Browning's love poems from my childhood, poetry about being held and comforted.

To lose the sense of losing. As a child,
Whose songbird seeks the wood for evermore
Is sung to in its stead by mother's mouth
'til, sinking on her breast, love-reconciled,
He sleeps the faster that he wept before.

That's what I wanted. *Nurture. Comfort. Security.* Those were the words I should have shared with Justus—the truth about women that he craved to hear.

The meek part of me screamed to be heard, to slow down and get off the treadmill, to find someone to clothe me and protect me. Someone to caress my forehead and bandage my cuts. I was bruised from unexplained falls, hand sliced, and spirits damaged from clumsy dinners, but had no one to patch me up. I sank onto the bench in the washroom and closed wet eyes, trying for the first time in years to listen for that gentle voice I'd buried for so long.

I hurt. Deep aches in my shoulder reminded me of last night's fall. My bandaged hand, free of the glove, burned under its dressing. And the wounded part of me, scabs ripped off by Xavier's self-centered comments, bled freely inside. For a moment, I wished I'd been pregnant. At least I'd have something on which to blame my string of misfortune. I craved someone to share it with. A partner. A loving mate.

Then I smelled leather. The scent of my motorcycle gear jolted me back to the present.

I reached up and fingered the smooth black of the riding jacket. For a long moment, I stood at the locker door, squeezing my eyes shut, focused on the narcotic allure of speed and work while I struggled to shut out vacuous desires for simplicity. And my desires for men.

It worked. The hurt part of me that had surfaced for just a moment—the part of me that loved poetry and barefoot walks in grass—escaped to the dark recesses of my shell. I compartmentalized my other half inside an emotional cave, buried away where it wouldn't be found.

I grabbed a tiny handbag and slammed the locker shut. Time to wrestle another corporate alligator for Xavier and make him look good. A new day lay ahead, and in it, a special opportunity to excel. There were big deals to be won today.

From hot wheels to a skirt and high heels, in five minutes flat.

I was ready.

◆ ◆ ◆

"Was that one of your famous 'Ice Slice' looks? The scowl you threw in the boss's direction just then?" Andrea asked a couple of hours later. We turned a corner in the hallway, headed toward my office. Xavier stood somewhere behind us and out of earshot.

"Is that what they call it?" I asked her, stopping outside the copy room. "An Ice Slice?"

"Yeah. Which makes you—"

"The Ice Queen. I could have gone all day without hearing that nickname. Again." I looked down at the floor. I hated office gossip, and this place had turned into another *Peyton Place*. Or *Sex and the City*. Funny how nicknames stuck. At least here I'd be a queen. The "Ice Princess" moniker had never faded in my last job.

"He deserved it, Andrea. After the way he treated me last night, what would *you* do?"

"Doesn't matter. He's an Executive VP now, Kate. That was *his* staff meeting, and he's not your peer anymore. He simply asked if you were ready for the Riddle presentation. That's all."

"I'm sure I told him this weekend."

"Don't read too much into that." Andrea pulled me close to the wall, out of the way of someone dropping off recycled paper. She waited until the intruder had passed. "You have to separate this thing with Xavier into personal life and office life, or you're gonna get burned. Don't assume that when you tell him something at your place that he'll remember it when he's here. He compartmentalizes. At your condo, he's in another world."

Compartmentalize. Like me.

Andrea had it nailed. I thought that Xavier would trust me more since we were close. But I'd come to realize our intimacy could work against us.

"Justus said you two had a long talk in the garage this morning." She looked up, straight at me. Her face was a mixture of pain and question.

"He really cares about you," I blurted out, pushing back memories of his skin against mine. "He asked my advice about some stuff. And I told him I'd fill you in about dinner."

"That's it?"

"That's it. I ran off to get changed."

Andrea raised an eyebrow, and then looked down at my dress. Her eyes stopped at my middle, then tracked back up.

"What?" I asked, looking down. *What's on my skirt?*

"Are you?" She nodded in the direction of Xavier's office. "You know. 'Preggo'?"

"Pregnant?" I gasped. "No!"

"You're sure?" she asked, pressing too hard. "You fainting anymore?" Her eyes bored into me.

"No. Not pregnant. And not dizzy. Just fine, thanks." My pulse rose with the temperature of my face. I suspected I'd turned beet red. "I peed on a stick this morning, Andrea. To make sure."

"Rumor mill's going full tilt, Kate. Someone overheard Xavier at Canlis last night. And—well—you know this place. Word travels fast."

His three words: "Are you pregnant?" The damage was done. Here I stood: Kate Pepper, the office mistress. Human Resources would stalk me for sure. I drew a deep breath, thankful that Andrea had been so blunt about what she'd heard, but unsure what to do next.

"You had to know this would happen. Eventually," Andrea said with a schoolmarm's tone. "Now what?"

She wanted to help, but I didn't deserve it. I felt dirty in Andrea's presence, afraid she could read my thoughts about her boyfriend. I forced myself to concentrate. To focus on work.

"What's next? Do my job. The Riddle briefing's in an hour."

"Is he ready?"

"He who?"

"Bill Naudain. Have you talked with him?" she asked. "You told him to build the Riddle presentation. Have you seen it?"

"No. I tasked him last Friday. We were busy, remember?"

"Yeah. Busy getting ready for the boss's charity dinner. But did you pull the files off the server last night and check them out?" She touched my bandage, holding my wrist for a moment. "That's all Xavier wants to know. He's not busting you. Just checking." She tried to smile, something to lift me up, then added, "'Trust but verify.' Xavier says it all the time."

Trust. I failed on that count.

I shook my head. "I meant to. But last night . . ." I snapped my mouth shut; I wasn't about to fuel her concerns about my problem. Whatever it was.

She pushed away. "Gotta run, Kate." She motioned her head in the direction we'd just come from. "Go find Bill. Close the loop with Mr. X. And ignore the looks. The rumors will pass. They always do." She turned and smiled, then started to walk away. "This time next week there'll be someone else they're talking about."

Headed down the hall, she waved over her shoulder. "Smile. You'll get through it."

I nodded, unable to speak. Kate Pepper. A traitor and a tramp.

✦ ✦ ✦

My stilettos made a *clack-clack* on the cherry wood floors of Consolidated Aerodyne as I headed to the main conference room. I loved that about this shoe. The staccato snap of a heel was a woman's gunshot. Less bloody but no less deadly. Someone once suggested that stilettos are a metaphor for sex. I prefer to say they're about power. Perhaps there's no difference.

This much is true: Power matters. Women who act like men get ahead. Women who act like women get trampled. Stilettos send my message loud and clear: Don't tread on me.

Riddle Incorporated came to us as the world's leading manufacturer of miniature plasma computer screens. In an era when flat screen meant big, they'd found a way to make huge profits by putting high resolution in a tiny package. In our hands at Consolidated Aerodyne, combined with my new concept for virtual e-mail—what I called 'v-mail'—their screens in our airline seat backs would make every plane a wireless, video-based, keypad-free remote office, for a third the cost of the competition. As the technology commercialization executive for Seattle's fastest growing aerospace firm, this account—and this technology—was in my sweet spot. But I'd taken a big chance, delegating the success of this big presentation to one of my staff. I snapped the power heels louder and picked up the pace. We'd win this one on substance, not glitz—if Bill had prepared the way I hoped he would. And if he wasn't ready, I always had a backup plan.

Xavier met me three doors from the appointment, matching my stride. It wasn't hard to find me. *Just use your ears.* His Italian loafers clacked alongside my power points.

"Ready?"

I didn't look at him, but kept my gaze set straight ahead, increasing my pace. "Double ready."

"Sure? Maybe I can help."

I wouldn't look at him, even if he begged. "I tasked Bill. If he blows it, I have a backup."

"You'd better. Management will crucify you if you lose this deal."
We walked in silence the rest of the way to the room. A part of me yearned for him to say something—anything—about last night. I wanted him to at least acknowledge me, not just match strides with my staccato shoes. Expecting an apology from Xavier was fantasy, but surely, he could try.

I forced myself to snap out of it; I had to rattle my own cage and get back in the game. Riddle's people would arrive in half an hour. Andrea knew our boss well; "Trust, but verify" was written all over Xavier's face, draped in a stony silence. He would let me fail on my own, or help me win if I asked for it. But for assistance, there would be a price. His offers always meant some form of control.

I blocked the entrance when I stopped outside the conference room. Xavier waited behind me as I'd hoped. My eyes met Bill's— a middle-aged man seated on the far end of a blond oak table. No fancy conference rooms for me.

"Are we ready?" I asked.

Three sets of eyes darted about the room with a guilty avoidance, finally settling on Bill, a key business developer on my staff. His gaze shifted from me to the projector, and then to the floor. Andrea had been right; he wasn't prepared. Andrea was *always* right.

"I'm sorry. I . . . I sent you a text . . ." he began, fumbling for his Smartphone.

Ready to scream but determined to win, I bit my lip and flipped a finger-sized data drive across the room toward no one in particular. Eight gigabytes of material, including a month-old draft briefing I'd prepared for today. I'd have to win this one on guts.

Let's see who grabs it.

Bill stuck his hand out like a professional goalie snagging a hundred-mile-an-hour puck and stopped the data stick in midflight. His nose twitched, and then a smile broke on his face.

"Just kidding," he chuckled, and looked around the room. The rest of my business team busted out laughing, most of them pointing at me.

"You were worried," he said, clutching the data drive between his thumb and forefinger. "Weren't you?" He tilted his head a little and frowned. "You know me better than that, Kate."

The flush I knew had to be crimson warmed my face. I nodded. All the power, speed, leather, and stilettos were useless if I didn't do my job. Bill had saved me. With a business deal on the line, and me distracted, he'd come through.

"I've got your back, Boss," Bill said, extending a palm with the thumb drive, then waving me to my seat. "Let's run through this once before the Riddle guys arrive. You'll love it."

✦ ✦ ✦

Two hours later, we'd landed a big one, a thirty-million-dollar seat-back display deal for four major air carriers. And it felt great. We'd won their business, but not the usual way. I always close the deals . . . on any day but this. Today it was all Bill. Nevertheless, a win was a win.

Xavier acknowledged me at last; the nod and thin smile from my chrome-headed boss almost made up for his gaffe last night. His *faux pas* faded to a distant memory as he escorted me from the conference room. Perhaps he'd say something, apologize, or just hold my hand.

"Good job," he said in a low voice, his eyes diverted down the hall by the passage of one of the short-skirted girls from Graphics. Then he was gone. Behind me, the noise level rose with the celebration of our win. But Xavier's two scant words and his wandering eyes set the tone for the rest of my day. My party balloon popped.

"Kate?" A voice called out from my right. I spun about on the heels to face Carla, our Human Resources manager. All three hundred pounds of her, arms crossed.

"Do you have a minute?" she asked in her signature throaty gravel voice born of too many cigarettes. It was the classic opening line of an HR inquisition. No doubt she knew about last night. She liked to bat the mouse around before she bit its head off.

"Actually, no. This is a bad time, Carla," I said, fidgeting. I pointed to the revelry in the conference room, a festive mood I far preferred to being moored in the corridor with Battle Axe.

She glanced at the jubilation, led by Bill, as they hoisted coffee cups to each other in mock toasts. One of them motioned for me to join them. Carla shook her head. "That can wait. But this can't." She pointed down the hall in the direction of her torture suite. A few doors down from Xavier's.

"What's this about?" I asked, my pulse quickening. This woman was easy to run around, but you couldn't run through her. She'd been gunning for me for months.

Carla shook her head with that wicked "got you" smile I'd seen before. She rubbed the front of her ample belly in a slow circular motion, then pointed at me.

"The word's out on you, Momma. We need to talk."

CHAPTER THREE

MY THIRD obsession is coffee. Excellent, top-flight, expensive imported coffee. Nothing by Juan Valdez and his scabby donkey. I go for the award winners like Kenya "AA" *Gachatha* and the famous Kenyan "black currant." Panama *Elida* or Sumatra *Lintong*. Starbucks might satisfy the "unwashed masses," but for me, it just won't do. I seek out real baristas and strong drink. Some people indulge in caviar, others in diamonds. I prefer black gold laced with caffeine.

Right up there with coffee is something to do while I'm drinking it. My e-mail is inextricably linked to a cup of the finest java that money can buy. I've conditioned myself to read messages only if I have a hot cup of joe in my hand, and lately I find that e-mail and the office just don't mix. The coffee reeks at work, disgusting brown tripe that my office mates load up with artificial creamer in carcinogenic Styrofoam cups.

E-mail consumes your life, so you may as well enjoy yourself while dealing with the drudgery of electronic messages. I do both at ISIP, where they serve up the best coffee in the world, and the fastest Wi-Fi in Seattle. It's the perfect business combination—Kenyan java and ripping-fast Internet. Hiram Berry started this place for coffee snobs like me who can afford a five-dollar cup and come back often for half-price refills. But at that price, his place didn't really catch on until he went wireless. Now Starbucks is racing to catch up with the digital end of his business. The coffee competition may have gotten their start in Seattle, but compared to Hiram's magic, Starbucks and Seattle's Best will never quite measure up.

ISIP sits in a confusing little building in an equally confusing triangular block at the intersections of Taylor, Fifth Avenue, and Vine. With all the one-way streets and crazy traffic flow, you'd miss this place if your nose clogged up and you didn't smell the roast. I caught a whiff one pre-dawn morning months ago while tooling through Seattle on my Ice Rocket. I can smell a quality Kenyan roast a block away, and I followed my nose all the way from downtown to that little shop, traveling on foot after I'd secured my bike at the garage.

ISIP is an odd acronym for a coffee shop, but I like it. Someone told me that "the brew there is so hot that *I sip* it." Thus, "ISIP." But I suspected there was more to the story. I dropped off a case of ice-cold Rising Moon Spring Ale at Hiram's place one day, determined to figure out why he'd named my favorite coffee shop something so nebulous. He craves beer like I crave espresso, and curiosity was about to kill my cat.

Hiram blushed after he'd polished off two Rising Moons in less than five minutes, burped something deep and stinky, then wiped his face with his shirtsleeve and confessed. "I had a computer technician job at Boeing and I hated it," he said, popping the cap on a third bottle. "I figured I'd open a shop that catered to my two passions—computers and coffee. After a six-pack of this stuff," he said, hoisting the colorful bottle of wheat beer, "I'd found just the name."

"At the bottom of a bottle?" Surely, the alcohol was talking.

"Maybe," he said with a laugh.

"So? What did the magic bottle suggest you name this place?"

"I Speak Internet Protocol—I Speak IP. ISIP" He laughed again and swigged half a bottle in a single gulp. "You know, it's kind of funny what people think the name means. Something about sipping coffee. That crazy rumor started after a woman sued a fast-food restaurant because she spilled hot stuff in her lap. I took advantage of the newspaper buzz and turned up the temperature on my brew. Been glad I did, too. Coffee's like steak, Kate. The longer it stays hot, the better folks like it."

He tipped a bottle in salute to me that day, and then swigged another six ounces. "No pastries here, Miss. No sodas, no energy drinks, organic juices, or hand-shaken iced tea. No frou-frou vanilla bean frappuccinos with double shots of mocha and whipped cream. We only serve the world's finest coffee. Very hot coffee. And very strong." He tilted the bottle to its limit, draining the last drop, then lifted it toward the ceiling, inverted in triumph. "To ISIP! To computers and the magic coffee bean!"

So here I was, in ISIP on a Friday night after work. Somewhere across town, Xavier was celebrating with the Riddle corporate reps, polishing off heavy drinks and finger food at a party in the Warwick hotel. He had invited me to come along, but after the HR manager's obligatory tongue lashing about office romances and personnel actions, I preferred to be alone. Alone, with a cup of something warm and the company of my lovely laptop.

I didn't think Xavier wanted me with him anyway. Celebratory events were his idea of a boys' night out, and knowing how X behaved when he got some liquor in him, I'd be the butt of some sexual joke or a grab bag for some drunken client. The silent fellowship of my laptop—obsession number four—and a cup of hot java were preferable to any event that featured Xavier and a mixed drink.

Hiram opens the shop early in the morning for people like me, but he also closes early, around ten p.m. on weekdays. The Berry family lives on the second floor of the little pie slice of a building, smothered all day long in the rising aroma of roasting coffee beans. His kids were probably addicted to caffeine in the womb.

Hiram's odd in lots of ways, but he has a wicked sense of humor. He's always smiling, brown eyes peering through retro glasses framed by brown matted shoulder-length hair. Tie-died shirts, faded jeans with holes, and Birkenstock sandals round out the hippie look. A true information technology weenie.

Hiram has lots of quirks, but the one I've never quite figured out is his soft heart. He hires the most unlikely people. It's his foible, but his customers tolerate it. "Mentally challenged employees," some people call them. You certainly don't need to be a rocket scientist to work in a coffee shop.

Candice is one of those idiosyncrasies he's hired, maybe a relative, or a friend. She doesn't know the difference between a computer and a television. She smiles a lot. She owns one shirt, a light-blue polo that she wears every day, winter or summer, with dark-blue cotton Dockers. I'm sure she weighs more than I do, but she's shorter by a head. To Hiram's credit and hers, every table she busses is spotless, every mug and piece of silverware shines, and Candice greets me with a huge smile every day. I confess that Hiram's quirks have been growing on me, Candice included.

Mother would be so proud that I've opened my eyes to people who aren't like me.

That thought made me squirm. I wanted, least of all, to be my mother. Even to be *like* her. But she would, in fact, be proud that I occasionally talked with Candice. Mother loved these kinds of people. Candice was pure. Nothing but good thoughts and nice words for everyone. Simple as white bread. An adult toddler. What Mother called "people with special needs."

Come to think of it, Mother had never met a person she didn't like. I don't know why, but I loathed that about both my parents. No matter what crowd you were in, everyone instantly became their best friend. "Love one another," Mother would say, calling it "an object lesson" when she pointed out gang bangers, prostitutes, and homeless people. Faceless masses teemed on New York's sidewalks, and she professed to love every one of them. Even simple people like Candice, adults whose minds were eternally stuck at age six. I shook my head to dislodge the memory of Mother and her sermonettes.

How can you love someone you don't even know?

The aroma of roasting beans wrapped me in its embrace as I opened the door to ISIP. An olfactory blanket draped itself over a throng of college-age kids armed with mugs of hot brew and open laptops, heads down, wired into the net. People here spoke to each other with animated gestures, but they never made eye contact; all eyes were on their computers or their cups. Candice saw me looking around for a table and headed straight for me.

"Hello, Miss Kate!" she squealed. The shop had already filled by six on a Friday evening, yet no one blinked when she yelled my name. They all got the same magical treatment. Candice was everyone's best friend.

"Hi, Candice. Table for one?" She knew my habits better than I did and pointed to a lone spot in the back. Perfect.

"I'll take it," I said, pulling my MacBook Air laptop from its shoulder bag while I walked. Candice ambled away, probably to get some tableware. I'd order the java later. Tonight, tabletop real estate at Hiram's mattered more than the drink.

Candice must be dropping the ball. The top of the table sported a pile of spilled sugar and a ring of water when I sat down. I moved in search of a napkin to clean it off.

"I'll get it, Miss Kate!" Candice hollered above the din of the shop. "Be right there!" She waddled in my direction with a rag.

I waved back. I could take care of myself. With my blade-thin silver MacBook Air balanced on the corner of the table, I grabbed a spare napkin and swept the puddle of water away.

The next moment my feet flew out from under me. I clutched at the tabletop, but my arm slid helplessly to one side, with no grip on the smooth surface. I pawed at the tall table with my hurt left hand, pushing it over as I collapsed on the floor.

"Miss Kate!" Candice screamed from somewhere close, but I lost sight of her and everything else at ISIP. My head filled with images of someplace far from coffee and the Internet.

I saw water, towering mountains of waves. I bobbed in some kind of lake, in the midst of a terrible storm. Water hovered above me, the liquid sky a massive ocean that crashed down to drown me. I fought for breath in a mad frothing sea as two watery hands clapped together, smothering me in the middle.

My head connected with something solid and I tasted blood.

Everything went black.

Again.

◆ ◆ ◆

"I think it's a fractured hard drive," I heard someone say. My head throbbed, and my eyes felt glued shut.

Hard drive? I wondered. *What? My computer has a flash drive.*

"She's with it, Hiram. Wasn't out more than a few seconds, I reckon," said a gravelly voice to my right. A large hand touched the small of my back.

I must be sitting up.

I jerked away, reflexively, and forced my eyes open. An older man, rough like a stevedore, knelt at my side.

"Miss Kate?" I heard Candice above me. No one else talked like that.

I nodded. I had to appear in control or everyone in the place would descend on me. I just wanted some privacy. When my eyes focused, I realized it was too late. I'd become the star attraction.

"This yours?" Hiram asked. He came into focus, standing above me, holding what looked like letters. Black plastic from the shattered keyboard of my only computer. His long matted hair hung down in front of him when he leaned over, a hand to my forehead.

"You took a nasty spill, Kate. That was our fault. I should have made sure Candice had that floor dry before you sat down."

I shook my head and heard Candice start to cry, repeating my name over and over.

"No. It's not her fault," I said, my tongue thick in my mouth. "I . . . I'm going to be fine."

Then I saw it. My hyperthin laptop lay under the next table, shattered. An elderly woman swept up plastic parts into her hand like she'd grabbed scraps of glowing metal from an alien spaceship. Even with the letters on them, she had no earthly idea what they were.

I thrust out my hand. "Please. Let me have those."

The woman shrugged and I took the salvage. Seven or eight keys were missing, and an ugly crack stretched across the delicate screen in all colors of the rainbow. It was either obscene abstract art or the smashed vestiges of the lightest laptop that money could buy. Candice howled all the louder and came close, her halitosis more than I could handle.

"Let me help, Miss Kate!" she sobbed, dripping big crocodile tears on me. She fumbled with coarse pudgy hands, failing in her attempt to pull me up.

I shrugged her off. It couldn't be any worse—humiliated at ISIP in front of the regulars, and my fifteen-hundred-dollar laptop in shambles. Gigabytes of data storage—with all of my special v-mail development code—lay scattered across Hiram's floor like broken china.

More crocodile tears dripped on me from the leaky waitress. The vertigo returned, and I had a hard time focusing on her as she stood above me. Candice leaned down, pushed her sodden face in mine while her breath knocked me back. "Miss Kate—" she started. I cut her off, turning my head for fresh air.

"Leave me alone!" I shouted, louder than I'd intended. If there really was such a thing as an "Ice Slice," I threw a few around ISIP before I crawled to my feet and stumbled out. Even Hiram's hot coffee wouldn't melt my last glares. Candice trundled to the door bawling. She tried to follow me into the night, but Hiram pulled her back inside, his arms wrapped around her.

"Kate?" he implored. I stomped out, stuffing parts of the busted computer into my bag with my good hand.

"Later, Hiram. I'm okay." I lied. My office had locked up for Friday night, and I couldn't get a loaner laptop until Tuesday. Monday was a federal holiday. I'd just lost my most valuable business tool, shattered ingloriously on a hard tile floor.

I shook my head and headed straight to a cab that waited under a dim light at Vine Street. Time to go home and get a shower. A long hot one.

Or better yet, go straight to bed.

+ + +

"Did someone die?"

I turned around, surprised by the young voice. I thought I was alone. A redheaded boy, about six years of age, stood near me at the base of the Fisherman's Memorial. Clanging rigging, the caw of gulls, and occasional horn blasts made the harbor a noisy place on a Saturday morning. I was surprised to see a little boy out by himself so early with no parent in sight.

I knelt by a bouquet of roses I'd just set at the base of the monument. My shoulder ached as I bent over, still recovering from the fall in the shower and the spill at ISIP. I looked up, twisting a sore neck to see the statue soar skyward, well above an early morning sun that rose in the east. Far above me, a bronze fisherman pulled in a huge catch atop the cylindrical stone pillar. "The roses are for my grandfather," I said, still looking up. I wished the child hadn't intruded. I wanted this to be my time.

"Why?" he asked.

I started to laugh, remembering how Mother used to complain that I overused that word. "Why?" had been my favorite childhood question. I arranged the flowers at the base of the pillar, watching the commercial fishing boats in the distance while I framed an answer to his question. I knew there would be more.

"My grandfather was a fisherman," I said. I forced a steady voice; I couldn't talk about Gramps without losing control. "But that was a long time ago."

"Why?"

I smiled. My quiet time was shot, so I figured I might as well enjoy this. "He was a fisherman on the Grand Banks, off Canada."

"Newfoundland," the boy replied, startling me. "Newfoundland, Canada."

I smiled again, in wonder at this little geography buff. "How'd you know that?" I faced him. "You're what? Six?"

"Nope. I'm eight. But people say I'm small for my age. Every fisherman knows about the Grand Banks. Commercial fishermen at least," he said, his chest swelling with the last words. "My dad's a boat captain." He pointed at the hundreds of vessels moored at Fisherman's Terminal. "Over there."

The terminal harbored a fleet of more than seven hundred vessels, most of them part of Seattle's commercial fishing industry. While the tourists milled around at Pike Place Market watching the vendors throw fish, I'd come to the local source for the fresh catch, on the shores of Lake Union, a few hundred yards from the Ballard Locks. The plaque on the memorial that towered above me read "a tribute to the men, women, their families, and the members of the fishing community who have suffered loss of life at sea." It was my favorite landmark in this town, like some kind of a portal to the Gramps I knew when I was this boy's age twenty-one years ago. A window in time back to my wrinkled, salt-weathered mentor . . . and my best friend.

I could feel Gramps' hard calloused hands wrapped around mine, big hands that had flung poles, pulled lines, folded sails in his youth, baited a hundred thousand hooks, and sliced the bellies of ten thousand fish. I drew in a deep breath, smelling him and his pungent old waxed rain gear in the salt air of the morning. I touched the smooth stone of the pillar behind the flowers, imagining that my hands rested on his hard shoulders.

"Do you like to fish?" the boy asked, crashing my moment again.

I shook my head. "No. But I like sashimi. Do you know what that is?"

The child frowned. "I'm not stupid." He pointed in the direction that he'd motioned earlier. "We sell tuna to lots of sushi restaurants. Our fish is the best." He smiled, reached toward me, and took my hand. "Come on."

"Wait," I insisted, dropping his hand to pull a small wooden chain from my purse. Four interconnected links of white pine joined a tiny cage at each end with a rough marble-sized ball captured inside wooden bars. Carving a ball and chain used one of the dozens of nautical skills that Gramps taught me on cold, wet winter days in Queens.

I laid my latest carving at the base of Fisherman's Memorial with the flowers and then moved to join the boy, who walked briskly toward the docks. "What's your name?" I asked, jogging to catch up.

"Liam. It's Irish."

"Sure. My nephew's a Liam," I said with a chuckle. "He lives in Milwaukee."

"Are you Irish?" Liam asked, pulling me along once he had my hand. "You look like it. Red hair."

"Auburn."

"Auburn what?" he asked. He never turned to face me, headed someplace fast. The little fellow reminded me of Gramps before his stroke. With the smell of salt air and a sea breeze in his face, he'd soon be charting his own course, oblivious to the rest of the world.

"Auburn's a color. It's—oh, forget it. Yes. I'm Irish. Half Irish. My mother is Italian. I grew up in New York."

"Is your name O'Malley?" he asked. I wished he'd just stuck with the "why?" line of questioning.

"No. It's Pepper. I'm Kate. Kate Pepper."

"Kate Kate cuts fishing bait," he said several times, enjoying his rhyme. A minute later, he skidded to a stop. "This is our boat." He pointed proudly to a long troller docked in the marina. "The *St. Jude*." The boat sported a neatly painted white wheelhouse with long delicate outriggers that topped a black steel hull. I didn't see a speck of rust.

"My dad's Irish, too. We're the O'Malleys." Liam jerked at my hand again and yelled a name I couldn't make out. A face peered out of the wheelhouse door near the front of the boat.

"She wants albacore, Mom," Liam stated loudly.

"I didn't tell you that!" I exclaimed, surprised that he indeed knew what I'd come for.

"Doesn't matter," the boy stated matter-of-factly. "It's all we sell. My dad catches it. He trolls all over the East Pacific for the best tuna." The boy invited me aboard the boat, and a woman approached. Probably his mom.

"Looks like you found Liam," she said with a smile, tousling the lad's hair. "Welcome to the *St. Jude*."

"He found me," I replied. Liam waved and took off through a hatch, headed into the bowels of the boat. His mother's handshake was strong like that of a woman unafraid of work. My mother's hands once had the same rough feel when I was very young and she held the only job of her married life—cleaning houses to bring in some extra cash. "Were you looking for fish, or did he catch you window-shopping?" she asked, her cheeks ruddy in the early morning cool.

"Actually, he's right. Liam's right, I mean. My hobby is catering fancy sushi dinners. I came to the terminal to get some tuna. For a party in a couple of days. I need the best. It's a big deal . . . a charity event." Surely, they wouldn't have what I needed. You don't wander up to just any fisherman and get Japanese-grade fish.

"I think we can help," the woman responded. She handed me a flyer. "Joe trolls for young albacore. We brain-stun them, handle them on a padded platform to prevent bruising, bleed them, and flash freeze the fish. We've got whole albacore and loins. Quarters." She turned when Liam rounded a corner with a frosty sample. He'd pulled out a chunk of tuna just for me.

"Liam. Take it back down below. I'll help Ms.—I'm sorry, I didn't get your name."

"Kate. Kate Pepper. And yes, Liam, that's just what I came for. How'd you know?"

He grinned. "She's Irish, Mom. Her granddad was a fisherman, too. On the Grand Banks." He darted back into the hold with the frozen albacore loin and left us on the deck. The wind recommenced, carrying with it spits of rain, leaving dots of moisture on his mother's face and mine. I shivered, despite my rain slicker and heavy liner. I winced reflexively with each drop, losing my focus with every spatter, as though looking through wet glasses.

I wiped my face with the sleeve of my jacket and felt somewhat better. "He's right. I need fifteen pounds of sashimi-grade albacore." I pulled out my wallet. "The boy's a good salesman."

"Like his dad. We troll exclusively for tuna. Young fish, a high fat content, and very low mercury."

"Perfect." I stuck the flyer in my purse and put a hand to the boat's railing, feeling the salty bumps in multiple coats of paint. I could see Gramps standing there, brush in hand, telling me stories about chipping paint on WWII destroyers as a young man, or painting Maine trawlers in his thirties, while he paid me pittance wages to slop white enamel on his old New York harbor tug. I loved the smell of paint, the locker with a dozen half-used cans of pungent marine black, yellow, oily varnishes, and buckets of thick black grease for the anchor chain. Gramps had been a patient man, even that terrible time when I made a horrible mess of his dock cleaning brushes. Layers of paint seemed permanently ingrained in my grandfather's rough hands, like the coarse layers on the rail under my fingers.

"Your hand okay?" Liam's mom asked, pointing at my cloth-encapsulated mitt. She handed me a bag filled with a box of frozen quartered tuna. "These are four-pound loins. Lots of fat in this catch. You'll like them."

I looked at my bandage, now a week after the slicing incident. "I made myself part of the meal last Saturday," I said with a laugh.

"Join the crowd. It happens every time we go to sea." She flashed a bandaged thumb I'd missed when we met earlier. She took my money and thanked me, calling for Liam. "Ms. Pepper needs an escort, son. Care to help?" The boy appeared out of nowhere, clambering through some lines like he'd been born at sea. No doubt, this was a seafaring family.

As I took a step off the boat with Liam, his mom yelled from behind. "Wait!" It surprised us both. "You're the lady who does the charity sushi dinners, aren't you?" she asked, her eyebrows raised in realization. "Sashimi Kate?"

I frowned. I'd heard that nickname and despised it. Half-sloshed men at parties threw it around like I'd modeled for the naked woman painting on the nose of a World War II bomber. If Mrs. O'Malley had heard it, the slur had finally made its way out of the martini bars and Xavier's upscale wine clubs. An ugly infamy.

"Yes, I guess that's me." Poor Liam looked puzzled.

His mom jumped off the boat and thrust a business card at me, wrapping her arms around me in a quick but awkward hug. "Come back soon. Please? We've heard about your charity work. That fundraiser you did for the children's hospital? We'd like to find some way to help, too." Her hand lingered on my forearm for a long time, her eyes connecting with mine. They were a curious combination of green flecks and gray that radiated peace. I felt this twinge, like we had some connection, far back. Maybe a common relative in the family tree back in Ireland, or we'd crossed paths at a coffee shop more than once. After all the strange events of the past days, that electric connection bothered me. But in a good kind of way.

She had tears in her eyes, the same tears I'd seen in the eyes of many parents who came to that charity dinner for hundreds of kids with cancer a few months ago. I didn't press her, sure there was a story there. For a moment, I wondered why the tears of patrons at that dinner hadn't affected me, yet hers pulled so strongly at my heart.

Why now?

Reflexively, I wiped at my face again, at the damp film of sprinkles covering my cheeks. As soon as I did it, my vision improved. I could see her tears so much more clearly, and something deep snapped again. Like with Xavier over the dinner, but different. This time I felt angst. Compassion. It was a deep pain, but the loving kind. Not the rage that drove my knife through albacore a week ago.

What's happening to me?

I hadn't cried in public in years, but the part of me that welled up inside threatened to gush out in a torrent. I thought I'd bottled that up for good yesterday in the executive washroom, but here it came again. Like a fight that raged inside me, the poetry writer and grass-skipping flower-lover screamed to be set free. I fought it back, closing my eyes a moment to regain my mental balance.

Focus!

I took a deep breath, seeing her talk when I opened my eyes but somehow not hearing.

Get control, Kate.

I wiped at my wet face again and that seemed to help. I resolved not to fall out on this dock like I had in the kitchen, the shower, and in the coffee shop.

Get a grip! Whatever it takes!

I heard her voice once more, unsure what she'd said while I bottled my old self up and shoved it away.

"Maybe—" she began, wiping at her eyes with a quick nod toward Liam, "maybe we could get together sometime . . ." She hesitated. "I know Liam would love it if you came to visit again. You've got a fan club." She smiled, waiting on an answer.

I nodded, unsure what to say.

Her wet cheeks sparkled in the morning sun. "You've done more than you realize, Kate—for so many people. You may not have heard it, but your support with those special dinners at the hospital has changed lives." She looked back toward Liam. "Including the life of our son. Thank you."

I shriveled on the inside. When I did that fundraiser, I didn't have any connection with the cause, just the sponsor—Xavier and Consolidated Aerodyne. Charities had never been my passion because I had no connection with the needy—until now. Liam, this little ball of energy, was a cancer survivor, and his ebullient mother was an emotional saint.

She reached out and took my good hand, her cool fingers gripping mine with a confident strength. The connection energized me, and I didn't want to let go, even if the soft, weak part of me escaped forever from its emotional jail. I'd never had this kind of connection with another person and I wanted more.

She squeezed for emphasis with her last words.

"We need you, Kate. And if you ever need *anything*, we want to be there to help." She held on for a long time. "We all struggle sometimes. Please . . . don't face that struggle alone."

CHAPTER FOUR

CANDICE KEPT her distance, her tattered rag in hand, standing like a squat blue pillar in the midst of Hiram's noisy coffee shop late on a Saturday morning. She usually ran to embrace me, but now remained stiff as the stone column I'd just left at Fisherman's Terminal. She feared me—Kate, the hotheaded woman with a heart of lead.

How could I have done this to her?

Much as I dreaded the confrontation with her lettuce-wilting breath, and much as I wanted to be alone, I had to patch up our relationship. I put out a hand when she started to retreat, her trademark cotton wiping rag raised like a shield when I approached.

"Candice. It's okay. I'm sorry I was so mean." I extended my hand again. "Friends?"

Candice didn't shake hands. Come to think of it, I'd never seen her shake hands with anyone before. In an instant, she wrapped me in a tight damp hug. Soft pudgy arms gripped me hard.

"Yes, Miss Kate! Friends! Friends for life!"

Candice smelled like cabbage. The odor reminded me of my grandmother, the cabbage-and-potatoes queen. Boiled cabbage, steamed cabbage, cabbage soup—and every night, potatoes served a new way. I used to kid her that she'd forgotten she left Ireland and could at last buy real food in America. Each comment earned me a painful rap with the back of a huge wooden spoon, her primary culinary instrument and disciplinary tool.

I associated the cabbage odor with people who didn't bathe often, and I suspected Candice was no cabbage cook. Her blue polo shirt and pants were dingy, like she'd worn them for several days in a row. But no one cared, least of all my soft new squeezy friend.

Her hug was genuinely strong. At last, I wiggled her away to an arm's length, her eyes gleaming. "Thank you," I said. "I'm glad to see you, too."

"Sit here!" Candice exclaimed, and pointed to what I knew was her favorite spot. Some child had once carved the rough figure of an elephant in the top of one of Hiram's round oak coffee tables. A few years of spilled coffee and the doodle etching of patrons' ballpoint pens had filled the indentation with a curious palette of blue, black, and red. She called the engraving a "funt," which I presumed to be her abbreviation of *elephant*.

I took the crudely engraved table, and she polished the top with ceremony, flourishing her white cotton rag. Five minutes later, I'd warmed up with a deadly hot cup of strong imported roast. She wouldn't let me buy it. Free coffee—my favorite Sumatran blend—made the ignominy of yesterday's fall worthwhile.

"I got this for you, Kate," Hiram said, sneaking up behind me a few moments later. I nearly tossed hyper-hot java on both of us. He handed me a crudely wrapped package, something the size of a coffee-table book bound in last Sunday's comic strip.

Dilbert. My favorite.

"For me?" I asked. I couldn't remember the last time someone gave me a gift. Not even Xavier. This was like Christmas, but better. People give at the holidays because they have to. Hiram, all six foot two of a walking hairy mop, cared about *me*. I lowered my eyes, afraid they might give away the pain that tried to swim out, then wiped at them while he spoke to Candice. His words to her drifted out as a gentle breeze; he was ever her loving mentor, never the boss.

"It's the least I could do after what happened last night, Kate," he said later with a smile. "Besides, I'm desperate for your business." Brilliant white teeth emerged under the cover of brown, his beard and long curly locks a hairy frame that surrounded an orthodontist-perfect set of pearlies. He watched with anticipation while I unwrapped the package. Candice took a place at his side, bouncing on her toes and clutching her rag in giddy silence. She watched him, waiting on his signal to scream with joy.

As I ripped away the funny papers, I could see it. For Hiram, this was the equivalent of donating his right arm. Or worse. He had the arm, but money was as scarce as instant coffee in this place. A shiny white MacBook, probably a used one he'd cobbled together from the bright plastic parts of others that he'd restored in his spare time— but a welcome window back into my digital world. He handed me a business card.

"The password's on the back, Kate. Free Wi-Fi for my friends," he said with another poster-child smile. "Sorry about yesterday. Maybe this'll get you online until you go to work Tuesday."

What was it with this day? A little boy befriends me and takes me to my dream boat. Then a big boy lays an even bigger gift on me, just at my point of need.

What was it Mother used to call this? "Tiny blessings"?

"Thank you, Hiram. And Candice. I . . . I don't know what to say."

"Say you'll bring all your friends to ISIP," Hiram joked. "That would be a nice start." He extended a hand. "Thanks for coming back, Kate. This means a lot."

I stood and extended my good hand, but Hiram threw his arms open and pulled me into a hug. Even taller than Xavier, Hiram felt solid and warm. Like a cup of his powerful coffee on the way down, his tight embrace made me tingle. I'd not felt that way in a long time, and I confess I hung on to him much longer than I should have. He tensed at last and released me.

"Anyway . . . gotta go. Candice will bring you whatever you need. Now, get online, girl. Probably a thousand e-mails waiting for you out there." With that, Hiram headed back to what he did all day—roasting beans or grinding a new blend in the back. Candice rocketed off to intercept a new customer. I was alone at last. With a much-needed coffee, a "new" laptop, and my blessed Wi-Fi.

Wireless Internet is a curious thing. A signal surrounds you nearly everywhere in Seattle with the instant ability to transport you anywhere in the world. It's like a mysterious electromagnetic fog, harboring strange digital wonders. That little signal could carry me to the office or across the world to someone's living room and their own computer. I loved it. Best of all, Hiram's wireless—his Wi-Fi—beat anything else in Seattle. Like broadband over the air, I could surf anywhere as fast as I wanted.

I opened the laptop gingerly, remembering too well the crippled feel of my shattered MacBook Air and its keyboard confetti.

Consolidated Aerodyne had closed for a three-day weekend, but thanks to Hiram, it was a short digital trip into the server that controlled our e-mail. A few keystrokes later and I'd joined my account with its three hundred messages. A few more keystrokes and I was "in the office," with full access to all corporate files. Everything digital that spilled on last night's coffeehouse floor waited safely in a duplicate file just five floors above the parking lot. Auto-backups work so well these days that I forget I'm using them. Sometimes the stuff you take for granted saves your life when you least expect it.

Hiram's place is no restaurant, but he does have one food item that he serves to special friends and family. Long after noon, perhaps two hours into a mountain of office work, my hairy friend brought out his simple but exquisite specialty. He cooks Seattle's finest grilled cheese sandwich: a three-cheese phenomenon flowing over thick chewy slices of San Francisco sourdough, smothered in real butter and grilled to a golden brown. Just what the heart doctor might ban, after I'd just slammed three cups of eye-popping imported caffeine. He set it down without a word, winked, and left. Hiram loved privacy. He was a computer weenie, after all. We had a lot in common.

Eleven years ago, I stood in his shoes. I was a budding computer nerd at the threshold of my career, living on the edge of the economy while I hung on for dear life. Three thousand miles west of Mother and Father, in a mouse-and-roach-infested one-room garage apartment in Redwood City north of San Jose, I'd declared my independence at the raw age of eighteen. As far from my parents as I could get yet still be in the continental US. On my own, with no sermonettes from Mother, no cramped family brownstone in Queens, and no gossiping noisy relatives. I earned eight dollars an hour and loved it, as a part-time secretary for a software company, with thirty hours of New York junior college and two programming courses to my credit.

I was in heaven.

Hiram rounded the coffee bar as I watched, on a beeline back to the kitchen and his wife. He pecked her on the back of the neck with a kiss, and she whirled around into his arms with a funny nasal laugh. Then she pushed him away, giggling, and shoved a grinder into his empty hands. Hiram shrugged and turned back to the kitchen while she watched, eyes sparkling.

I wish I had that.

This couple couldn't put together enough nickels in a year to make a month's payment on my Ice Rocket, yet they were happy. My old life in Redwood City, poor as it was, had that same magic sparkle, like the lilt in her laugh and the joy in his quirky smile. Forgotten fingers lingered on the steaming sandwich, still so hot in the center that it would sear skin off the roof of my mouth. I eyed the bubbling butter, counting the calories, mentally measuring my midriff. Fat lost the standoff; my stomach won as teeth tore into toasted sourdough and hot cheese.

My mind wandered back to California.

✦ ✦ ✦

"Can you do it?" my tall bearded boss asked eleven years ago during the heyday of his startup business in Silicon Valley. "I need someone who can program this thing." I jumped at the chance, with no earthly idea what I faced, but was determined to break out in this office. Measure up? I'd jump higher than anyone else, to prove that the programming could be done.

Dr. Thomas Cook's business in Sunnyvale, California started small—just me and three oversexed college boys, all of them in jeans, sandals, and Hawaiian shirts, our eyes glued to computer screens for twelve to fourteen hours a day. We loved it. The token girl, they pegged me as a hungry and independent college coed, the office fax queen, and a dependable copy mistress. But I could program computers, too. The butthead boys in Birkenstocks hated that.

"Software's for guys," one of the "testosterone team" remarked early in my career. I think he felt threatened, but I loved the compliment. They knew I consumed every programming course I could squeeze in at night—and I wore a skirt every day because I wanted to. That wardrobe choice drove them nuts, but not because of bare legs or libido. The red cape of my hemline taunted the bullish macho in those three male nerds.

Dr. Cook took me in after we met one Sunday over a free-sausage-sample table at a Whole Foods store in Redwood City, the commercial cornucopia where I cruised every weekend to make a meal. I alternated trips to big supermarkets where sausages, crackers, and cheese were the fare of freebies, and then to the mall's food court, where a couple of laps around the plaza would fill you up on toothpick-skewered samples of chicken. Grab a free cup of water and leave well fed.

Apparently, Dr. Cook had dined like that often enough during his college days to recognize a fellow "grazer," and he offered me a job cleaning his tiny office so that I could afford to eat. "Can you type?" he'd asked one day just a week after he hired me, when he caught me diving into a jar of mints.

Type? Who can't?

"Sure. I'm a programmer," I'd answered, stretching the truth to the limit. I had six measly credit hours in computer applications, but I'd say anything for the big break. "And if you need a secretary . . ."

"Don't have one, so I guess you're it," he replied with a huff. That was eleven years ago. Until I came to Seattle, Dr. Cook could claim to be the only employer I'd ever had.

"Can you do it?" he'd asked that lucky day a year after I fell into the typing job, throwing me into a programming task that changed my life.

I bit into Hiram's luscious butter-toasted cheese, three layers of delight mixing into one as I pulled the melted strings away from the sandwich. I fought back mental images of Xavier peering over his hawk nose at me, eyeballs-become-lances that shredded my pants to pull a virtual measuring tape about my too-soft belly. I squeezed my eyes shut to block out his face, my ears ringing from tensed muscles, then I peeked through partially open lids to make sure he'd run away.

I wondered why Dr. Cook ever gave me that magical chance to excel. He had no reason to share his success, but he did. Freely. He gave me a ticket to the enchantment of Sunnyvale and San Jose, where the recently rich arose from the most humble and unlikely beginnings. Some of them simple people like me. Plain California girls who crashed the breakfast bars at Hampton Inns to save spare change, and smashed roaches in their apartments at night to save exterminator fees.

But even simple people can spout great ideas. Ten years ago, I came up with a doozy.

E-mail is a pain. You have to open it, read it, reply to it or forward it, then save it or delete it. So many actions that it's hard to hold a running conversation with a girlfriend. It's not social at all, an impossible medium in which to keep a dozen conversations going at once. I used to complain loudly about that problem when I'd flip from one computer application to another, multitasking between a friend's story about a neighbor's break-in and finishing a boring typing job for Dr. Cook. There had to be a better way. I believed I could solve that annoying multitasking challenge.

I was nuts.

What began as a personal struggle to network with my friends eventually turned into Dr. Cook's golden egg. No. More like a golden goose laying lots of golden eggs. My idea for social networking eventually caught the ear of the boss, a brilliant Rice grad who'd always been on the lookout for the breakout opportunity. When I got frustrated one day and drew my idea on a white board, angry I couldn't talk to five people at once, he understood me. We birthed a networking software that ran smack dab into another startup in the same town. The other company grew famous and won that market, but Dr. Cook walked away with several zeroes worth of cash in a sale of our intellectual property. My fledgling software venture actually worked, through sheer brilliance and dumb luck. Dr. Cook peddled our software to an MIT dropout on the rise to stardom, and the sale changed my life. Money can do that.

Sharp cheddar warmed my mouth, its soft tendrils sticking to the gaps at the base of my teeth. I could probably afford to buy Hiram's coffeehouse now, along with his sandwich recipe, but somehow getting the meal for free made this dining experience all the more special.

Ten years after I'd left New York, I was running on the frantic front end of a roller-coaster software business as secretary, programmer, and then web developer, and life eventually lost its glamour. No balance and no roses. Just money . . . lots of money . . . and endless software deadlines. No relationships, no personal life . . . and a desperate need for a change. Dr. Cook hated stress more than he loved the money. That's why he sold out. Annual Christmas letters remind me each year that he moved to a little ranch near Austin, Texas, to rebuild old Farmall tractors and work with the Boy Scouts. I opted to change locale and move up the ladder. Life had to be easier somewhere else, somewhere slower-paced, like Seattle. Dr. Cook knew better. I should have followed him to Texas.

I polished off the last of the sandwich and hit Send on my last message. The digital day was done and now I could play. As the loaner laptop slid into my bag, I could imagine Dr. Cook's hearty laugh and deep gray beard during our early days at the cramped office in his garage. Dr. Thomas Cook, the world's hardest-working man, quit cold turkey and headed to a Texas Shangri La to repaint antique tractors. To his credit, he still had the first dollar bill he'd ever been paid. It wasn't cliché. Unfortunately, my money discipline left something to be desired.

I had a condo, a motorcycle, and a closet full of Fendi stilettos to pay for—and no idea where to find the last dollar that I'd earned.

I couldn't afford to quit yet.

CHAPTER FIVE

THE BLUE fleck paint job of my Ice Rocket matched the azure tint of Lake Wenatchee as I rode through the mountains east of Seattle, late on Saturday afternoon. The bike is a sky blue with a tinge of purple, and what you see depends on the sun and the time of day, like with sea ice. The painter got it just right. At noon, you might see deep sapphire, but the purple deepens as evening overtakes you. And chrome frames it all, flashy silver that runs from one end of the bike to the other.

Other than standing under a steaming showerhead, my favorite place to be is wrapped in tight black leather, reclining on my monster—a horsepower wedge slicing through air. Hugging my contoured metal steed, there's no sitting back. You lean into it or it will kill you. I'm a pulsing extension of its power, and it thrusts me forward at speeds that blur thought. Once, as a little girl on a field trip in northern New York, I lay down on a giant fallen spruce, wrapping my legs and arms best as I could around the monster. Strapping myself on the Ice Rocket reminds me of straddling that tree. I'm leather skin on a cobalt-blue metal beast.

Stevens Pass Highway climbed through the Cascades, where I headed east from Seattle. It's a winding road, and I occasionally roared past a car on a curve and scared both of us. In a few wide-open stretches I opened her up. I raced from a dead stop to a hundred in a few seconds, anything along the road was just a smear. Towering gray granite ridges dotted with green spruce and fir made a wall on both sides of the road as the highway rose two thousand feet up to Coles Corner and Lake Wenatchee. Snow still topped the peaks, melting into tumbling streams that ripped away at the sides of the mountain. Near the base of some slopes, emerald grasses covered sandy loam, highlighted in the red and orange of wildflowers still in bloom. The rugged beauty of the landscape complemented the pummeling velocity of my ride. If you could harness a killer whale, or strap yourself to the top of a log in a lumber flume, surely it would feel like this, a tiny black leather body wrapped like a leech around blue and silver road rocket.

Toilets in gas stations are generally sorry experiences wherever you live. No different here, at a tiny fuel-and-snack stop deep in the Cascades. After two hours strapped to the Ice Rocket, every rumble vibrating a strained bladder, any convenience was welcome—filthy or not. I needed relief more than the Ice Rocket needed gas. The bell on the gas station door jingled as I exited, hands dripping wet, wishing for a hand towel. I immediately felt the hot spotlight of someone's eyes.

"D'you ride that thing . . . or does it ride you?" a driver asked with a lecherous glance as he jumped off the running board of his logging rig. The man must have loved cool weather, clad only in a T-shirt that proclaimed his allegiance to red razorbacks. He was a long way from Arkansas. And it was too cold for T-shirts.

"I ride it. Sort of like strapping yourself to the hood of that rig," I said, casting a glance at his Peterbilt. "But it's a lot faster."

Funny how, when men insult me, I always think back to my father. I compare every man to him, and, generally speaking, my parent loses. But not this time. One thing my easygoing father was not—a leering womanizer, what Justus once called a "man whore." He treated Mother with the greatest respect, and he honored me in every way. You could barely get my father off the couch, but he did have one hot button I could depend on. He'd "go native" and rip the eyes out of any ape who mistreated me. I loved that about him. Too bad that quality didn't rub off on more guys. It certainly didn't on this loser.

"Ever lay it over? I mean, in the driveway?" another voice asked from a distance. It was an older man, about my father's age. He watched me from the station's one gas pump as he refilled a dusty maroon Suburban.

"As in 'fall over?'" I asked, pulling my helmet on.

"Yep. As in forget the kickstand. Ever do it?"

"Nope. I'd never get it up."

"That's what I thought." He went back to his gasoline and looked away, but kept talking. "You headed west?"

"I am. Headed back to Seattle." I looked up at the sun, rays of gold, purple, yellow, and orange firing through a base of scattered clouds. I had about an hour, perhaps more, until the sun set over the city. It was a two-hour ride home.

"Pretty sloppy back that way. Storm's movin' in."

I love to get wet.

I zipped the leather up to my chin. "Good. Rain hits like paint balls when you're going a hundred."

"Have it your way, little lady. Just a warning."

I nodded as I slung a leg over my blue beast. The clientele in the gas station ogled out the window, waiting for the "little woman" to climb on her mean machine. I could imagine the catcalls, and jiggling bellies with belt buckles the size of saucers.

Five seconds later, Coles Corner and the leering eyes disappeared behind me in a flurry of dust. A hundred miles of curves lay ahead, and two hours of blessed mental rest. I lost myself in thought atop the blue metal steed.

✦ ✦ ✦

Control. The word was tattooed on my mental horizon as I raced back to Seattle.

H_2O

Life revolves around control. Mother controlled me, dictating skirt lengths and the duration of phone calls to boys. Her loving but voluminous instructions about food, hygiene, makeup, and school were all part of her insatiable focus on her only child, a precious daughter. She'd been nice enough about it, but gave me no room to be myself. What else do you call that if not control? Yet, her structured environment never seemed to include my father, a man over whom she had *no* control. They were polar opposites—a woman dominated by the determination to get things done, and a loving but lazy father who did nothing. Perhaps my role was to serve as the only human in our home whom she *could* control.

Father didn't seem to care. He loved television. He lived for television. His home? A chair the permanent shape of his butt, and the right arm of his leather recliner permanently dented with the weight of an arm that forever held a cola, a sandwich, or the remote control. I can't remember when I saw him sit without food in his hands. He gripped the next bite like smokers clutch a forgotten cigarette, a perpetual counterweight as he filled his head with the latest images on the boob tube. We had drawers full of old remote controls and extra batteries. You could never have enough. Television and life were synonymous.

Dark clouds snuffed out the red and orange darts of a setting sun ahead of me. My special headlight oscillated gently left and right like a locomotive headlamp. It would scare the pants off drivers coming my way, and no one ever veered my direction from opposing traffic, fearing that perhaps they'd wandered onto a train track. In the gathering dusk, I could see Mother with her apron and the dreaded willow switch. "You come in this minute!" I was out way past my playtime, and Mother would never approve of this. Loose in the wild mountains, riding a light-speed blue gazelle.

The wind is a memory, vivid as it hits you, then blowing past and gone. I could smell the approaching storm front rolling in from the west. Warm downdrafts mixed with cold tubes of wind, burbling down from gathering black clouds above me. The ride home threatened wet. And wonderful. I loved the rain.

Memories, like the wind whipping me in the curves toward Skykomish, always flood back when I'm prone on the cycle. There was something about moving, running away from the past as I raced through the present. I could see my youth fleeing fast behind the bike, my gangly days as a skinny girl in a class full of short, fat boys. Pimples and freckles and red-hair jokes. My nubile young body changing faster—much faster—than my parents' old-fashioned traditions. Mental images sifted through brain files of boyfriends and telephones, car keys and car wrecks. Broken hearts and that horrible senior prom, failed friendships and the treachery of a girlfriend who stole away the only boy I'd ever loved. Life in Queens, New York? A massive disappointment.

I raced on, veering around slow traffic as I approached the slopes of Mount Index, towering to the left. A setting sun peeked out from behind the mountain, barely visible. Rain pelted me with occasional spatters. Low black clouds draped over the curves of the road. I accelerated, reveling in the grip of squeaky-clean tires as the torque threw me through a mini–rain squall of spray thrown up behind a truck's tires. I could pass faster than any vehicle on the road and corner better on wet pavement than any race car. I used both gifts to my advantage as I dove headlong into the approaching liquid gray.

Lightning flashed ahead, a brilliant blaze somewhere to the west. I careened down the slick descent, flying through the foothills of the Cascades as rain enveloped me. My black skin shed the storm, icy needles pricking thick leather. I hugged the Ice Rocket even tighter and made my body one with the metal as we shot into wet blackness. The pelt of raindrops on my visor grew to a roar, drowning out road noise and conquering daydreams. The odor of ozone swept under my chin shield, reminding me of the smell of my uncle's copy shop where a dozen laser printers cranked out countless reams of paper. It was the smell of rain. I became the windshield of a jet fighter in a downpour, the leading edge of a space shuttle roaring off the pad into the throat of a hurricane.

I overpowered the tempest and my control became complete.

✦ ✦ ✦

Xavier's face filled my vision, somewhere just beyond the smashing drops that exploded by the thousands on my visor. His bald dome, shaved so carefully each day, glistened in the wetness. Straight thin lips made a perfect horizontal line, the base from which sprang a perfect nose, bifurcating at the top into two perfect eyebrow lines like a palm tree above his eyes. He waxed his eyebrows once a week, plucking them into a fine black arc. I've never understood why.

The blue unnerved me, his eyes so cerulean I'd once been convinced that he wore designer contacts. Black pupils dotted irises so perfect they could have been painted on white eyeballs. But they held no pain, no warmth. They stared like an eighteenth-century canvas of stuffy people bereft of emotion. Perfect eyes that were his eyes but held no zest for life. Dead blue.

Not a wrinkle broke his perfect face. No smiles and no crow's-feet. No frowns and no lines beyond his mouth. No surprise or horizontal lines on his forehead. His was a digital face, just a smooth continuum, broken only by straight lips and the sprouting palm of brows that framed two ponds of penetrating blue. That, and a finger or a hand always held to his chin. He always appeared in thought, but not a thread of emotion ever stitched in his face.

Do I love him?

Xavier never hugged me except in bed. I thought of Candice, shivering at the remembrance of her intolerable breath, but warming at the memory of her strong embrace. She cared for me. I let myself relive the feel of Hiram's sturdy body and warm muscles rippling beneath my hands as I wrapped myself around him in a hug. Xavier held me on occasion, in moments of passion, but I couldn't remember enjoying it the way I had when I'd held Hiram.

I thought of the laptop, Hiram's extravagant sacrifice to make up for my accident, a loaner Apple provided yesterday by a java pauper. Aside from obscenely expensive dinners, I struggled to remember anything that Xavier had ever given me. A car zipped past in the opposite direction and disappeared—like my memory of any gift from him, if there ever had been one. I warmed again at the remembrance of Hiram's *Dilbert* comics and the crude wrapping paper, of bubbly Candice as she waited for me to unwrap the surprise when I returned to the coffee shop. These were simple people who dripped love. Contented people.

The memory turned sour on the pivot of another word I despised. *Content.*

Contentment tasted of mediocrity, and mediocrity meant weakness. I refused to be mediocre, the accommodation swamp of "good enough" that had sucked the life out of my parents and almost claimed me as its next victim. Until I escaped Queens.

I lifted my head and gunned the bike, determined to outrun average, to veer away from "middle of the road." A gust of wind grabbed me and lifted my torso ever so briefly. I grabbed the handles hard, jerking myself back toward the bike in a struggle against the torrent and blast. It was my one danger, ballooning off the bike like a sail at high speed. Gold Bar, Washington, raced past as I hugged the bike and crossed a double yellow in front of a big rig, with just enough clearance to zip in front of the eighteen-wheeled monster as we entered a downhill curve.

As I accelerated away from the truck, I felt a rivulet of water trickle down my neck. Rain pelted me in the highway gale as I rode on, and more of the wet intruder that ran down my spine slipped in a second time when I turned my head. I could feel the cold now, stabbing aches in joints stiff from too long a ride. Soon, the seep of water breeched my leather neck wall and ran unabated, a cold stream wriggling down to the small of my back, where it spilled left and right to encircle my waist. Shivers grew and my joints felt sandy, grinding as I shifted on the bike to swerve around cars and trucks that slowed for the rain. I roared under an overpass, a concrete sign of approaching modernity, and nodded at two bikers huddled under the bridge against the storm.

Perhaps I should stop.

Monroe—the outskirts of Seattle—lay just a few miles ahead. I'd press on.

◆ ◆ ◆

I don't remember coming off the bike.

I recall the sensation of flying, and I know I left the Ice Rocket because my hands flailed. One moment I was speeding across wet highway, and the next: no grip on the handlebars, no more cold steel of the gas tank under my chest, no warm thrum between my knees as blazing cylinders fired me forward into the maelstrom.

I saw colors. Brilliant tints and shades filled my vision. A bold arc swept from left to right, rays of red, orange, yellow. Of green and blue. Faint arcs of light purple, then darker violet. Hue lay upon hue, blazing from left to right as though a massive light show pierced me. I could feel radiance boiling up within me as brilliant geysers of light erupted from my face, blasted into my visor, and then reflected back into my eyes. There was no sense of sound. The deafening spatter of rain was gone. Everything whispered, "Quiet."

No—it was not quiet. A high-pitched tone, like a bad case of tinnitus, rang all about me. My joints screamed with cold, stiff pain, but they weren't moving. I tried to raise my hand, but it lay asleep, beyond my control. I knew that I had some connection to life, but could command no movement. I tasted wet copper on my tongue.

The lights grew in their intensity, and I forgot the pain, if only for a moment. Deep blackish red like venous blood morphed into the bright red of maraschino cherries. There was the pink of salmon flesh in perfect slices under my knife. Orange juice bubbled up, frothy delight filled with pulp, swelling in a glass in slow motion. Yellow brilliance engulfed me. I slid on a mountain of banana peels, dazzling yellow like summer sun. And then the pale green of stylish skirts in a San Jose dress shop, fading to the deep green of grass in spring as I lay in a park in Queens. Soft green, deep-verdant blades. And blue. Xavier's eyes, skies, and fragrant crayons. I held a box of blue Crayolas kept hidden during the day, smelling their perfect color at night when the lights were off. Images of navy, cobalt, and azure danced before me when I couldn't even see my hands. And purple so deep I could taste it. Royal robes on the priests at mass, Easter eggs, and ripe grapes. Miles of vineyards on weekend getaways from work. I could see wine, pungent Merlot. Merlot with a bite. Bitter wine. My mouth burned.

Then a Voice in my head rumbled with a timbre I felt certain I knew, but for which I couldn't place a face. "... My promise ..." the Voice said, precious words lost in the milieu of my distraction. Then the arc of brilliant colors disappeared, snatched away by the Voice with the Message.

I hurt.

✦ ✦ ✦

I smelled cigarettes. Like in a bathroom where acrid smoke mixed with the steam of the shower in a wretched stench. But this was different. I shivered. The pungent stink made me want to retch. Someone breathed the stuff in my face.

"Don't move," someone mumbled above me. A spot of red glowed above my eyes, but I could see little through my rain-and-mud-spattered visor. I tried to move, ignoring the injunction, and pain shot through my neck.

"Stay still!" the voice commanded, spitting the red glowing thing away. I saw a white light behind the head, like a flashlight or bouncing headlight. It came closer.

"She alive?" a voice asked from somewhere behind the smoky head.

"Yeah. She's lucky. Bike's a wreck, though."

"Shame."

"D'you call it in?" the first voice asked, just in front of me. The reek of cigarette smoke grew and it filled my helmet. But that made no sense. I tried to move again and felt a hand on my shoulder, another under my neck.

"Ambulance is on the way," the second voice said. "Any bleeding?"

"None that I can see. Bring that light closer."

I heard steps, but the light dimmed, replaced by nightmares, sketchy snatches of horrific dreams, and a wave of nausea. My last memory was of cold wetness, dark soil soaking through my back. I imagined that its icy fingers penetrated the leather of my jacket, slid into my organs, and clenched them in a fist. I screamed as an unseen hand drew me down into frigid muck.

◆ ◆ ◆

"You've been out of it for a long time, Ms. Pepper," a tall physician said. "Do you remember the wreck?"

I'd traded my bike for a hospital room at some point. It was all a blur. I couldn't remember anything except cigarette smoke, the vivid colors of a rainbow . . . and a Voice. But beyond that? I tried to shake my head, but it hurt.

"No. Nothing. I . . . I've been blacking out lately. A lot."

"When?" the doctor asked. Young guy, probably a resident. Bags under his eyes, a white coat with a stethoscope hung around his neck, and a name stitched in cursive above the breast pocket of his lab coat. Something Indian I couldn't pronounce that ended with "M.D."

"Fainting here and there. I fell in the shower a couple of days ago, and slipped at a coffee shop. Got dizzy a few times, too. I thought maybe—maybe I might have been pregnant. I took a test. It came up negative."

He took a few notes, not looking up. I hated that about doctors.

"Was it a home urine test?" he asked. "Or a blood test?"

"Home test. Three of them. All negative."

He nodded as if he knew exactly what it meant to be pregnant and unmarried.

He has no idea.

"Nurse, get me a couple more tests with those blood samples, please." He passed a slip of paper to the woman at his side, and then put a light to my eyes. My neck screamed when he touched it, but the rest of me seemed fine.

"You were just the other side of Monroe," he said. "Going pretty fast, according to the truckers who found you. Said you'd swerved around them too fast in the rain. They found you and the bike about a mile beyond where you passed them illegally. Lucky for you."

"Lucky?" I asked.

"Yes. They were both EMTs once. Miraculous. I mean, how many truckers out there used to drive an ambulance?" He raised an eyebrow. "Count your blessings, Ms. Pepper."

"My bike? What about it?"

The doctor looked up at someone I couldn't see. I tried to roll left, but it hurt too much. A hand took mine. Long, bony fingers. It had to be Xavier. My heart leapt. He'd come!

"Bike's messed up pretty bad, Kate."

I craved to hear his voice.

Say more.

"You went off the bike and slammed into a pile of really soft stuff. Road sand, leaves, that kind of thing. The bike went straight ahead into a rock ledge. If you'd been on it—well—you wouldn't be here." He squeezed my fingers, moving into my line of sight. The doctor stepped aside, instructing me to follow his movement with my eyes as he wagged a finger from left to right.

"Have you ever been under anesthesia?" he asked. "Any negative side effects?"

I tried to shake my head but failed. Good thing I couldn't—my answer would have been a lie. I mumbled something and he asked me to repeat it.

"No—I mean—yes. I have. But no negative side effects."

"What kind of anesthesia?" he asked, his eyes still glued to the stupid report.

"An operation."

He looked up. Of course it had been an operation. He shrugged with that look of "go on."

"A long time ago. I'm sure it doesn't matter."

"Let me be the judge of that, please," he said, making eye contact for the first time. "What kind of operation? General anesthesia—where they put you to sleep? Or local?"

"I asked for a general. For some female stuff."

"Ms. Pepper, I really need you to be more specific. How long ago?"

"Twelve years." I paused. "I was seventeen. In college." I held his gaze for a long time, and he got the message. I didn't need to say more. The doctor turned back to his clipboard and made another note. As he did, Xavier's grip seemed to weaken, his fingers slipping from mine.

No! Don't leave. Not now!

I tried in vain to look up at Xavier, swords of pain stabbing me if I made the slightest move.

H₂0

"The MRI says you're fine, Ms. Pepper," the doctor continued, setting the report aside and placing his stethoscope to my upper chest. Xavier moved away. I wanted him to pull me off the bed into a bear hug, no matter how much that hurt; I was desperate to feel his long fingers intertwined with mine, his arms wrapped about me. But he moved out of range. Always out of range.

"You'll hurt in the neck and shoulders for a few days. You have a bad strain. But there's no sign of any damage. Again—count it a miracle that you survived, and had such good medical care on the way here."

"Thank you, Doctor. When can I—can I leave?"

He chuckled and then turned to Xavier. "Is she always in such a hurry?" he asked, as if they knew each other and had shared private guy jokes.

"Always," Xavier quipped.

Was I? Always in a hurry?

I'd craved to hear Xavier's voice, but not his sarcasm. Not now.

"Encourage her to rest, Mr. Morton. She can be discharged, but I recommend that she stay home for one week. Have her come see me in seven days."

Before I could slip in a question, the doctor with the strange name shook hands with Xavier and left the room. Not so much as a good-bye to the patient. I was invisible.

"I have a charity dinner to prepare!" I protested. Just raising my voice made me hurt everywhere above my neck. My forehead felt like it would explode.

Xavier grabbed my hand. My protest brought him to me.

"It's tomorrow, Kate. But I can reschedule, or get someone else to prepare the meal. You need the rest."

His voice hummed with strength. He'd put the event aside. For me. Tears welled in my eyes, and immediately the familiar shower dizziness returned. I dreaded fading out again.

-71-

H_2O

Not now! Not with him here!

I squeezed his hand as hard as I could, struggling to clutch reality. To hold on to this moment—and, for better or worse, the only man in my life.

"Will you be there for me? To help?" I pleaded, eager for an extended answer, a long-worded profession of his deep caring in this dire moment. I'd lost control; my heart raced, craving his response.

He moved in front of the bed and smiled, a rare pursing of his rigid straight lips, revealing a beautiful dimple in his cheek. The deep blue of his eyes sparkled in the purple fluorescent light of the room. His reply was terse, but heartfelt.

"Yes. I'll be there for you. I promise."

CHAPTER SIX

PHOENIX. A mythical firebird rising from the ashes of a fire of its own making. That's me. A two-legged phoenix standing at the sink in a stranger's kitchen on Sunday evening, sushi knife in hand.

A legend I remember from my tugboat chats with Gramps told of a rare bird from India. A tall bird with eye-popping red plumage, building a nest out of cinnamon twigs. "After five hundred years of life," he told me, "the bird will ignite the nest and burn itself to ash. From those ashes, the egg and the young life of its renewed self will rise."

If I had a fire of my own making, it would look like racing in the rain at night on the Ice Rocket, flying at seventy miles an hour into a pile of dirt and suffering a mental blank until the truckers-turned-EMTs shook me out of my daze. Now, despite my hopes, I was in my second life, back at my cutting board only a day after the accident. Despite the fire, I suspect that the charred Phoenix had felt a lot better than I did. Every muscle in my back and shoulders burned like those cinnamon twigs.

"You're nuts. You know that, right?" Andrea whispered to me, her shoulder brushing against mine where she stood to my left. "You have serious issues, girlfriend." She chuckled and swirled a rag through the deep sink, flushing out the last of our vegetable trimmings. "But, so do the rest of us. What gives? I thought he said he'd cancel this event."

I sighed. She was right, but I refused to admit it out loud. I'd lose my Phoenix status with Xavier, who'd lauded me to all his friends when I'd reluctantly agreed to get out of bed and support his charity event. He told me that I was the "sushi talk of the town," but I wondered if he'd really tried to find another chef. I had to travel halfway across Seattle to cook in another woman's obscenely expensive kitchen. More than anything, more than coaxing burning muscles out of spasm and more than rest, I wanted him. I wanted to be noticed. To be held.

"I've had issues for a long time, Andrea," I confessed.

A friend in Redwood City once told me, "You're a paradox. Strong, brave, and determined to break free. Yet, you slide so easily back into old habits. You let guys mistreat you." That friend, like Andrea, stuck with me through my issues. But they were both right. I was a mess.

I sighed and nudged Andrea in the ribs as I sliced carrots into tiny sticks. "You're a mess, too, by the way."

Andrea huffed. She knew exactly what I meant, my poking at her habit of trolling along dreamy-eyed in Justus's wake at work. But when Justus occasionally worked up the nerve to get more serious, she always played hard to get. A bizarre mating behavior, two sane adults in their weird cat-and-mouse game, repeated every day. Our own TV sitcom.

"I'm done," I said, and scraped the last carefully sliced carrots onto a serving dish. I picked at a thin slice of *gari*. The delicate shaving of pickled ginger was perfect now, a week after I'd made it. Five platters of my special sushi roll assortment sat ready to go. Some blending of rice and slicing of fish was all that remained for the final snack presentation. I handed my cutting board to Andrea and winced as I twisted at the hip. Every part of me screamed "lay down," but I'd progressed too far into the dinner preparation to quit now.

"Hand me the rice and we'll finish this up," I said to Andrea.

H$_2$O

"Ready to go," she replied, passing a bowl of sticky white stuff. Miles of granite countertop and a hanging rack of gray Calphalon pots surrounded us—like on a television set for some famous cooking show. But I didn't like it. Give me my wooden board and tiny kitchen. I didn't need all this glitz, though I did lust for some of the hostess's hyper-expensive cutlery.

"Two hundred of these rolls and we're done, Kate," my friend said, shoulders slumping. We'd both been there for four hours on a Sunday afternoon, slaving away and, until half an hour ago, working alone. Xavier breezed through the kitchen, headed to an early start at the host's wine bar. I'd be asleep in half an hour if I joined him, alcohol my certain sleeping pill. Fatigue's tendrils pulled at every sore muscle. I promised myself a massage day tomorrow—a day of rest, away from the office.

Sushi preparation is more complex than most people think, a combination of fish and rice blended in an art form all its own. Andrea set a bowl of water to my right. She'd slice the fish in quarter-inch-thick portions, and I'd press raw meat and rice together in a tiny roll. If we worked fast, and we usually did, we could each knock out two snacks every minute. Less than an hour from now, we'd be done. I couldn't wait.

"Platter's ready. Let's rock," Andrea announced. The guests would arrive in ninety minutes, whether we were finished or not.

I dipped my hand into the water bowl to moisten my fingers. Palms lightly watered, I could press the sticky rice and fish together without becoming part of the meal. As my fingers slipped into the bowl, I felt deep fatigue gnaw at aching shoulder muscles, the part of me that suffered the brunt of the attack when I'd hit the dirt traveling at a mile a minute. I rolled my shoulders, mentally tallying the minutes until we'd be done. Andrea sliced the first slab of fish for the snack presentation, handing it my way, while I spread water on my palms and reached for a dollop of rice.

Andrea gasped, her mini-scream pealing in my ears though I could see nothing.

I remembered seeing the white of cooked food in her bowl, imagining the sensation of sticky grains as I would squeeze them in my palm to make an oblong ball, forming the viscera beneath a pink slab of Liam O'Malley's special albacore. I remembered the cool drip of the water on my fingertips when my hand reached out to the water bowl. Then blackness consumed me.

A crash of splintering porcelain hit my ears as her bowl smashed on the tile floor of the ultimate kitchen. Andrea yelled my name. Blind, I reached out, a modern Helen Keller seeking to locate a familiar face or point of reference.

In that split second of blindness, a lightning bolt ignited in my head, the explosive herald of the strange images that followed. On the heels of a searing light, I could see a river, black and brown baskets floating in the water, filled with crying babies. No, it was a single baby. A hungry baby who reached up to touch me. And water everywhere, a broad expanse of roiling brown that surrounded the child. In my mind's eye, I imagined I reached down to pluck the baby from the water. I stumbled blindly into Andrea, clambering like a babe. As we touched, it was as though a switch turned on in the room and I could see again. The image evaporated, child and all.

Andrea's eyes were wide with fright.

"What's the matter over there?" Xavier yelled. He had that aggravated tone, the kind he got after a little wine loosened his famous temper. I touched my fingers together on my right hand, feeling the familiar gum of sticky rice grains. It all came back.

"What happened?" Andrea asked, grabbing at my hands. "Are you okay?"

"You broke her bowl!" Xavier yelled, his voice thrown like an uppercut. I knew that tenor, the "I'm going to show you how to behave" tone as he rushed to correct me. He had no idea how to squeeze a ball of rice and a slab of albacore into a dinner delight, but he'd let me know he could do a much better job if somehow I wasn't up to the task.

"Dizzy again," I said, unsure what had distracted me. I lied; I hadn't been the least bit dizzy. My eyesight had failed for only a microsecond, but long enough to knock a thirty-dollar ceramic mixing bowl to the floor and reduce it to shards. And I had no idea why.

"Kate?" she asked again, gripping me above the elbow.

"Clean it up," Xavier demanded, umbrella eyebrows scrunched in a fierce scowl. His breath reeked of red wine, his face too close. "How'd you manage to do that?"

Andrea's grip tightened as she came to my defense, ever my protector.

"She shouldn't be here," she hissed, moving to separate us. I hoped that Xavier would get the hint.

"Fainting again?" he snapped. "I thought you were over that."

Thanks for nothing, X.

He looked at his watch, ever ruled by his obsession with time, then looked back up at me. "The early folks might be here in an hour." He stood still, penetrating blue eyes all business. The gentleman I'd fallen for always vanished when money came into play. Tonight promised a new contract if Xavier could raise the cash for their favorite charity, and the presentation had to be good. Very good. The higher the stakes, the better the meal, and the meaner he'd grow. Dollar madness.

"I'll be fine, X. Just a little tired, that's all."

"You're exhausted, Kate. You said so two hours ago." Andrea's tone bled raw, and she turned to shield me from him.

"I can do it, X. Just let me freshen up a little. I admit, I'm tired. But we're almost done."

"No we're not."

I faced Andrea, throwing an Ice Slice in her direction.

"I'm serious, Kate," she said, and then turned back to the boss. "Call Kyoto Bar and get some help, Xavier. She needs the rest."

He stood in silence, gritting his teeth. Jaw muscles danced beneath a fresh shave.

Say something, Iceman.

He shook his head, then turned and picked up his near-empty wine glass. "Go on. Get cleaned up. I need you at full strength." He waved his hand toward the bathroom, adding, "If that's possible."

Andrea let go of my arm and spun around, tossing her knife into the sink with a clatter. "This is stupid."

"Please, Andrea," I pleaded, looking away from Xavier to retrieve the knife. "I can do this." I motioned to the bathroom with my head, and she relented. Xavier set down his glass, and much to my surprise, grabbed an empty sack and scooped up bowl fragments.

"Get some more rice ready," I said to Andrea, as though there'd never been a standoff. "I'm going to go wash up."

While Xavier gingerly lifted razor-sharp porcelain fragments off the tile floor, I headed to the half bath near the hostess's den. Some water on my face would make me feel better. I struggled to focus on the task—two hundred servings of sushi. Only the soft warmth of my bed would make this evening all worth it. But try as I might, the images of a howling hungry baby, wrapped in brown and floating in a basket on a broad river, dogged me all the way to the toilet.

Xavier's hostess made her money in the soap business, or so the story went. When the only way to wash your hands came packaged in a bar of soap, local legend says she convinced her husband to buy up all the plastic pump dispensers in the world. "Liquid soap," she told him, "is the future of the industry." The old man had the guts and the money to do it, bought up every pump device on the market, and launched the soft-soap phenomenon. As I suspected, plenty of liquid hand soap waited in the bath.

Her decorations were ultramodern; a freestanding deep brushed-silver sink floated magically above the floor without visible support. A tall gooseneck emerged from the wall above the suspended pot, and a lever at knee level was the only contrivance I found to start the flow. Hands under the long silver spout, I pushed hard with my right knee and cupped my hands, waiting on a stream of blessed wet.

The cool shocked me, more frigid than I'd expected, and I bent over the stainless bowl, immersing my face in water as it swirled below me. I longed for refreshment, and for a clear head.

As the water hit my face, my vision failed for the second time that day. As if I had shoved my face into pitch, my eyes were sealed in an instant. I could feel the water, cold sending shivers down my spine. But the bathroom and its modernity evaporated, replaced by an ebony void.

I gasped, alone in a place I'd never been before, and I spun about, hands extended, groping. Blackness consumed me as I stumbled forward, in hopes I'd find a wall or a door. Wetness dripped from me as I hovered in free space, flailing in the large powder room to touch something firm. Part of me wondered if I'd stepped off a threshold into a dark pit, falling away forever.

"Andrea!" I yelled, panic rising in my throat.

The dense black began to glow in the center of my vision, like a fire burning somewhere deep within it, rising up to meet me. I tripped on a bath rug and stumbled into a wall, sliding down it to the floor. I groped along the cold baseboard, seeking a portal to this cavernous washroom.

The red blaze at the center of my sight grew, like frothy arterial blood that gushed on black velvet. It filled my vision, rivers of life force coursing in front of my eyes. I followed the junction of wall and floor with both hands and began to scoot to the right.

"Andrea!" I screamed again, hoping my voice's volume would wash away the blood in my eyes. The river began to flow, its bright red darkening to a venous purple-black. I saw people standing at the edge of the crimson flow, moaning. Their hands were raised to the sky; their fingers dripped bloodred as they groaned in deep pain. I screamed again and at last heard her reply.

"Kate!"

She's behind me!

I was on my knees and spun about on a loose rug. With my good right hand firm on the floor, I pushed up as I came about, determined to stand and get out of this place. I could hear her running, her shoes clacking on tile, then on the wood of the den floor.

"Andrea!" I yelled again, sure she'd soon reach the door. Following her sound, I pushed upright, my left hand touching what I hoped would be a door handle. I grabbed at it, despite the clumsy bandage, and the lever gave way, the portal swinging in toward me.

There were thousands of people before me, lining the edge of the ochre mental river, their screams and panic now my shriek. Clad only in white, drenched in red, they moaned at the water's edge. Dunes of sand stretched out in the distance behind waves of grieving brown people with dark eyes, their tunics soaked in sticky blood.

"Kate!" I heard Andrea scream, no more than a foot away. I could feel a rush of air in my face.

The door!

Before I could react, the heavy door ripped free from my tenuous grip. The red of the river and the moans of thousands were silenced instantly as something massive smashed into my face. Red transformed into the white blinding flash of a concussion, and I fell back, a taste of blood and its thick wetness on my tongue.

"Kate!" Xavier's voice boomed. I could smell his distinctive cologne pungent on air that rushed in as the door opened. I felt his mass behind the brutal impact with my jaw and forehead as the door cracked into my head. The flash of light in my eyes faded as sharp pain engulfed my teeth and cheek. I fell back on the cold tile, run over by a perfumed charging bull in the black of night.

My last image was of green. Summer in New Jersey, where my parents took us on picnics to the countryside, away from the concrete jungles of New York. Carpets of thick grass lined dark ponds where lilies floated like flat leaf boats on mysterious waters. I recalled my favorite playthings at those ponds—slick green bundles of croaking magic that drizzled on me when I squeezed too hard. I could hear them, their throaty bellows chirping around me now.

In a strange confluence of imagery, the red river swirled before me, the screams of white-robed figures piercing my heart. The slimy creature in my hands at the Jersey pond suddenly multiplied times over and leapt toward the people on the shore. Thousands of the creatures erupted from my hands in an instant. The blood-red river spawned teeming masses of croaking creatures. They overran the river's bank and thousands of white-robed people fell over, suffocated by a wave of slimy green.

Frogs.

CHAPTER SEVEN

"THERE'S NOTHING wrong with her," the doctor said, his voice tinged by the lilt of a native tongue. The young Indian at the hospital was up to his old tricks. He never looked at me when he spoke. Xavier stood above me, pretending to be my protector . . . but I didn't need it.

"I've run a series of scans of her skull. She took a nasty chop on the forehead and jaw when you threw that door open. But fortunately there are no fractures and there's no concussion."

"What about her blood work, Doc?" Xavier asked. "She's been getting dizzy, too. Frequently."

He shrugged, like he saw women every day that fell apart when they washed their faces or rode a racing bike in the rain. "She's not anemic. Blood sugar's normal. Regular lipid profile, far as I can tell."

"But is she *pregnant?*" Xavier demanded, never looking in my direction. I shuddered and closed my eyes.

The doctor paused, and I wish I'd seen his face. My eyes sprang open, and at last he paid attention to me. Somehow, in his silence, I felt he understood my pain. He shook his head, then lowered his eyes to the chart and headed for the door.

"Ms. Pepper has no obvious medical problem that we can find. We can discharge her today, but I recommend bed rest. I sent her home for a week last time." He looked at Xavier at last. "Try to follow doctor's orders this time," he offered as an afterthought, and then walked out of the room.

Xavier stood still, watching as if the physician would return for one last question. Like a master waiting on his dog to return at his command. But no one came. Finally, he turned back to me, where I sat on the bed white-gowned and upright.

"Do you remember any of it?" he asked.

I shrugged.

"I had to call Kyoto," he said with a tone of disgust.

"That's good. What time is it?"

"About eleven. You fell apart around five."

"Fell apart? Is that what you call it?"

He raised a waxed eyebrow in that weird Mr. Spock kind of way and then shrugged. "We found you in the bathroom. You were out."

"I don't remember much, but I do recall thinking that a bull ran through that door."

He nodded but said nothing.

"I want to go home, X." I reached down, checking to see if I still had on my underclothes. Someone had brought me here, dressed me, and cared for me. I'd lost all track of six hours of my life. I put my face in my hands, remembering the moments just before my vision faded the last time.

I don't know why I'd missed it when I looked outside earlier, but when I glanced back at the window, I saw daylight. It wasn't night. The sun was out, near the top of the sky. Time was slipping away without me.

"What time is it again?" I asked. "What day?"

"Monday. Monday at about eleven. You were out all night. Scared us to death."

Days were slipping away. Not just moments.

"I've changed my mind," I said, rotating my shoulders to stretch and work out the kinks. I could feel the pain of the cycle accident more than ever. "I want to stay here. If they'll let me."

"That makes sense," Xavier said as he grabbed a coat off the back of the one chair in the hospital suite. "I'll go arrange it."

"I need to check on something. Can you go to my condo and get my MacBook? Please?" It was the least he could do.

"Sure. Let me work out the hospital thing, then I'll head over. You stay here."

I nodded slowly, watching him, in hopes he'd make eye contact with me. Just once. A nod or a blink my direction. Any sign of recognition, a shred of care or concern. But his gaze locked on to something outside the door, some movement.

White. A skirt. As she passed, his eyes followed her. I slipped out of the bed, my humiliating gown gaping behind me, feet shivering on cold linoleum, before he finally turned and acknowledged my presence.

In that moment, watching his eyes follow the nurse in too-tight-white, I vowed to myself that I would stand on my own. I'd confront this problem—whatever it was—alone.

I could no longer depend on X.

❖ ❖ ❖

I'm seeing things.

I typed those words into the search bar of Google, my laptop laying beside me in the hospital bed. Doctors—at least the young Indians—weren't answering the mail for me. I had to take control of my health care in this place.

"Hallucinations. Delusions. Delirium." I read aloud the major headings of suggested web pages that answered my search.

Great. I must be crazy.

A friend of mine once took too much of a bad drug in college. I remember one particularly crazy night as she ran around the dorm lobby naked, convinced that someone clung to her shoulders. A lunatic meth-head, scratching at her arms, boils breaking out on her face. Somewhere in the back of my mind, I think of her every time I have an itch or think I've seen something. But I've never touched meth.

Hallucinations?

I read aloud again. "Arise from fever, or other illness involving a fever. Also extreme fatigue, dehydration, sleep deprivation, bereavement, depression, narcolepsy, dementia . . ." and a host of things I knew I didn't have. Mania. Migraines. Brain tumor. Kidney failure. Stroke and cataracts. Postpartum depression. That last one certainly wasn't my issue.

Was I seeing things? I had to be. I could still sense the river of red and the robed mourners on a muddy shore, stark against the backdrop of sandy dunes—and the nauseating wave of slimy-green frogs. That mental image chilled me, despite the warmth of the bedroom in the hospital. The pictures in my head were linked inextricably to the sharp stab of a heavy wooden door that slammed into my face. A door that caved in under the impact of Xavier's heavy body.

Somehow, I'd come through a crisis again, unbroken. Unscathed after two serious accidents, my sound body that defied logic and probability. What was it a nurse said, tending me after the bike wreck? "You're blessed." Any other time I would have said I was lucky. But not this time. Maybe the nurse was right, about my body at least. But not my mind.

I propped the laptop on my knees, sitting up in the hospital bed, and surfed in search of an answer, with no idea what that might be. Half a dozen "ask-the-doctor" and "find-a-nurse" websites later, I had all the information I needed. Either I had a serious physical problem, or I stood on the threshold of insanity. I felt fine . . . so the logical choice suggested I'd gone nuts.

"Will that thing tell you what's wrong?"

I looked up at an older man standing in the doorway. Long gray lamb chops extended down the side of a wrinkled face, and reading glasses rode low on his nose. His hair unkempt, and his doctor's smock a little soiled, he was a rumpled old man compared to the starched precision of my youthful Indian resident and his crisp clothes.

"No," I responded. "It hasn't. Not yet." I looked back down. "But my own diagnosis is no less conclusive than what I'm getting from this staff. They're nice people, but no one seems to know what's wrong with me."

He smiled and entered the room, then perched himself on the foot of my bed. It seemed a little bit intimate, but the doctor was sitting at my feet before I could do anything about it. He leaned into me, his hand taking my wrist without so much as a "May I?"

"You're not hot, so I doubt it's a fever. You weren't feverish when you crashed the bike, were you? Sweating? That kind of thing?"

"How do you know about the bike wreck?" I asked. This oddball in a lab coat seemed to know all about me.

"I run this place," he said with a wave and a long laugh. "I'm sorry, I'm Dr. Lin. Chief of Medicine, humble servant of the sick and ailing." He smiled and looked back at his clipboard, but only for a moment. His warmth was hard to miss. The man cared more about me than he did the stupid paper, a sure change from what I'd seen of the other doctors in this place. He scooted closer, taking a gander at my white laptop. My thin gown gaped in all the wrong places.

"You like Macs?" he asked, pulling his stethoscope from his shoulder and leaning toward me again. "May I?" he added, gesturing to my chest. There was no privacy here.

"Why not? If you think you can hear the crazy movie that's been playing in my head, I'm all for it."

A few probes in sensitive places, a few knowing glances and wise utterances like "uh-huh," and an index finger waved in front of my eyes seemed to satisfy him. At least he listened.

"There's another option you might consider," he said, his wide smile a sign that he liked me.

"Another option?" I asked. His eyes locked with mine. His lamb chops and the glasses that rocked on his nose gave him a gentle sort of look, the antithesis of control and coercion. He wasn't here to pry information or decisions out of me; he radiated an "I'm here to help" kind of warmth. A welcome change.

"It's entirely possible you're *not* hallucinating."

I frowned. "You mean I'm crazy?" Maybe this guy was a shrink. No wonder he made me feel at home.

"Nope. Not crazy. But I've seen enough of this kind of disorder here in Seattle, and in this hospital, to tell you with some certainty that you're not alone. Not by a long shot." He lifted the chart and clipboard, adjusting the stethoscope on his neck as he stood and walked toward the door. His smile radiated care, dotted on each end with a strip of gray fur. Just hearing his voice, conversing with him, gave me a sense of peace that everything would be all right, even if I waded in the swamp of the most unusual trial of my life.

"I'm not alone?" I asked, suddenly aware of what he'd just said.

The doctor stopped at the doorway, leaning into the frame in a natural pose. I could see his stitched name now that he stood erect, a ragged blue of tattered thread that had been washed a hundred times too many.

Dr. Lin, Chief of Medicine.

"Correct. You're not alone. Not in this rainy city. I've seen your condition a dozen times in the last twenty years. But now's not the time for me to talk to you. You're not ready to hear what I have to say. Not just yet."

"Try me. Please. Don't walk out on me now!" I had to know, but he shook his head.

"Nope. You rest up." He turned and walked into the hall as I cried out, despair launching a deep cry that surprised even me.

"Please!"

He stopped.

"Give me some hope. Tell me I'm sick and not going nuts!"

Dr. Lin's hand caught the doorjamb and he spun around, that furry smile wrinkling layers of well-smiled skin. A strange peace radiated from him.

"Answer the phone, Kate," he said, his smile infectious. "Someone's trying to give you a call. Sort of like Captain Kirk getting an incoming transmission on the bridge of the starship *Enterprise*. But it's not Kirk. It's someone far more important."

"What?"

"I told you that you weren't ready to hear this. But you will be. In a few weeks, if my guess is right. You'll call me, at your wits' end, and tell me in tears that you're open to any option. Happens that way each time." He winked with a strange half smile—half frown. His brown eyes locked with mine, while waiting for me to take the next step.

My doctor is rude, and his hospital boss has flipped. There's no hope for me here.

"You think I'm crazy." He said it with a matter-of-fact tone, like he could read my mind. "I hear it all the time, Kate. You certainly won't be the first." He turned into the corridor; somewhere under that rumpled doctor coat and comfortable exterior lurked Santa Claus.

"Answer the call, Kate. It's collect, but someone you need to know is trying to reach you. Only you can accept the charges, and you'll be glad you did."

✦ ✦ ✦

"We missed you, Kate," Hiram said as he opened the door to ISIP four days later. At six on a Friday morning, I'd be his first and only customer. That's the way I wanted it.

"Bed rest," I said, not anxious to get into a prolonged conversation. Sunday's face-smashing episode—followed by Monday's hospital stay and the bed rest Tuesday through Thursday—had separated me too long from Hiram's coffee. Folgers in a can and cups of hospital Starbucks didn't do it for me. I wanted something exotic this morning, something distinctly African. I needed my import jolt.

"Been sick?" he asked as he pointed to the familiar "funt" table. It was too early for Candice, so I was on my own. Fine by me.

"Maybe. We're not sure. Wrecked the bike—I guess you heard about that."

"Yeah. Bet it hurts. To lose the bike, I mean."

"It does. I feel like I lost my right arm. It was a part of me, you know?"

"I've walked that path. I'm that way about my bike, too," Hiram said with a furry smile. "My bicycle, that is. I love it."

I imagined my brown hairy friend, whiskers whipping in the breeze as he pedaled away. He stood there, waiting for me to finish, like he too could read minds.

"Then, last Sunday, I fainted again. Like I did here. I've been thinking, Hiram—"

"That's dangerous."

"Maybe. So here's the deal. I only faint when I've had your coffee in the past twenty-four hours. Is there something in your roast that you're not telling us about?"

He stopped midstride and turned, a hand to his chin in thought. "Sorry to hear that, Kate. But no. Ever since the jail time, I've stopped doping the beans." His brief smile faded. "Seriously, we've been worried about you. So, sit tight. I'll be right back." He turned toward the kitchen and jogged away. I could hear him yelling at me from the kitchen just moments later. "Your usual will be ready in five minutes!"

"Don't want 'usual,'" I yelled back. "Need something exotic. Rwanda maybe."

"Got it. Back in ten."

ISIP served up the rocket ride of wireless providers, and at this time of morning, with no other customers, I had the rocket to myself. I read once that the new world—the flat world of globalized Internet commerce, free video downloads, free book downloads, free music downloads, and free Wi-Fi—was the model of things to come. It amazed me what I could find in such a short amount of time, sitting at the "funt" and cruising around the world on a borrowed laptop. This last day of designated bed rest would be spent on my time. No office. Just ISIP in the morning, five hours or more of research into these stupid fainting spells. And all afternoon at the spa.

Internet. Coffee. Massage. In that order, and lots of each today.

+ + +

"You've been at this since six this morning. It's time for lunch. Hungry yet?" Hiram asked. He waved at his wife in the kitchen, sharing one of their private codes for orders. Sometimes I wondered if she could read his mind.

I rested my chin on my hands, elbows propped on the table. "May as well," I responded without much emotion. "Nothing to show for all this." I waved at the laptop screen.

Hallucinations?

I needed a fever, or drugs, or some severe problem like chronic fatigue to hallucinate. I'd prefer one of those problems. Everything else screamed "cuckoo."

Dementia? Delirium?

I had to be old or going nuts for those, and I wanted to believe I was neither.

I dreaded the last option. Not crazy or sick, but somehow I was becoming my mother, the "seer." An oracle like I lived with for seventeen years at home, every day punctuated with my Italian-American mom's latest spiritual insight, every breakfast tedium another blow-by-blow replay of her latest dream. One of my girlfriends had a mom who swore she saw blood running from the wounds of Jesus on the crucifix in the church sacristy. Her mom had nothing on mine. Every day revealed some new spiritual handiwork in my mother's life through the magic of her vivid imagination. I'd rather be sick, or insane, than be her.

"Three cheese, grilled, on the way." Hiram tarried at the table. "Not finding something you need?" he asked. I knew his tone, his "information technology consultant" role. Poor Hiram couldn't keep his hands off computers. "Can I help?" he asked as he peered over my shoulder.

I shook my head but wished it were possible. Deep inside I desperately wanted—*needed*—his help. But for now, I liked just having him here, asking me questions. He cared what I had to say, which was more than could be said for the doctor . . . or for Xavier.

"The doctor says I'm not sick. But I've fainted four or five times, nearly killed myself on the Ice Rocket, and I have these incredible dreams. I mean really vivid walking-in-a-rainbow-and-touching-it sort of dreams."

I waved at the laptop, and then slammed it shut. "I'm crazy—the only conclusion I can reach with the available data—or I'm sick and hallucinating, yet the doctor says I'm just fine." I drained the last of my fourth cup of the Rwanda special, with no idea what he called it.

"Are you just Googling stuff?" he asked, fingers lingering on my computer, anxious to learn more.

"Yes. Got a better idea?"

"Mmm-hmm," he said with a strange smile. The beard turned up on the ends and seemed to make a halo around his face with his long matted hair. "I still have a few tricks up my sleeve."

Hiram was like this—a human Rubik's Cube taunting you to solve him. He waited, eyes locked with mine. He wanted to be asked.

"Okay, Hiram. I'm onto your game," I said with a shrug. "Help me. Please."

His teeth flashed as he smiled, blinding white orthodontic perfection. "Great! We'll do a latent semantic index search. That'll help us narrow some things down."

"Excuse me?"

"LSI. It's the latest thing to read any kind of text input and find the common denominators, the core themes. Folks discover amazing things with it. We'll put in all your symptoms and let the system mine through the net for a few days looking for common threads. That'll show us every connection that's out there." He watched me closely. "Get me a file with all your problems, all your symptoms—"

I shook my head, pushing back from the "funt." "No can do, Hiram. It's too personal."

"Do you want to get well?" he asked with a wry twist of the beard and his mouth.

I nodded. He had me.

"Then write it down, Kate. At least do it for your sake. It'll be cathartic." He started to walk away, then faced me again and finished his thought. "If you change your mind, bring the document to me. I can tell you all the common themes of your disease, even connect it to standard diagnoses. Who knows? Maybe you're not sick. Maybe it's a message or something. Perhaps you're fainting and seeing things so that someone can get your attention." He shrugged and turned away, talking over his shoulder as he reached the kitchen. "Stranger things have happened!"

That did it. More talk about "someone" trying to reach me through a spiritual telephone. I tossed the laptop in my shoulder bag. "Whatever," I huffed.

The moment that horrible word slipped my lips, I froze in place, one leg off the tall chair and my bottom halfway out of the seat.

This can't be! I'm talking like my father, and I'm crazy like my mother. The Irish couch potato and his Catholic prophetess.

I slid off the chair and dashed out of the shop without even saying good-bye. Hiram probably never noticed I'd left until he returned
with the lunch. Five blocks south, headed to downtown on foot, I
realized I'd stuck him with the coffee bill and the grilled cheese.

It didn't matter. I had to get away. Somehow, my parents had
found me, yet they weren't even here—the worst of outcomes. I was
fast becoming my visionary mother, and had expressed my most
hated word—"whatever"—the nauseating watchword of my emotionally absent and slothful father.

I ran.

CHAPTER EIGHT

THREE DAYS LATER.

TAXICABS ARE portable toilets on wheels, filthy mobile germ pits that consume and disgorge humans like a disease vector. That's Xavier's view of it: Seattle's gasoline-powered mosquitoes and rats, spreading infection with raunchy seat covers, virus-laden handles, and tobacco-tainted air.

Frankly, I enjoy their convenience—like a portable toilet; when you need one, you're glad you've got it.

A taxicab was my only form of conveyance. After the Ice Rocket was totaled, slamming into a rock wall at a mile a minute, it would be a long time before I went on two wheels again. If ever. I stopped the cab a block before Consolidated Aerodyne, just in case Xavier might be watching. He'd delouse me and demand that I bathe in bleach if he ever found me in the clutches of a cabby.

"Welcome back, Kate," someone said from across the lobby as I walked into the main reception area early on Monday. The place seemed so shiny, so new. I realized I'd not entered by the front door in so long that I barely recognized my own company. Was my memory fading, too? I couldn't identify the receptionist as she approached me.

"What are you doing back so soon?" she said, gushing with the energy of a hyperactive Wal-Mart greeter. No wonder they gave her this job.

"Back to work. Why else?" I looked around. I didn't recall any of it, but the logo over the desk *did* say Consolidated Aerodyne. I shrugged, forced a smile, and dashed into an elevator that threatened to close. I raised my hand in a little wave. "Bye!"

The reaction to my arrival repeated itself on the fifth floor, a location I did know. What had Xavier told them? I might have been at home, but I didn't die. Andrea met me halfway down the hall, skipping across the carpet like her best friend forever had just returned from the hinterlands.

No hugs, please. She read my mind and spared me that pain.

"Thought you were out again today," she said, casting a glance over her shoulder. Justus trolled a few paces behind her. Nothing had changed.

"This is my world, Andrea. It's where I belong." I kept walking, and she matched my stride. "The doctor said one week bed rest. One week, not two."

Andrea lowered her voice. "Xavier's pretty wound up, girlfriend. Better watch out," she warned, nodding in the direction of the corner office. "He asked about you this morning, and we told him you were still at home." She pulled me back, leaned near me, and whispered. "Just watch your step."

Andrea served as the aural version of flypaper. If news buzzed, she caught wind of it and it stuck. I could depend on her intuition when bad vibes ran strong in the front office. On occasions like today, when trouble threatened, she forged ahead into the wilderness of Xavier, my ever-dependable scout. I'd keep my eyes open.

Again, something inside, like a little alarm clock going off told me I had reason to be concerned. That mental alarm warbled away that a product or presentation might be due. My "inner voice"— what Mother used to call it—always got it right. I couldn't shake the feeling of something amiss as I set up my laptop and went about the business of the day.

Xavier ruined it all, just as the memory of the forgotten task hit me. I wished, at that moment, I was lying in the bed back in the hospital.

"Where have you been?" the familiar voice asked in the gruff tone that I knew meant business. You'd think he'd forgotten every curve in my body at times like this, so easily did he shut off intimacy and transform into my boss.

"I spent the last week at home, Xavier. Doctor's orders. But you knew that." I tried not to look up, afraid my eyes might give me away. I could feel the hot wetness of an uncontrolled tear. He'd not set foot in my condo since he drove me to the failed sushi dinner a week ago Sunday . . . and that hurt.

" 'Bout time you're back. Who's got the nine o'clock pitch with Boeing?" he asked.

I shrugged, my head down, pretending to fiddle with some problem while docking my computer. "I'm ready." I lied. "You'll love it."

Xavier's scalpels sliced across his watch's face, splitting seconds. "I'd better. The Boeing deal is too big to lose over some stupid head problem."

I stood up to confront that comment, but he left my office as he said it. Andrea calls that kind of appearance a "drive-by shooting." Drop in, discharge the verbal weapon, and run. My head pounded and I felt red flushing my cheeks. I took a deep breath to slow my heart, ready to scream, but the boss escaped. I slammed the door, glancing at my watch. I had fifty minutes.

A couple of heartbeats later a gentle knock at the door announced Andrea, who poked her head in and waved a sheet of paper. "Go away," it read, our solution to drive-by shootings and office gossips. She winked, pasted the sheet on my door, and closed it. I had forty-nine minutes left.

If Boeing was an animal, it might be a dinosaur. The huge ones with the long necks and monstrous bodies that move with glacial slowness. Their managers thrive on long presentations, mountains of words, and armies of bloated process teams. I had forty-eight minutes to build something that would impress them. That would be hard to do. I was too direct.

Acid rose in my throat, and my stomach roiled as I booted the computer. A gut-busting nausea and burning throat wrapped up in one, my classic reaction to stress. Anyone else would call it panic. I plowed into my keyboard with a vengeance, sweat beading on my face as I clicked "dismiss" on my daily task and meeting reminders. No time for e-mail, for staff meetings, or for the Consolidated Aerodyne "word of the day." At the precipice of crunch time, I had to show Xavier my worth.

I would stand alone. Independent. And I'd win.

◆ ◆ ◆

"I'm going out, Andrea," I said four hours later. "A long lunch."

"Thigh and calf massage, or just a shoulder quickie?" she asked with a laugh. "You earned a full body job today, by the way."

I smiled. She was right. Xavier had stood speechless, Boeing had departed here thrilled, and before he could ask how I'd wowed them, I slipped out for a well-deserved break. Another one of my guilty pleasures, reserved for special occasions. Like today. Even if it was just a Monday.

"Shoulders," I replied, tossing a copy of my presentation on her desk when I walked out. "I'd probably sleep all afternoon if they gave me the full body works." Today, with the aerospace dinosaur vanquished, I intended to play. Play a lot.

There's something about panic that brings out the best in me. Some people work best when they have a long time to prepare, with days and weeks to think through a problem, to form and critique a solution. I can honestly say that working under pressure is one skill and personality quirk that did not come from my parents. Dr.

Cook had brought it out in me. He used to say, "I've done so much for so long with so little, I can do everything forever with nothing." It became his preamble to the impossible request of the day, the passionate demand that we needed a new program or web interface or graphics design completed for a customer that very minute. In the web-centric "dot-com" world of Sunnyvale in which we lived at the time, we probably did need it that fast. And I always delivered.

Give me too much time and I flounder. I try thirty different paths and have a hard time deciding which to follow. When there's no deadline—and I mean DEADline: a challenge that will kill someone or cost me my job—then it's almost impossible for me to focus. But put my neck in a noose, threaten my job, or put millions of dollars on the line and measure success in seconds . . . then, I can work magic. I'm the best there is under pressure. Today, with forty-eight minutes to go and tens of millions of revenue on the line, I'd found instant clarity. Boeing discovered, in that same clarity, a vision for their new v-mail-enhanced seat-back designs. Three hours of discussion later, we were on the road to a sole-source forty-million-dollar contract. My focused panic won us about a million dollars a minute. At this point, everything else at the office could wait, paling in comparison to this win.

Now I could recharge.

◆ ◆ ◆

"Kate?"

Xavier's gruff tone—his raw "how dare you" voice—set off my mental alarm. My muscles tensed and I looked up from the coffee shop table that afternoon.

Xavier's little worm was up to its old tricks, his temples leaping in a fit of vibrating arteries. His face and scalp shone red and wet—mad with sweat. Not the kind of perspiration you get in a workout, cascading off in rivulets while on the exercise bike or the spa treadmill. This was furious sweat, explosive beads that squirted out of their pores and hung in place like giant salty pimples. Gramps used to say that people at the point of a meltdown could squeeze body juices out of their pores from the stress. Xavier was near "critical mass," and I backed up, just in case he took a nuclear swing at me. He'd tried that once before.

"What are you doing here?" he asked with a clenched, twitching jaw, the little globules of perspiration swelling at each pore of his bald pate, none of them yet on the run.

I wanted to laugh. I was drinking coffee at ISIP late on a Monday afternoon. People go to coffeehouses to drink coffee, and this was Seattle, after all. Coffee capital of America. The I'm-thrilled-with-the-Boeing-deal Xavier had been hideously transformed. Laughing at his ridiculous question would only inflame him more.

"I'm celebrating, I guess," I said, hoisting a glass of a special roast from the mountains of New Zealand. A new taste for me.

"Celebrating what?" he asked. "Your stupidity?"

How to respond?

I looked down at my watch on impulse. Had I missed something? Was I dreaming again, slipping into one of those dreaded hallucinations that the web doctor said came from excessive stress or drug overdose? I grabbed the coffee cup, staring at the dregs of my New Zealand caffeine experience. Maybe it was the coffee, not hallucinations. Every cup seemed to be followed by some disaster.

"I'm sorry, Xavier. I—"

"Shut up. Don't apologize. The damage is done, and there's nothing you or I can do to repair it at this point." He spun about and stomped toward the door without an explanation.

Clueless, I jumped up, leaving laptop and coffee at the table, and ran him down at the door. I grabbed at his black overcoat, but he shrugged me off, his powerful frame quivering beneath thick wool material. Xavier shed people like a grizzly shaking water off when he stood on the verge of "killing mad," ready to tear a person's head off. He could do it. Fortunately, he kept walking. I followed him into the cold afternoon air.

"Answer me," I yelled. "What have I done?" I struggled to come to grips with whether this moment was another of my crazy-woman mental disasters. As the last words slipped my lips, he turned on me and pinned my arms against my side. His hands were vise grips on my upper arms, and I tensed, ready for the backslap, the hard bony hand across my face I'd suffered before. Anger surged, shoving my doubt aside. If he dared hit me tonight, in public, I'd jam a knee into his groin. He'd remember that for a long time.

"The Japanese?" he screamed. "Their special invitation to Consolidated Aerodyne? Does that ring a bell with you?" His eyes bulged and flecks of spittle struck me in the face. White froth lined his quivering lips.

"They're here tomorrow. I'm ready. What about it?" My heart pounded as I said it. Something didn't add up. I shook my head, trying to knock out the cobwebs as I raced through mental math. He barked the answer as fast as it came to mind.

"Tomorrow in Japan is today, Kate!" Xavier yelled as he pushed me away with enough force to knock me down. I grabbed at a stair rail and kept my balance, but couldn't look him in the eye. I'd blown it through gross stupidity; they had arrived a day before they left, one of those disconcerting truths of travel across the International Date Line.

"You set it up. You invited them," he screamed with no concern for the patrons arriving at the shop. I didn't care either at this point.

"We paid their way, arranged all the events, and their itinerary started with you. Today. Remember? We talked about it at staff meeting before your accident. You said you were ready—"

"I said I *would* be ready—" I objected, trying to salvage some self-respect. I had my days mixed up. It could have happened to anyone. Especially after this past week.

"But you weren't! They came, all six of them, ready for 'Kyoto Kate.' They have a nickname for you, for crying out loud." He ran his hands over a sweat-laden bald head, slinging his arms down into balled fists. I backed up the stairs two risers—just in case.

Realization fell like lead rain, washing my anger away. "X. I am so sorry. I . . . I just lost track. It was dumb—I don't know how." I fished my phone out of my pocket. It had been with me all day, and there was the dreaded news. A dozen missed calls, all from the office. Silenced since I'd entered the Boeing meeting. My heart fell into my shoes and oozed onto the sidewalk.

He put up a hand, half turned as he walked toward his Mercedes. "Don't! Don't apologize; don't make excuses. I don't want to hear about your stupid visions, your sickness, your bike, or your head. I don't care about any of it. I want the old Kate, the on-time-works-her-butt-off-Spiderwoman-sushi-cooking-webmaster-motorbike-riding super-Kate." He slammed his palms against his temples. "*That's* the woman I want."

He spun in a complete circle, shaking his fists at a leaden Seattle sky. I could smell the rain on the way. "Who are you, anyway?" he screamed. "*What* are you?"

"X. I need to—"

"No! Don't start. I don't care, remember? You have no idea how much I don't care. I depended on you, even consulted you when the schedule changed and asked how it would impact your bed rest. I gave this to you to win, and you blew it."

"They'll understand—"

"What?" he fumed. "Understand? Yeah. They get it. You stood them up. They're furious. They flew ten hours to come see you, and you were nowhere to be found." He pointed to my left with a bony finger that punctuated the now misty air.

"Know where they are now? Headed that way. To SEATAC. They'll be on the first flight back home to Tokyo. At our expense. *Your* expense!"

"No—"

"Oh, yes. Gone for good. The offense of being stood up runs deep with these people. Go find a sword and sacrifice yourself. It's the honorable thing to do at this point." He stomped toward the car, sweat and the first drops of rain glistening on his shaved dome.

No words would do. Nothing I could say would help. I remembered too late his talk with me in the hospital. I'd been completely consumed with the MRI and diagnosis. Bad timing . . . and I'd forgotten to tell Andrea to put the event in my Outlook. It was a bigger opportunity than the Boeing deal. And, from the sound of it—an opportunity lost.

Xavier opened his car door as rain started to fall in earnest. He looked up briefly, and then back at me with a glare that would have melted any Ice Slice I could throw. "Don't apologize, Kate. Go fix this. Get them back any way you have to. Get on your knees . . . or do it on your back, for all I care. I must have this win." He paused, staring me down. I'd become a statue.

"It's yours to lose, and I don't do losers."

+ + +

Rain fell as Xavier drove away from ISIP. Misty drizzle became drops. The cool of mist became a damp cold, sinking clammy fingers into my business suit. Drips of rain ran down my hair, soggy in the Seattle dew, now frizzing in the wet. I'd find any excuse to stand in the rain, my favorite shower, on any day but this. Not feeling luxurious seemed fair at this point. Completely at fault and deserving of nothing, I sank lower than the sidewalk.

Spatters of rain bounced off the street ahead of me. Dimly aware of the water, I sought out the phone in my jacket pocket. How could I have forgotten to turn the ringer back on, have missed so many calls, the desperate pleas from Andrea to come in and stave off impending doom?

Poor Andrea. I'd promised her it would be a short massage trip; I'd promised I'd be back soon—and I'd lied. I took the works, the full-body massage. I went Roman all afternoon, in celebration of the Boeing win. I deserved it, I told myself. The phone waited, its desperate messages queuing up in my spa locker while I played hooky.

From spa to ISIP for a caffeine jolt before heading back to the office for a late night of e-mail catch-up free of the interruptions by well-wishers who were glad I'd returned in good health. I thought it brilliant, skipping the chitchat of people with too little to do, a night of mining e-mail, and all caught up before Tuesday, when the Japanese arrived. Until this. My deadly one-day miscalculation.

Drips of rain ran off my hair and dripped down my neck, ticklish trickles of cold that sent shivers down my spine. My focus slipped; my incredible self-loathing was replaced by some odd mental image of a jar. Water overflowing in jars. I shook my head, determined to get back in the game, to hate myself for what I'd just done to Xavier and to my clients. Hate myself for the damage to my reputation and my job.

The imagery wrapped me in its shroud. I saw jars of water carried by women in robes, scurrying into little mud huts. I saw gray bricks and dimly lit rooms, food preparation and densely-packed people. I could smell them.

"No!" I screamed aloud, running my hands through wet hair as the rain began to pelt. My suit would shrivel in this downpour, but I didn't care. I deserved it.

"Focus, Pepper!" I screamed at the night. "You messed up. No more daydreams!" I yanked at my hair, milking cool rivulets from each hank.

Red! I saw red splashing in ugly swaths from bloody reeds that were sloshed against some kind of wall. Water washing feet and hands. Water for making meals. People singing and eating simple, bitter food.

"No! Not again!" I yelled. "Leave me alone! I want my head back."

I jerked at my hair again, squeezing out more sky juice as the flash of red engulfed me. I stood still, sure I'd fall over in this rush of color that sought to sweep me off my feet. More water, more jugs, more sounds like moans and screams. Women ripping at their clothes. Men wild with rage.

I turned and ran.

"*Kate?*"

A voice came to me in the midst of the red, a cool voice like the burble of water cascading from the stone flasks of my daydream. A Voice calling my name. I followed the sound, blinded by rage and this nightmare. I stumbled and fell, a thin cold handrail jamming itself under my right armpit as I tripped.

"Kate!" the voice said again. Hiram grabbed me under my left arm, throwing something big and warm over my head. He pulled me up, his thin muscular arms strong but not quivering like the furious ones that had shoved me away only moments earlier.

"You're soaked!" he exclaimed, pulling me to him. He smothered me in a warm cover, thick like a huge beach towel. I rubbed my hair instinctively, vigorously scrubbing to dislodge the mental pictures of water flasks, the screams of unknown bodies, and the slop of single red strokes on something like doorjambs. I rubbed harder. The more I rubbed, the clearer my vision became. Hiram pulled me into the coffee shop.

Candice waited inside, another towel in hand. Her face radiated a strange mixture of empathy and glee, as though she was terribly glad to see me—and in great pain to see me so wet. I began to understand in that moment that Candice possessed some kind of "human X-ray vision," the penetrating purity of a simple heart that allowed her to feel my deep hurt. It was like she knew me, could see deep within me. What hurt me also hurt her. It wounded her somehow to sense the pain that ripped away at my insides. The rage and the mad blackness inside me scared her. Candice recoiled as she handed me another towel.

I shivered, aware in that moment how much I needed help. My head was a mess. I'd botched a ten-million-dollar consulting deal with some arrogant Japanese traditionalists, and I'd let my boss down. A week ago, I would have called him "boyfriend." I might have even hoped one day to say "fiancée." That bond was severed for good.

I couldn't focus, so caught up in my failure that I'd begun to see things again. I took Candice's towel and wiped my face, then wrapped it around my shoulders. Hiram's hand lingered on my arm, and I brushed it off. I needed to be alone, to go home.

"Can I call you a cab?" he asked, his voice loaded with the same empathy I'd observed in Candice. Who were these people with eyes that saw pain? I couldn't describe why, but I knew we were connected. Struggling to understand, I nodded to Hiram. Yes. A cab would be good, and I sank into the chair he pushed toward me. My eyes didn't leave Candice.

"Blue is your color," Mother told me once. She'd taken some class at the YMCA on colors and women and something spiritual. I can't remember much more than that. But I do remember her pronouncement. "You are water blue. Aqua. Light and delicate." I thought she'd gone over the edge again. Certifiably nuts.

Before me, Candice knelt quietly in front of my soaking-wet form, a frumpy pillar of blue. A dingy blue polo shirt with the ISIP logo and vestiges of someone's coffee staining the linings of her shirt pocket. Blue, like me. But not me.

She reached up, placing a pudgy hand on my wet knee, her eyes staring at her hand as if the sensation was one she'd never experienced. It was a warm hand, electric. I could feel her heart beat in her palm like the thrum of a hummingbird.

Scared.

It occurred to me that I'd never actually taken her hand on purpose, never connected in a personal way. I'd spent months, maybe years knowing this person, but never touching. No skin to skin, no connection. Her warmth flooded me as her hand rested on my wetness. After what seemed minutes, she looked up, her eyes glistening. She reached and took the tail of my towel in her hand, dabbing carefully at my soaked blouse. Anyone else doing that would have earned a slap. But her simple spirit and her mothering care gripped me in a way I can't completely describe. I wanted to be wiped and dried by her. She dabbed in silence for several moments and then smiled, eyes brimming. She spoke for the first time since Hiram had hauled me in from the rain.

"It's okay, Miss Kate. Jesus can make you clean."

CHAPTER NINE

FOUR-THIRTY in the morning—my alarm belted out its screechy bark like Rocco, the neighbor's obnoxious bull terrier. I hated that stupid dog, the same way I felt about my alarm clock, Rocco's digital counterpart.

I forced myself out of bed, feeling every minute of my hour of lost sleep, brutally sacrificed at the altar of preparation. No palatial tours of dreamland this morning. After yesterday . . . the missed meeting and the fight with X, I was determined to make today as flawless as it could be. I'd find the old super-Kate and bring her back to life.

Did I really want the old Kate back? How about a new woman instead?

I rubbed sleep from the corners of my eyes.

Get a grip, girl.

Minutes later, teeth freshly flossed and electric toothbrush buzzing, I stepped out of the bathroom, ticking off a mental checklist of the items on my glass-and-chrome-plated desk in the bedroom. I had triple-checked my schedule and phone the night before; I wasn't about to make the same gaffe twice.

My work laptop, complete with all of the presentations, winked blue LEDs, ready to roll. My iPhone lay tethered on the desk, powered up and ready for action. And my tiny crocodile tote beckoned, its gold-rimmed jaws propped open. Not a proper purse, only large enough for the phone, some keys, and a few sundries, but supple as butter. It fit the bill.

Back in the bathroom, I stared at my reflection in the mirror. There stood "old Kate"—the "super–Kate" whom Xavier missed—a woman in control, focused on what she needed and wanted, with the world by the tail. But somewhere deep inside lurked a "new Kate," a mental midget who forgot things—important things—and suffered screaming matches with her boyfriend-boss. A softy who cared what other people thought about her. A psychotic who saw things.

I couldn't deny the mental imagery. The rainbow of colors that flashed before my eyes on the Ice Rocket. Pregnancy had nothing to do with it. Home tests and blood tests confirmed that the problem lay elsewhere. In fact, the docs made a big deal over the fact I was a miracle case, in far better shape than I deserved . . . flying off the back of a racing bike, and suffering a facial beating from a swinging door.

But I couldn't deny the reeds in the river, and the frogs, and the blood. The jars of water, the red swaths above crude doors. Those were real—at least as genuine as my mind would allow. The mirror reflected the real me. Green eyes bored back into themselves—hard.

Beside me, my cell chirped. Five a.m.. Time for a shower and a taxi ride to work, then drown the dread of my mental fragility in a frothing sea of self-pity.

My precious bike is trashed, I lost a huge business deal, and I'm crazy.

+ + +

"Temperature one hundred and ten," my computerized shower stated in its programmable British voice. The pronouncement brought me out of the funk, heralding the opportunity to indulge in my morning baptism of wet heat. I hung a plush white terrycloth towel on the chrome bar outside the plate-glass door and stepped into billowy steam.

I didn't have time to fully close the glass behind me.

No time to scream.

The moment I touched the hot stream, I fell.

The world roared bright and wet like a brilliant waterfall. I felt the warmth of morning sunshine, saw clouds, sensed wind and mist and something that looked like the whitecaps on a river, or foam atop waves. Everything stood askew, all at the wrong angle; the waves ran vertical, not horizontal. I tumbled, disoriented, but I could make out what might be a horizon, tinged with smoldering fires. As I got my sense of "up," I realized that someone had turned the ocean on its side and poured it onto rocky ground.

I fell, a plain of bare earth dotted with smooth rocks rushing up to greet me. I screamed but no sound emerged as I slammed against rocks and flowed over them, caught up in a massive wave of froth, bubbles, and rushing chaos. For another long moment, everything went dark and I had no sense of up or down, right or left. I spun out of control, wobbling toward some kind of wet doom.

I raced faster than I could ever go on the Ice Rocket, consumed by a thrumming power that surrounded me, as though a million horses forced me forward and I'd become nothing more than breath from their heaving nostrils. All around me flowed watery darkness, the sort of bluish-green I remembered from diving classes off the coast of Monterey. I leapt over boulders and raced across bare sand faster than I believed possible.

Before me lay my quarry. Thousands of insignificant forms stumbled feebly before my fury. Something deep inside drove me toward them; I could taste their end as death splayed out before me in a blast of misty spray and hoarse throaty screams. I slammed into their backs and swept them away in the ferocity of my flood fury. They ceased to exist, weak human forms disintegrating before my frothing jaws.

A gyre of drowning carnage lay beneath me. I could see them for the first time, frail things. Dark-skinned men with terror etched across suffocating faces. Horses chained to chariots struggled against my raw power, harnessed to blasted pieces of splintered iron, wood, and gold in a maelstrom of wet destruction. I raced toward little men garbed in dirty white tunics, my watery hands ripping them in half. Men with painted eyes were torn in two, churning in a wet cloud of red, screams bursting forth from their mouths in blood-tinged bubbles.

The whites of each man's eyes stood in stark contrast to the black lines painted around them. Each thrashed and gurgled as I consumed him. Time and again, I punched through a mask of crimson bubbles and rammed myself into a gaping mouth. My watery body shuddered as I drove deep into the heaving lungs of little brown-skinned men.

I fell. My back slapped against the cold white tile of the shower and I screamed, clawing at slick walls for some grip, for a brittle hold on reality. The vision fled, but as I was immersed in the hot shower stream my next heartbeat birthed yet another nightmare.

Bright, piercing sunlight from a noonday sun shone through me. A shadow, cast by dusty hands and a bearded face, fell across me, blocking the warming sun. A man dipped his hands deep inside me, his filth rinsed away by my cool darkness. A portion of me taken away, he drew me into himself, his eyes suddenly growing wide with my hidden surprise. He spat back into me and cried an unintelligible word to someone whom I could not see. The hairy shadow departed, and I again enjoyed the sun's full stare, rejoicing in its renewed warmth upon my liquid skin.

A hand and arms appeared overtop me a second time, draped with a threadbare cloth, much like the sleeve of a robe. I could tell that this hand was far different than the dusty hands and shadowy face from before. This hand was steady and full of fervor, its strength apparent in calloused fingers. Those fingers held a large stick above me. The figure spoke a single word and the hand dropped the wood onto me. It slapped my surface with a loud smack.

I smashed into the partially opened glass door of the shower stall. My head reeled from the vision; searing pain clawed into my body through every pore. Somehow, I knew that the door to the shower wasn't fully closed. Disaster loomed, and over my own jagged wails, I heard it.

The plate glass cracked.

Light scattered across a thousand slivers. A shower of glass shards sliced into naked flesh. I gagged, my cry aborted before it could achieve life. I caught a glimpse of my wet body refracted in the mirrored walls of my bathroom. In a garish blend of fun house and slaughter house, I saw the reflection of feeble fingers snatching onto terrycloth towel.

The fingers were mine.

My blood splattered across a pale tile floor, and I heard the whoosh of air as it fled my lungs. My back slammed hard against the tile, but my right foot remained hooked on the sill of the shower. Pain had its way with my body, and I tried to scream but my mouth just opened and closed. Water spritzed my foot from the hot shower, and the electric arcs of yet another vision sparked inside my mental eye.

All around me, darkness—yet I sensed movement. I felt like a cork bobbing on the surface of a raging sea. No, not on the surface. I went down, plummeting into frothing blackness with a dwindling lifeline of bubbles leading my eyes up to the shadowy footprint of a boat on the surface. I turned my head, peering down. The bulk of something huge vanished below me into the abyss.

Panic rose from somewhere deep inside.

A huge maw, no other word for it—a mouth as big as a car—headed my way. It intended to consume me, to swallow me whole. The whitish line of the mouth closed and my world went black again. My insides rumbled as the thing that had eaten me let go a throaty, gushing growl. My whole world trembled.

My eyes flicked to the left. Six inches from my face lay my iPhone.

I lay shivering on the floor of my bathroom in a pool of watery blood and shattered glass. My terrycloth towel, stained with splotches of pink and red, was gathered feebly beneath my head.

The display on my cell flashed "14 missed messages," and it started to walk, vibrating on the floor with yet another incoming call. Someone wanted me bad.

It was nine a.m.

CHAPTER TEN

LYING ON the floor, I reached for the phone out of reflex. Other than 911 or Andrea, there was no one I could call for help. That says a lot—and none of it good.

"He-hello?" I replied, my voice cracking. Terrified, I'd just come a wrist-slice from death, falling through a glass shower door in my worst hallucination yet.

Xavier's harsh voice—his argument voice—launched a string of profanities that made my ears ring. He never bothered to ask about me.

"Kate, I'm outside the conference room hanging in the wind! Again."

"Wha . . .?" I mumbled.

"The Ellsworth meeting, stupid. You're fifteen minutes late. I've got no briefings, no strategy, and no idea what to talk to our clients about. Did you just wake up? Did you—"

I hung up, tears stinging my eyes. Lying in a pool of blood, my sanity on the fritz, I was in no mood for his whining.

I'd rather bleed to death than ask Xavier for help. I'd do this on my own.

✦ ✦ ✦

Three and a half hours later, I'd managed to pluck the glass shards out of my skin and bandage dozens of small, shallow cuts. Thankfully, the terrycloth towel beneath me had spared me a worse fate. Doctored up, I slipped into some clothes and called a cab. I tried to congratulate myself on getting dressed, my "big accomplishment." I finally made it to the street.

Two weeks ago, my major event of the day would be landing a multimillion-dollar account, or breaking new ground with the insertion of a new media application into a previously untapped market. Now, it felt great to simply be alive. I looked like the loser in a Jersey knife fight.

The mental image of a knife conjured up impressions of Xavier, which did little to strengthen my grip on reality. How could he not even ask what was wrong? And so carelessly dismiss me over a meeting? Almost four hours later and he'd not even called to check on me or see how I fared. Clients always came first.

In anger and despair, I punched the power button on the phone and slid the power bar to "off." If X couldn't find the time to call me back by now, he'd just lost the opportunity. I blew a stray hair from the corner of my tear-rimmed eye in frustration.

Mother would say, "count your blessings" at a time like this. Waving at a cab, I sucked in a breath and paid for it; every movement hurt. The cut on my right side ran long and deep—but it would heal soon enough—unlike the issues with Mother. The cab puttered to the curb, and I crawled inside, an arthritic spider, then whispered some directions to a wispy-haired cabby and laid my head back on a cracked seat.

Part of me wanted to curl up into a little ball and sleep for days, listening to the rain pattering down the long narrow windows of my bedroom. Another part of me wanted to understand and grapple with whatever had just happened inside my head. Xavier entered my mental bedroom. He did that often—it's hard to loosen the knots of sex once they've been tied tightly in your subconscious. But I didn't want him in that way; I just hoped he'd come and sit beside my bed as I lay there, sleeping. Maybe put his hand on my forehead and stroke my hair.

The face in my mind's eye cared nothing about caressing me. It leered at me like a ravenous wolf. He meant only to devour me; I was his passion meal. A frothing fanged mouth morphed into his thin-lipped, spittle-flinging countenance from yesterday. My arms still ached from the memory of his tight hold.

I wonder what my father would have said, what he would have done, had he been there for that encounter outside ISIP. But I didn't have to wonder; I knew. For all his sloth and television addiction, Norman Pepper would kill anyone who touched me in anger. If he'd been here, Xavier would have plucked fragments of Mercedes bumper out of his face for days. I chuckled but regretted it in an instant, the gash under my ribs ripping me back to reality.

My little yellow submarine on wheels bumped to a stop, and I paid the stunted driver. After an arduous climb out of the back-seat and onto the curb at the corner of North Fifty-Fifth Street and Meridian Avenue, I glanced up at my destination: Beehive Acupuncture. The business logo depicted the profile of a woman, lying prone, with hundreds of tiny needles poking out of her skin. A cutesy bee smiled where it hovered nearby, its stinger resembling a thin acupuncture needle. The business, recommended by Andrea when I'd first started getting dizzy, reminded me of a gypsy dive in the Bronx, painted in garish eye-catching stripes of black and gold.

I was desperate.

✦ ✦ ✦

"You say you're from Queens? You don't sound like a 'New Yawker.'" The rice-paper-and-bamboo screen between me and my "doctor"— the esteemed Moon Dance, NCCAOM board-certified diplomat of acupuncture—did little to hide her bad attempt at the twang of New York's Midtown boroughs. I chuckled, slipping into the flimsy gown I'd been provided. The material could barely be classified as clothing, and it itched.

"I did my best to lose that accent when I moved to Redwood City," I answered as I stepped out from behind the screen. In the dim light, I picked my way down several steps into a darkened, candle-strewn "regimen area." It reminded me of the sunken den at my Uncle Tony's place back in Queens, crammed with crummy sofas and loveseats, a huge television, and decorated with metric tons of empty chip bags and popcorn bowls.

Moon Dance obviously worked hard to make this area pleasing to the senses. Long satin burgundy curtains muted all the right angles in the room with soft slopes. The room's few pieces of furniture were low to the ground and upholstered in warm, cozy colors and textures. The floor was covered with rich Oriental rugs, and the only lighting came from about fifty short, stubby candles. Calm New Age music wafted into the space from somewhere. It reminded me of a formless womb. She'd deposited a clean creamy-colored towel atop a narrow, stunted couch; it was to be my only covering. Moon, seated in a lotus position on a thick embroidered rug, made a small motion toward the towel as if we'd done this together hundreds of times.

"You lived in California? Ah . . ." She closed her eyes, clear blue and in stark contrast to her flowing mane of ripened gray, as if entering into some sort of trance. "Karmic circles are truly wonderful, aren't they? I lived in California, too. Several years ago, in the San Jose area, in fact."

By this time, I'd pulled off the itchy paper-robe-thing and lain face down, naked, on a luxurious towel. She draped the other towel across my buttocks, then stiffened as I rolled my head to look toward her. She kneeled by my side, frozen in place.

Moon's eyes were huge. She stared at my body, or more accurately, at the dozens of bandaged cuts on my ribs, arms, and legs. Her words were laced with fear. "Are . . . are you all right?"

I craned my neck to look back over my shoulder at my bare back and legs. I smiled at Moon Dance. "I fell out of the shower this morning," I quipped, as if everyone did that every now and again. "The glass door broke."

Maybe I *was* crazy.

+ + +

Needles slid with barely a prick under my skin; Moon Dance knew her craft. I felt a spidery-legged burn under my flesh after each tip slid in, but the burn quickly dulled to a dusky smolder. I knew after the second needle, however, that I could easily get hooked on this. It wasn't the acupuncture, the New-Age talk, or the posh setting. I loved her touch—plain and simple. After each shaft of metal dove into the waters of my fragile hide, Moon would gently rub the area around the insertion; she called it "coaxing out the healing energies." I had no idea what she did, in a medical sense, but I knew it felt wonderful. Her hands were warm and smooth. Best of all: she accepted me.

Ruthlessly, unabashedly accepting.

I so craved that sort of touch from a man. Just a simple gentle touch. Not a touch that was the first step in a long and sordid master plan of getting me into bed. Not the numbing, mindless touch of a massage, which I also loved. Moon's touch had purpose. Something deep-seated and subconscious inside me desired to be held and caressed with some purpose other than for Xavier's physical satisfaction or my own.

I needed touch for my *soul.*

Moon's voice poked through the cloud of euphoria that encased my brain in a thick Seattle fog. "You know, Kate, this acupuncture will do nothing for your cuts."

"Sure."

She laughed, her voice filled with mirth. She'd gotten over her fear of my fresh slices once I'd dismissed them myself.

"So—why are you here today? When you called this morning, I sensed a frightened and hectic energy about you."

I peeled my face off a butter-soft leather pillow, hoping that I hadn't drooled on it in this touch-induced natural high. "It's my head, actually. I . . . I've been having—"

I paused, licking my lips as another solid steel shaft slipped into my shoulder. The burn sprouted like a mini-sun beneath my neck, followed immediately by Moon's delicate fingertips rubbing in small clockwork circles, coaxing the flames toward a glowing demise.

"I've been having headaches," I said, not wanting to sound like a kook. "And I've been blacking out."

X's sarcastic voice mocked my answer in my head. *Smooth, Kate, smooth.*

"I see." A quick three-needle succession along my upper vertebrae dazzled my nerves and made me gasp. I winced from the cut beneath my ribs. I'd not expected that trio of piercing sticks, and I certainly wasn't prepared for what happened next. It felt like the skin along my shoulders started to shift toward the center of my spine.

"Hmmm. Very strange, indeed, Kate. Are you sure you're telling me everything?"

I dabbed water from the corner of my eyes with the towel below me. "There's more . . ." I tried to speak, but the words dried in my throat. I dared not cry.

"Kate, it's okay." She placed a warm hand on my shoulder, not in a cold, clean, clinical sort of way and not in a weird, rub-away-the-sting sort of way either. Just a simple human gesture of care and concern.

I thought my heart would break.

I began to tell Moon everything: the dizzy spells, cutting myself, the bike wreck, and my precious Ice Rocket—smashed beyond repair. I told her about the lost time at work, the arguments with

Xavier, falling at ISIP, the lost sense of cohesion, and all the things—all the crazy, confusing things—that ran through my head.

The touch of her hands coaxed out my pain, and she sat silent through it all, like she was watching water pour out of a pitcher. In truth, when I'd finished the tale, that's the way I felt: emptied. She rose and retrieved some tissues for me. When she returned, her resolute look spoke care.

"Kate, I don't say this to many people these days because there's so much confusion and turmoil that people can get caught up in . . ." Her words trailed off into silence, and for a moment her lip trembled, as if she drew on some inner reserve before she continued.

She sucked in a deep breath. "There's no denying that a historical and metaphysical precedent exists for the sorts of things that you're dealing with." The gray-haired matron took my hand into her warm fingers and looked deeply into my eyes. "Kate, have you considered that these things you're seeing and these experiences you're having could be . . . real?"

I squinted in disbelief. "What do you mean?"

Moon searched for clues, for some sign of whether or not she should continue. She might have been looking for some chakra, a force center of energy that emanated from my body. Quack science. She nodded as she surveyed me with her fake inspection, her gray hair floating in slow-motion rhythm to the music that permeated us both.

"Kate, I'm asking, have you considered that what you're seeing could be a sort of spiritual communication?"

My skin tingled. Like that moment during the mystery movie when you think you've figured out who the killer is, but you're not quite sure. I opened my mouth to speak, but Moon ignored me.

"Have you considered that you might be having visions?"

Visions. *I hated that word.*

I immediately rose onto both elbows, and the towel slipped off my butt. I didn't care. Something from the small reptilian part of my brain that controls assertive dominance told me I needed to be looking down at Moon when I spoke next.

"Get these needles out of me. Now!"

Reduced to a naked female porcupine, I wasn't about to pay someone to insult me with gibberish about a message from the great beyond.

This quack on Fifty-Fifth Street had been the wrong choice.

I needed *real* help.

CHAPTER ELEVEN

I TRIED MY best to slam the condo's automated door. A gash under my ribs protested when I forced the malfunctioning portal shut. I was furious. Furious at Moon for implying that these mental images were some spiritual communication, furious at the cabby who made passes at me all the way home, furious that I had to walk the last two blocks because I didn't want the jerk to know where I lived.

My iPhone dinged. Surprised by a call so soon after I'd turned it back on, I answered the phone by mistake. I wish I'd checked the caller I.D. first.

"Kate? Kate, honey? It's Mom."

No!

Just when my day couldn't get any worse. Dumbfounded and furious, I clamped my lips shut.

"Kate, are you there? I'm worried about you, Missy . . . " She sounded older. Weaker.

"Yes, Mother, I'm here. What is it?"

"I'm worried, Kate. I've had some terrible insights, frightening ones. About you."

"Visions?" I blurted out. "Don't you have some sort of prayer group you can talk to about this? Why call me?" Angry words spewed like hot lead.

Mother continued unfazed. She never heard me when I talked. Not in my twenty-nine years.

"Kate, you know, these visions are unlike any I've ever experienced. I'm concerned for you. For your safety."

"What is it this time, Mother? Are serpents crawling up my dress again? You know Charlie Walker and I haven't dated for years, right?" It was a vicious jab to my mother's emotional solar plexus, but I didn't care. My poor ninth-grade boyfriend—*almost* boyfriend—never had a chance. She imagined black snakes, vipers that spewed from his mouth and tried to crawl up my legs. Charlie had been my one-and-only chance at high school normalcy. The first boy who wanted to take me out, but he was too old—a junior. Mother stood her ground, refusing to let me be with him. Once Mother spilled the beans with another parent, telling her about Charlie's tongue snakes, I became the pariah of my class. No one would take up with "Viper Girl" and her mentally unstable mom.

"Kate, you do know what happened to Charlie, don't you?" She said it without malice, like she knew I'd protest and had her next response all queued up. Her tone shocked me. No doubt, I'd been conditioned to expect contempt and deliberate hurt in Xavier's presence.

"No, Mother, I don't know. Did he become New York State's official snake charmer?"

"Charlie passed away six years ago, honey. From AIDS." No judgment in her tone, just a statement of fact. Mother broke my silence and continued. "But that's not why I called, honey. I called about you. The Spirit is warning me. He says that you're being tested."

The flower of anger blossomed once again in my chest. "There are no such things as spirits."

I almost choked on the last word, but I spit it out in a flare of rage. I caught a glimpse of my reflection in Shogun's tank as I talked, a face of fury much like Xavier's when he'd railed at me outside ISIP.

"Kate Joanne Pepper! Do not blaspheme the Holy Spirit!" Mother had used "the middle name." She really meant business.

"Look, Mother. I'm not in the mood to discuss this right now. It's been a hard day." A day that had spiraled downhill fast. "Let's talk later. Please."

Mother's voice regained its calm. She never changed, a small, slow-moving brook, content to simply be. I ground my teeth, desperate to end this call.

"That's fine, Missy. Just know that your father and I, and everyone at church, are praying for you."

"Don't bother," I spit out.

A long silence followed, a weak-sounding cough, then Mother's voice. Suddenly sad and tired, she replied, "Okay, Kate. Just know that we love you. So does God."

"Whatever." I hung up.

✦ ✦ ✦

Wednesday: back in the office on "Hump Day." I'd heard that term all my life and never really understood the meaning until today. Today, the worst of Wednesdays—the worst Hump Day in history. The office routine refused to end. My unintentional time off left me with a miniature pink mountain of telephone messages and an Outlook in-box straining from the added weight of unreturned e-mails.

A small part of me was thankful for all those messages—a good reason to avoid Xavier. As far as I knew, he had no idea about the shower incident, and didn't care enough to ask. That fact summoned the smaller, far more volatile part of me—a trembling volcano that ached to confront him and spew molten fury in his face. It was good—for both our sakes—that he had to travel to Portland just before lunch. No talk of Japanese or missed meetings—and no confrontations over his utter lack of concern.

My mind was made up. The mental abuse from Xavier was at an end. I'd let myself be walked on for much too long.

Lunch faded into dinner and a call-in pizza. Pizza cooled and morphed into vending junk. I kept fueled up, knocking out work faster the later it got. No distractions in the evening office, and three days worth of work completed in one long stretch. Around eight p.m. I took a stroll up and down the hall to confirm I'd outlasted them all, then changed roles.

There had to be a solution, some answer to my mental dilemma. With no one peeking over my shoulder to watch me on a late night in the office, I opened a new folder on my laptop and got to work, desperate for fast Internet and some peace of mind.

Time to hatch my plan.

I created a "spider," a software sub-routine that crawled the web site by site, seeking terms and documents that matched my symptoms. A solution as powerful as Google but different, ferreting out only a few key terms. With a couple of hours of effort tonight, I could program the code. Even run some tests using our company's web connection. But I dared not launch it from work, sure it would suck up hours of processor time. ISIP was the ideal host, and I suspected Hiram would buy in, willing to rent out his servers when the shop closed. With Hiram's servers as my network home base, no one at Consolidated Aerodyne would discover that I'd gone nuts.

Hours later I rested, my work complete. The "spider" functioned just as I'd planned, but true to form, it proved to be a network hog. Zipping off into a digital netherworld to search billions of home pages, dropping a few key terms and checking for logical pairs, it proved its worth in a few minutes of testing. No solutions emerged for my problem, but I proved I'd picked the right strategy. Next step: ISIP, and Hiram's powerful servers—the perfect host to my subroutine, humming away all night.

I packed up, said a terse good-bye to the last of the cleaning staff, and headed out, strolling through velvety dark streets toward the wharf.

Time to clear my head.

✦ ✦ ✦

I melted into one of Seattle's off-kilter evenings; the overcast of low-lying clouds reflected the orange sodium light of city streetlamps, neither day nor fully night, neither hot nor cold. Well after midnight, the deserted streets of Seattle's wharf district beckoned as I wandered aimlessly. Marooned on the far side of the moon, I strolled alone. Mother would chastise me for walking at night. Xavier would protest and pretend to protect me by driving me to his place, a hermit crab scurrying from the dark. But the avenues lay deserted, and I welcomed the solitude of an inky orange-lit night.

Thoughts from the last several weeks rolled around in my head like rocks in a tumbler, abrading their rough edges into smooth ones. Six months ago, I hadn't a care in the world . . . yet now my life lay in shambles. I scrambled to pick up the pieces.

The sharp tang of salt in the air and the clang of a solitary brass bell yanked my attention away from my thought tumbler. Predictably, I'd arrived, on autopilot, at the harbor. I stood still for a moment, soaking it all in. The reflections of pier lights and the black silhouettes of boats stitched together in a wavering, otherworldly softness. The air breathed thick, fresh, yet full of subtle taints. I loved the sea.

No one understood why my father ran away from his family roots in commercial fishing. Sure, with the unpredictable nature of the business and long cold hours at sea, it took a special person for that kind of work. But none of those obstacles hindered Gramps. My grandfather lived to fish, to venture beyond sight of land—and through him I came to love the ocean, the sheer untamed vastness of it. The lure of a solitary boat beneath my feet and the wide horizon beyond the bow intoxicated me. My love for freedom—the antithesis of control—grew from my love of time with Gramps. He meant freedom, and freedom came on the water.

But now, liberty drained from me, robbed by fear; uncommon mental imagery threatened to steal my mind at any moment. Fear that I might degrade to a psychotic shell of my former self. Two possibilities lay on the horizon: I drifted on the brink of insanity— a mind full of random imagery the precursor to complete mental oblivion—or I suffered what my mother and Moon threatened: honest-to-goodness visions, inspired by a strange spiritism and beyond-the-grave communication. I shuddered as Gramps's voice washed into my mind, a gentle wave on my cerebral shore.

"Kate, sometimes we're called to make hard choices."

Our nets once snagged an adolescent gray seal. It was two weeks after my thirteenth birthday, and we were fishing off the coast of Maine. Gramps had left it up to me to decide where and when we'd cast a net. He hated nets, the bane of a line fisherman. He knew I yearned for control even then, as a young budding woman. "Don't set it close to shore," he warned, pointing out the rocky outcroppings where the seals slept, sharp rocks that would rip the nets from our boat.

I didn't listen, determined to decide for myself. He stood silent, head bowed, when I pulled the lever to release a small seine, trolling close to shore in the calm of the bay. He watched, no judgment on his weathered face—only a shadow of sadness. Half an hour later, as I ran the winch to retrieve the net, I learned that actions have consequences.

We'd captured a harbor seal, still alive, but only barely. Nearly suffocated and tangled in the wet seine, the gray creature gasped.

I'd become that seal, snagged in a net I'd not seen coming, drowning in a sea of paralyzing imagery. Hopelessly tangled in an abusive dead-end relationship with a man who cared more about his next meeting than my well-being. And alone—a successful woman with few true friends. For all my wealth and accomplishments, I swam in a pool of misery. Many knew about me, yet almost no one knew me.

"You have to make a decision, Kate," Gramps had said, his voice low and broken. I could almost feel his rugged hands on mine as I watched ripples in the silky black surface of the harbor. I had to decide the fate of that seal, but Gramps didn't let me suffer through it alone. I needed that kind of love and support now.

"She's in pain, Kate. Don't prolong her agony." Sorrow gripped Gramps's voice—a lamentation for me and for the seal. In my mind's eye, reaching back sixteen years, I saw my small, delicate thirteen-year-old hand reach for a well-worn ball-peen hammer. I could imagine again the weight of the wood shaft and the metal head when I lifted it high. It wavered there for a moment.

I had to make a decision.

The hammer fell. I chose between a prolonged agony for the slick gray creature and a hasty death. A choice between misery and peace.

Standing at the water's edge at Seattle's downtown wharf, that rusty old ball-peen hammer fell again. I made a decision.

I am not crazy. That option must die tonight, in this harbor.

"Crazy" meant I'd lost all control. I swung the killing machine, eliminating the option that I might be nuts. I made the determination. I concluded the early diagnosis. I controlled the outcome.

Of course, that left only one other choice. If not crazy, then what? Visions?

I chose misery over peace, well aware of the implication: I had become my mother.

CHAPTER TWELVE

THREE DAYS LATER.

I'D TIMED it perfectly. Jogging toward the front door of ISIP, I didn't even break pace as Hiram opened the door. I traipsed right in, his first customer on Saturday morning.

"Early bird!" His bearded lips split into a wide grin. "You're pretty wired, Ms. Pepper. D'you win the lottery?" ISIP's owner asked, then pointed to a pair of piping-hot carafes on his "Blend of the Week" table.

I nodded, wagging a finger toward the Hawaiian Kona Peaberry selection. "Something like that." I unslung my backpack and pulled out my MacBook Air, ready to connect to ISIP's wireless web. It came up a dry hole, as if his Internet service had never existed.

"Hey, Hiram, what gives? The wireless has vanished!"

Hiram frowned, thumping a steaming mug down atop my table, then turned on a heel. "Tenth time this week!" he bellowed and stomped into the server room behind the counter.

Moments later my laptop pinged while I watched, steaming caffeine in hand. My screen sprang to life, filled with megabytes of fresh data to be allocated and analyzed. Digital Christmas. My spider script worked!

Moments later, as I bent over the new material, Hiram's voice snapped me out of my playtime.

"Kate, we need to talk." Hiram's smile had upended itself, a sour-faced parody of joy.

"What's up?"

"Your spider search, kiddo. It's choking my servers and crashing my network." He shook his head. "You're the reason."

"I . . . I don't understand, Hiram. You know a spider couldn't do that. It's designed to—"

"Yeah, I know what it's designed to do. But I can tell you that whatever search this thing of yours is executing has choked my machines the way wet grass kills lawnmowers. The wireless ran fine before your spider script, but it's worthless without a network, and that crashes three or four times a day. Thanks to your program." He shrugged and laid a hand on my shoulder. "Sorry, friend. No more searches during normal work hours."

A hard edge lurked somewhere beneath the surface of that last comment. I'd affected more than Hiram's bottom line.

"I'll shut it down soon, okay? I promise. Just let me run it a little while longer, and I'll let you charge me double to make up for the possible loss."

"This is what I do for a living, Kate. I love this place and I want to keep it. You know as well as I do that word of mouth can make or break a place. If word gets out that ISIP's Internet is on the rocks, then it won't matter how much coffee I sell."

I nodded. He had a point. "Make you a deal, Hiram. You charge me double for the next week and I'll tweak the script to make sure it won't crash your servers. Deal?"

The bearded mug before me softened a bit, taking on a much more familiar likeness. Hiram chuckled. "Okay."

I took a sip of delightful Hawaiian brew and went back to my razor-thin laptop. All of the e-mail, forum threads, reader feeds, and other information my script had garnered aligned themselves in an orderly list. Ranked by their relevance to my search, the list stood arrayed like electronic soldiers ready to deliver their reports. A "10" rating caught my eye, a response to an instant message query my spider script had generated and pushed out to social media networks.

H₂O

The response came from someone with the pseudonym WRKRJC. It reminded me of a radio call sign, not a Facebook tag.

The title reeled me in: "Have you considered the alternative?"

Hungry for answers, I dove at the keyboard. My fingers, honed from years of coding and secretarial duty, flew with a life of their own. "Okay, I'll bite," I wrote. "What alternative?"

Middle school girl-likes-boy butterflies fluttered inside as I waited. Was I really this close to an answer? The spider script had to work.

My laptop pinged in reply, and words appeared on my screen like magic. "Excuse me?"

I arched an eyebrow. That wasn't the response I expected.

I typed an emoticon smile. "You sent a message in response to my search for information on visions."

The response was immediate. "Oh yeah! Sorry. How are you?"

More fast fingers. "I'm well. Right now, but not all the time. And you?"

"Better than I deserve. So, what's up? You said you're seeing things?" WRKRJC certainly didn't fool around. I liked that.

"Yes," I typed, then paused, steeling myself for the next words. "The available evidence says I'm having visions. But I'm not even sure that's possible. That stuff's for movies." I rested my forehead in my palms after hitting Enter.

I really must be nuts. Before long, I'd be standing on a street corner in a trench coat with a sign that foretold doom and apocalypse.

"People can have visions," came back the quick reply. "You shouldn't be concerned with that. It's the *source* of the visions that you need to unravel."

The chatter grabbed me, words that rang with confidence and assuredness. No novice to the online world, however, I knew those characteristics could be counterfeit. I decided to test the veracity of my new friend, WRKRJC.

"How can a vision have a source? I mean, isn't the mind the source?"
This time there was a long pause.

"While it's true that a person's mind can 'see' things, like a dream or a daydream, a vision is a little different. Lots of people get caught up in self-created worlds and wind up drowning in a sea of self-induced experiences. Since you're questioning the validity of what you're seeing, I suspect you aren't headed down this path. Dreams and daydreams come from elements that are already inside your head—like memories. Visions, however, can contain messages and images inside them that you've never seen or experienced before. For visions, a person's mind is like an envelope. It holds and stores the vision inside it, but that's where the relationship ends. Just like the letter inside the envelope, a vision has to come from somewhere else. Then, there's the other alternative. Hallucinations. Those have a definite cause: drugs, fatigue, fever, psychosis . . . and spiritual possession. That kind of thing."

Impressive. This WRKRJC wasn't some New-Age flake spouting stuff about aligning with the cosmos, stroking crystals, and chasing chakras. I'd already waded through that drivel. I pushed the chatter a little deeper.

"Okay. That's believable," I typed. This felt good, to communicate with someone on an even footing. Xavier and I never communicated. We connected physically, even emotionally, but never mentally. No deep discussions and dialogue; he was a hunk under his shirt, but cotton candy in the mental department. I felt an immediate attraction to this I.M. friend, hoping I'd at last found someone with whom I could share my problems and my fears.

But was it a "him" or a "her?"

"I'm no druggie, I'm not sick, and I get some sleep. Scratch the hallucinations option for now. Let's talk visions. You said they come from somewhere else, like a letter in the envelope. Define 'somewhere else.'"

As if the chatter anticipated my question, the next message replied, "Let's just say they either come from the 'good side of town,' or the 'bad side.' Which side of town are you on?" He followed his question with a winking emoticon smile, indicating that something akin to a private joke just passed between us.

I had a feeling that WRKRJC and I would get along just fine.

✦ ✦ ✦

"I hate to say this, Kate, but you've got to go home."

Hiram stood over me, his rain jacket thrown over a shoulder and keys jangling in his hand. I'd been so preoccupied that I hadn't noticed the time. ISIP stood empty, a shell of its busy self. I'd grown so engrossed in the web and talking to my new I.M. friend about my mental failings that I'd lost all connection with the present.

"What time is it?" I asked, caught in the middle of a great article about recent hallucinations among Seattle residents, a post that WRKRJC sent to me. Apparently, I had company; a vision virus had made its rounds here in the rainy city. Just like Dr. Lin had said. That was some comfort, but not much.

"It's nearly six-thirty, Kate. Sorry, but we close at six on weekends." He jangled the keys again and smiled, curly brown sprouts of his beard turning up on the corners of his mouth.

"No problem," I replied, packing up. Nothing Hiram could say could ruin this day, after the success of my spider subroutine and meeting someone with what seemed to be credible answers. I pulled my gear together. "Give me a sec."

"Glad to. D'you bring a raincoat? It's gonna storm tonight."

I froze, today's success forgotten in an instant. I really had lost my connection with reality. I didn't own a car and had jogged down from my condo for a quick cup of java. But I'd stayed all day. That was a first.

"No. Didn't bring anything but this," I said, pointing at my work-out top and pants. They might stop a sprinkle but nothing more. In a full-fledged rainstorm, I'd get pummeled. My laptop, too.

"Can I stay and call a cab, Hiram?" I asked, my pulse quickening.

"Sorry, Kate, but I have a can't-miss date with the wife. We're barely going to make the show as it is. You can wait on the stoop, though. Okay?"

An uncovered stoop while I waited on an unreliable cab, a mad dash home with a bouncing laptop on my back, or hide out at Walgreens across the street?

This would be the great test. A vision now would be certain proof that water was the source of my anguish. Betrayed by my first love.

I decided to make a run for it.

Hiram let me out the locked door, and I checked my pack once more for keys and personal things. I was determined to not leave a pile of important materials at ISIP and lose them until Monday. He nudged me with a gentle push into the open air. Hiram had to go. I'd never seen him in such a hurry.

"See you Monday?" he asked good-naturedly as he dashed off.

"Yeah. Sure," I replied, not sure of anything. I stared up at the sky. Not typical Seattle; this looked like Wizard-of-Oz weather, a green-gray line of towering thunderstorms approaching from the Pacific. I didn't have long.

"See ya," he yelled when I dashed off the stoop into a brisk humid ocean breeze. I could smell it—the air laden with ozone. A cold front headed our way fast, and home lay ten minutes away at a jogging pace. A cab might take that long to show up.

Time to go.

Before I reached the corner, I heard the first clap of thunder. Like a rendition of the William Tell Overture, the storm let go a *boom* with a gut-rumbling crash. I cinched my backpack while I jogged, then ran faster, pulling the straps as tight as they'd go to prevent my feather-light laptop from bouncing in the cavernous pack.

Any day before the advent of my great "vision disease," I'd be loving this kind of weather. Bring it on, rain and all. I loved a storm, to be immersed in a downpour, and the wetter the better. A little hail made it even more interesting. But now, staring into the face of my mental disaster, a single drop might be an errant bullet, and a storm cloud an armed gang. Considering the last few days, and what I'd learned on the web, if I was soaked by this storm I might lose my mind.

My feet pounded twice the pace of my heart for block after block as I raced toward my neighborhood. At two blocks to go, within view of my condo, the first drops—big crocodile tears—slammed into a car windshield at my left. The temperature plummeted ten degrees inside the span of five houses. More crocodile tears pelted the sidewalk, some of them whizzing past my cheek, another slapping into the street when I dashed across an intersection. A block to go. Frigid air blasted my face.

Two big sloppy drops hit me on the shoulder and in the chest. My Gore-Tex shell knocked the water away; it was only a matter of time before I caught one directly in the face. I readied my hands, mentally assessing the pain I'd encounter if I fainted while running at speed. Road rash, torn-up palms, maybe a concussion when my head hit the pavement. It would be ugly.

Half a block to go.

I yelled at my door from as far as I thought the automated system would hear my cue. I owned the only voice-activated door on the block, a convenience for shopping days, not for escaping an approaching storm. Nothing happened. I yelled again, out of breath and fighting a pounding heart.

"Open!" Again, I yelled. "Open!"

Nothing. I was three doors from the condo, and I could see the sane freedom of a dry home beckoning me through the bay window on the front of my place. My stuff, dry and nestled away, waited for me.

"Open!"

Two doors away, my own portal started to swing. I would make it!

Then I heard the Devil himself, the cascade of rain that comes with a fast-approaching storm. A war zone raged only a hundred yards ahead of me, sheets of rain piling down on cars. The well-defined front stood feet away, and its early warrior drops blasted all about me. With a hand on my stair rail, feet on the steps, headed toward the safety of my open door, I took the first hit.

A cold monster drop slammed me in the face like a dragonfly smacking the windshield of a speeding car. It wet my entire cheek. It was like being hit in the face with a baseball bat; the force of the water's imagery knocked me back that instant. I grabbed hard at the black steel railing along the stairs, desperate for some stability. Only one step to go. I'd shifted from full speed to some horror film-like slow motion, overtaken by the weather front. Pounding rain swept up the street. I got a hand on the doorjamb as sheets of water drenched me, a frightening ripping rain and windstorm knocking me into the side of my open door.

My mind swam with a jumble of images. Every water drop in this maelstrom packed a wallop of mental mayhem. Through it, somehow, I managed to fall forward instead of back down the steps. I landed on a wet wooden portico inside my condo and lost all connection with this world as the storm raged outside. Sodden, wind-blown, and cold, I was transported to someplace far from home.

To a place of perpetual wetness.

✦ ✦ ✦

My feet were anchored in muck, a gray sticky mud-flat that stretched a hundred yards in both directions. I stood tall and straight, immobile but aware, a pithy stalk of green.

Ten thousand reeds like me stood to my left and my right. A broad shallow river stretched out to my left—cool, clear water flowing by me slowly as it coursed down the broad valley that hemmed us in. Ahead of me to the east, dry barren mountains of aged rock shot up from a salty desert plain. Behind me to the west, more mountains stretched to the sky—rugged stone, white and parched. Other than my sister reeds, I could see no green in any direction. A barren wasteland surrounded this blessed ribbon of water that I thrived in, my eternal home.

Loud voices headed my way, a crowd of people moving slowly, slogging into the mudflat and pressing down other reeds like me so they could reach the water. Somewhere within earshot, a lone voice rang out, crying aloud in the wilderness. The mass of humanity worked its way toward him, and mucky step by step, he slogged toward me. His voice carried far into the reeds about me as though amplified by some unseen force.

"You brood of vipers!" he yelled, stopping in a shallow bend of the river just downstream from me and pointing at someone on the bank. "Who warned you to flee?" He waved a heavy wooden staff at men who pulled their fine robes up about them to wade into the swamp. They feared the embrace of the mud.

The loud man wore a rough dingy robe, pulled tight with only a rope belt around his waist. While the finely dressed ones stood on the riverbank, flanked on all sides by my fellow reeds, he waded into the middle of the river with others who were dressed as he, a mass of common people who called to him. He welcomed these people into his arms and continued to wade upstream. He stopped abreast of me and dipped his hands into the cool flowing water that gave me life.

He cupped water and lifted it high above a boy, then let the water course over the lad's head, saying, "After me will come one who is more powerful than I." Another came to him, a woman weeping and holding her head down. He cupped more water and poured it on her, wetting her head and her shawl. "His winnowing fork is in his hand, and he will clear his threshing floor," he cried aloud. His voice carried to the distant hills, to sheep grazing on scrubs of plants that eked out some existence in the desert climate.

The water that surrounded me surged with power, as if the massive hand that guided it toward me and my sister reeds did so with a plan, a purpose in its existence. A hand moved the river slowly beyond my view, but brought it here for this very moment, for this man in the rough robes, for the men and women he immersed in its embrace. Each man and woman, every child, once immersed in the waters and wetted with his cupped hands, came out refreshed, a new creature.

The crowds parted and another Man approached, a citizen not like the rest. Although clad in common clothes, his dress was radiant—white and glowing. I felt his presence, as though the Man created or directed the river that flowed about me. He became One with us, part of our world of reeds. I felt I knew him, yet I'd never met him.

The loud rough-dressed man stooped, sinking to his knees in the water as the Radiant One approached. We embraced them both where they sank in the life-mud at our roots. The rough man spoke to the Radiant One in a quiet voice that I alone could hear. "No, Lord. I need you. Do you come to me?"

The Radiant One put his hand on the shoulder of the rough man, lifting him up from the cool waters. "Let it be so now." Then the Radiant One bowed his head, sinking to his knees near my roots.

The man in rough clothes cupped his hands, dipped, and lifted water toward the sky, then wet the head of the One who knelt in our flow. As the water poured over him, I felt incredible power thrum through our river, penetrating my roots and making me more alive than ever. His spirit became part of me, deep inside me somehow, part of my birth, an essential part of my inner being. I wanted to know this Man better, to be one with him.

As the Radiant One arose from the water, I watched in adoration and praise. A dove, shining white in the brilliant sun and desert heat, descended from a cloudless sky to alight on his head. He put his hand out, steadying himself by holding on to me as he arose. Standing, the Radiant One caressed my smooth stalk and spoke to me alone. Out of a million reeds drawing life from this river and mud, he chose to speak to *me*.

"I am calling you," he said, straightening one of my twisted leaves.

"Who are you?" I asked. I felt his pull and wanted to embrace him. He spoke only two words in response.

"I am."

CHAPTER THIRTEEN

FIVE DAYS LATER.

"SUNNY TOMORROW?" I wondered aloud. "On Friday?" I stared out the office window, its commanding view of the Seattle harbor always a welcome rest for weary eyes. Sleep had escaped me this past week, supplanted by constant worry.

"Yes. For one day. Then rain all weekend. Don't you hate that?" Andrea asked, leaning into the doorjamb of my office. "We'll be stuck in here drafting presentations for our boss and selling seats to airline companies on the day the sun finally decides it's going to bless us." She huffed. "The wrong day."

I shrugged, hoping Andrea would find something else to talk about. I felt like Hester in *The Scarlet Letter*. I just knew that everyone could see the giant red label on me, flashing like a Las Vegas billboard:

Crazy! Dangerous when wet!

Sunbeams, a Seattle rarity, radiated their "come hither" call to the outdoors, beckoning me to the safety of their embrace. No wet. I'd find some excuse to get out tomorrow—if for no other reason than to get home in one piece. Memories of last Saturday's deluge and my mental collapse had not faded. I came to Seattle to soak in the water that fell from the sky year-round. I loved rain. That is, I used to love it. These days, water had become my enemy.

"You listening?" Andrea asked with a knock on the jamb. I'm sure she reads minds. At a minimum, she could read mine. Or read energies. If my vitality had a color, it had become black as coal. Nothing shone bright in my life these days. When you don't know where your head is, it's hard to get a grip. My mind tripped out on water, and that made no sense.

"Yes. I'm listening," I replied, but I lied. Andrea could have been chatting for an hour, and I might not have heard her. My mind ran on a single track today, a total focus on staying dry. And sunbeams meant sanity.

"You're staying late tomorrow?" She probed again, her question some kind of code for a more pointed unspoken query: "What about Xavier? Aren't you guys going out or something?" Everyone knew he'd been gone all week, and maybe they just assumed I couldn't live without him.

I could. Live without him. For good. I'd turned over a new leaf. I just hadn't told her yet.

"I'm too far behind. Lots of work to do," I said, turning around in my chair. My back faced her when I looked out the window or worked at my station. I liked that; people weren't always trying to make eye contact when they walked by my office. "E-mail's a mile deep, and I've got briefings to build." I took a deep breath. "And then there's the issue of the Japanese. I'm still working to sort out that mess. My mess."

The e-mail glut could only be blamed on me. I'd spent so many hours trying to sort out this stupid problem with the pictures in my head that I'd let many customers and contacts lie fallow for too long. I had to get notices out tonight to the key buyers and customers whose invoices kept me fed.

Andrea stiffened and stepped back into the hall. For a brief moment, I wondered what I'd said to offend her. But her body language gave it away. Xavier was headed our direction.

"Boss man on the prowl, and he looks mad," Andrea whispered, then backed out of the office as if headed to another. "See you."

I nodded in silence. Xavier never came to my office unless he wanted something; my boss was certainly the last person in the world who'd drop in for a chat. I felt the dull thud of his shoes approach in the hall, a wooly mammoth stomping down the corridor to our showdown.

I could always feel his mad strides . . . and this one promised trouble.

I closed my eyes, breathing deeply again. Moments away from a reckoning.

✦ ✦ ✦

The invoice fluttered to the floor. Surely, Xavier didn't think he could throw a sheet of paper at me and have it fly across the room like a knife. But that's the way he launched it when he stomped into my office. If the sheet had some mass and a sharp point, it might have impaled me. But it fell harmlessly at my feet.

I picked up the printout, a mass of numbers and names. Somewhere in this jumble my credit card data and company employee number lay hidden—the source of his great distress.

"So you *did* use the corporate credit card, right?" Xavier chewed me out in my own space. My boyfriend, soon-to-be-"ex," played the bad cop in a routine we both knew very well. But no pretense here. His shaved head glowed crimson, and wiggle-worms did backflips under his temples. His forearm bulged beyond the cuff of a rolled shirt, arteries throbbing under the silvery band of his "power watch."

"Yes. I used it. It's a corporate card, and it gets me a discount on network access. I needed to do some research outside the office. Research that started when I broke my laptop."

"You're not being honest with me, Kate. I replaced that laptop long ago. Some of these expenses hit as late as Saturday. So—what gives?"

"I'm paying for some web searches, that's all. It's private, and I pay my part of the card off every month," I said, crossing my arms. "It's not costing you anything, that's for sure." I stood, determined to match him on this one. Xavier had a habit of backing down when someone got in his face. I'd try that, just for fun. I needed this charade to end; crowds had gathered within earshot, and I didn't need an office scene.

"Searches?" He fumed. "What's wrong with our network?"

"Nothing . . . I—" I cut it off, unwilling to tell him. Xavier would belittle these stupid visions of mine as some health issue, or try to convince me I really might be losing my mind. That kind of help I didn't need.

He stood in silence, his final stage before a mental meltdown. I'd seen it lots of times. If he stalked off, I'd gained the advantage, and a reprieve.

"Shut it down, Kate. No searches. No corporate cards. I have the audit department breathing down my neck and you've got a boat-load of charges to some offshore account that's doing network activity. Far as the auditors are concerned, you're running a telephone or gambling scam. And it's obviously not work-related." He spun about, his hand hesitating on the door. He looked back and lowered his voice; it was the first time I'd heard compassion since the early part of our dinner at Canlis. "What's happened to you, anyway? I feel like I've lost the old Kate. I just don't know you anymore."

I had an answer ready, but Xavier didn't wait. He let go of the jamb and was gone in a flash.

"I'll deal with it," I said, loud enough for him to hear when he stomped down the hall. His thuds echoed in the wood-floored corridor. A few seconds later, I knew for sure he'd heard me, his voice carrying down the long hall past rooms filled with my coworkers. He set up a gauntlet of embarrassment I didn't want to face.

"You'd better deal with it, Kate. For my sake. And for yours."

◆ ◆ ◆

There are days when I hate a ringing office phone. On the back side of my confrontation with Xavier, I didn't want to talk to anyone. Nevertheless, I've never been able to adopt that time-management technique of ignoring a call. Somehow, ringing phones are too tempting when the number is unknown—some special business opportunity looking for a home, or a client calling from "out of the blue." In marketing, no matter how bad your day, you take every call. I stared through three rings at the number displayed on my desk phone, debating whether to run into the hall and throw something at Xavier. I answered.

"Kate Pepper, Consolidated Aerodyne," I said, dragging the last vestiges of professionalism out of some cranny deep inside my dry shell. I held myself together with both hands, and there weren't any grips left for another person. This had better not be another request for a charity dinner.

"Ms. Pepper? This is Gloria O'Malley."

Who?

"We met at our boat, the *St. Jude*. I'm Liam's mom."

St. Jude?

"Ms. Pepper?"

That was weeks ago, an eternity. How long had this curse plagued me? The dizzy spells. The images in my head. Xavier barking at every move like some mad dog behind a too-short fence, ready to leap out and get me.

Liam?

The name struck at some part of me that still felt good. It radiated warmth, a stark contrast to the mental blizzard that gripped me. I realized she'd been waiting on the line to see if I remembered her.

"Liam?" I asked, trying to connect. The past seemed a fog. I'd forgotten nearly everything other than my mental anguish and my search for peace.

"Yes. We sold you a few pounds of sashimi-grade tuna. I'm the lady on the boat. My son met you at the fisherman's monument." She paused. "I hope you don't mind me calling. You left your card that day, and I wanted to ask you something. Well, not for me. For my son."

Liam!

The synapses started firing again and it felt good. The little red-head at Fisherman's Memorial, the boy who'd always asked "why." The warm spot inside me caught fire and melted my coldest recesses, a memory of the boy, and our brief encounter at the memorial when I'd laid the flowers for Gramps.

Gramps!

One memory spawned another. It felt good to be in the embrace of old thoughts, my grandfather's face in my mind's eye, his hand on my shoulder. My grandfather would know how to deal with all this—including the power-mogul boyfriend and boss who rapidly distanced himself from me. He'd have an answer to the source of the insane pictures in my head and the dizzy spells.

"Yes! I remember now. Thanks for calling, Mrs. O'Malley. I'm sorry; it took me a minute to make the connection."

"That's all right. Please, I understand, Ms. Pepper. I'm sorry to bother you like this, but—well—I needed to ask a favor, if I might."

Here it comes. The warm spot started to fade. Another charity, another dinner. I slumped in my chair, unable to shoulder yet another load.

"Yes?" I wanted to hang up.

"Liam brought me something. I feel terrible about this, because he's kept it a secret for weeks, and it's probably special for you. I'm so sorry . . ."

"I don't understand—"

"You left some flowers along with an item at the base of the memorial. Lots of people do, you know? Someone picks up the flowers when they're old, but, well, you see, Liam picked up the other memorabilia. Something carved, like a chain. He's kept it for a while, and I found it in his room last night and asked him about it. He told me where it came from, and I wanted to get it back to you."

The warmth came rushing back, a big wave crashing on my emotional beach, smothering me with hot tingles. I could imagine Gramps smiling at me in the doorway, dressed in an old wax-cloth rain slicker and his droopy fishing hat. His hand extended toward me in that memory, a shiny whittling knife and a carved wooden ball-in-chain thrust my way. It all started there, on my ninth birthday, two decades ago. I wanted to reach up and grab Gramps again, to be smothered in his fishy arms—and to cry.

"I . . . I remember." My voice stuck in my throat.

"Liam is my creative one," she continued. "He's always doing something with his hands, you know? Everything nautical. He's been after his dad for months to teach him how to carve a ball and chain, and—well—I guess the temptation became too great when he saw yours at the memorial. I'm so sorry. We'd like to return it to you in person, if that's okay. I want Liam to learn a lesson from this."

I stared out the window at the Seattle harbor, imagining they were in a boat just beyond the wharf. The sun would be shining Friday. I could go outdoors to visit them and remain sane.

"Yes. I mean, yes! I'd like to come see you."

"You don't have to—"

"No, please," I insisted. I had to get out of here. "And I want Liam to have the chain. As a gift. My grandfather taught me how to carve it, and I left it at the memorial in his honor." The words seemed to spill out of me, warm fuzzies flooding through me. It felt so good. "I'd really like to come see Liam again if that would be okay. So, please, don't apologize. I'm sure he meant well."

"If you insist—"

"I do," I blurted out. For the first time in days, I felt happy. A feeling I'd lost in the past weeks. I wanted to see the little kid, to tell him about my grandfather, to feel the warm sun, to smell salt in the air and remember days gone by. I wanted my life back.

"I'll come down Friday afternoon after school, Mrs. O'Malley. And I'll bring a present, if that's okay."

"It's Gloria, please. But you don't need to bring a gift. Not after what Liam's done."

"No. I need to do this. But don't tell him. I'll bring a whittling knife, if that's okay with you, and some balsa wood. I'll teach him how to carve the ball and chain. It's easy. Anyone can do it."

"Ms. Pepper, really. You don't have to."

"I *need* to do it, Mrs. O'Malley. I mean, Gloria. For my grandfather's sake. He'd want me to pass this skill on." I paused, wondering how much I should say. "And for my sake, Gloria. How about Friday afternoon? Liam's in school, right?"

"He is. This—this is so special," she said, her voice cracking. I heard her sniffle. "And thank you. For doing this."

"Great," I said. I felt a smile. Those were muscles I hadn't used in a long time.

"Four o'clock?" she asked.

"Four sharp." I'd be out of here early Friday. Forget my plans for a late night at the office and e-mail. The time had come for me to reconnect with my past.

✦ ✦ ✦

"We spent a lot of money to put this new carpet in," Xavier said an hour later, standing above me in the doorway of the office copy room. He didn't stoop over to help me, or offer to lift the black nightmare from my hands. It was just one sentence; another icy condemnation that stabbed me as I sat on the floor covered in black copy toner. He wagged his head as he left. A woman giggled in the background, standing just beyond him in the hall, unseen. I imagined my fingers, caked in powdery black, ripping out her eyes.

A crumpled sheet of paper ripped out of the inside of the copy machine lay at my side. My gray skirt, doused in dark powder, had become woolen midnight. No one came to the door to help. I sat alone, on my own, just like ten minutes ago when I left the office to get a copy made. No admin assistant would make a copy for me, presumably too busy with Xavier on a "special assignment" to be able to copy the bill he'd thrown at me half an hour ago. And no technician came to repair the copier. No one offered to help me insert a new toner cartridge, or to help me up off the floor, covered in the impossible mess of a busted cartridge, my clothing trashed.

More giggles rippled down the hall, gurgling out of delicate throats I wanted to slit. I tried in vain to dust off the blackness, but it rubbed into my hands and the fabric of my clothes with an inky permanence. The harder I tried to distance myself from the dry stain, the more it spread, like a virus, a dark powdery cloud growing around me.

I headed for my locker, and a new change of clothes. The detritus lay on the floor, a black bomb exploded at the base of a white paper-eating copier and its toner guts.

✦ ✦ ✦

This is going to hurt.

Hammered copper basins shone beneath polished gold waterspouts across the breadth of the granite bathroom counter in our executive washroom. A mirror the length of two people stretched across the room, reminding me that I looked like I'd been the only target in a paintball battle, or someone had dumped a bag of black flour on my lap and arms. I looked atrocious.

Granite stall dividers lay to my left, fancy walls of swirling red-brown rock grain. One more appointment in an overdone ladies' room complete with perfumes, mouthwash, puffs, soap and tissue dispensers. None of them any good to me at this point. Only the gold water spout could help, a menacing snake protruding from the granite, waiting to strike. My hand shook as I extended it toward the faucet.

I moved back, pressing against the fabric-covered wall behind me, careful not to place black hands on the expensive covering. My eyes never left the faucet, one of six golden serpents frozen in time over their metal basins. I imagined I was in Egypt, covered in the black of night, waiting to be sacrificed at the throne of Isis. The snakelike spouts beckoned me, hissing my name.

Sweat?

I could feel dampness under my armpits, a sensation I'd not experienced at work in years. My forehead beaded up; I resisted the urge to wipe it. Glistening sweat formed on my brow in the mirror eight feet in front of me. My hands shook, and I laced blackened fingers together over the worst of the damaged skirt, desperate to steady myself.

I'm alone.

I came to Seattle to get wet. Dry San Jose, with its stucco cookie-cutter homes and mind-numbing traffic, had been good to me financially. The endless dry horizon of buildings and eucalyptus trees stretched for miles, a flat land of technological wizardry, squeezed in between the mountains south of San Francisco and the coastal hills to the west. I used to escape to Santa Cruz and the towering redwoods for nature and for damp . . . until I came here, to worship water in the land of wet. That all seemed so long ago now, with me plastered to the wall, petrified of the thought of a simple hand-washing.

I must get clean.

Xavier is the germaphobe. I'm more sane, just a "clean freak"—in Andrea's parlance. I wished she were here; I felt desperate to share this incomprehensible fear of water with someone who might understand. I could tell her anything, and she'd rarely judge me. I wanted someone with me because I knew I had no other option. The stain on my hands was a powdery virus; it would spread wherever I put my fingers. The black had to go.

Washing is the only option.

I advanced toward the sink, sweat running down the insides of my arms, trickling onto my elbow. More beads dripped from my brow down my nose. I couldn't wipe at anything, or the blackness would multiply.

And then the visions returned. Even sweat discomforted my unstable mind. Mixed with my sight of the real world, I could see steam. Drops of rain. Soaked earth. Icicles. Snow. I shook the water free of my face with a snap of my head, and most of the dancing pictures departed, if only for a moment.

I stood over the hammered copper bowl, its snake-god spout poised above the basin in lust for the coming sacrifice. That's what I'd become—a lamb led to slaughter at the altar of water. I reached out a shaking hand to turn on the flow, a lever each for hot and cold. I dared not sample the temperature of the stream. I wanted this to end as soon as possible.

Steam rose from the basin as it filled, fogging the mirror. Perhaps a blistering hot wash would hurt so badly that I'd never notice the crazy pictures in my mind. That was my only hope. I shoved my hands into the water, biting my lip hard as I did it, desperate to find some other focus than the insanity I knew lay only a moment away.

The snake bit me, striking with the force of a thousand vipers. Instantly, I became liquid in the mouths of soldiers, a blessed wet that doused the faces of dusty, sweaty warriors. I lost sight of myself in the mirror, and I bit harder on my lip to force blood, desperate to maintain a hold on reality, but aware of two worlds—one real and one imagined. I knew the basin lay below me, and its heat singed my hands. In my mind's eye, the part of me still sane, I could imagine my palms and fingers turning beet red in the scalding bowl. The serpent struck at me repeatedly as vision after vision drowned my mind.

A spring lay all about me, a half-moon of rock eroded out of a hillside above, and I gurgled from the base of a mountain across stones, headed into a dry, parched plain. Men dressed in ancient battle garb stood in me, all around me, dipping their hands into me. I ran cold and wet, gurgling from the rock into a pool.

Some men knelt in me, others squatted. They all came thirsty. Some drank fully, were satisfied, and left, while others took a brief sample of me, then shook me from their hands and stood to leave. I flowed all about them, washing their sandaled feet with my coolness, slaking their thirst. In the distance, a shorter man, arrayed in fine armor, stood quietly and counted as they drank.

They all had beards, and I dripped from the black hairs of hardened warrior's faces. Some gathered me in their cupped hands and drank, while others knelt with beard immersed, sipping like an animal from my surface. But they all drank. The short bearded man counted each one, directing some to the left as they stood up, sending others to the right. There were so many splashing in me, grabbing at me, drinking me in, yet I continued to flow, bubbling from the mountain, headed from the pool to the plain, into a stark dryness where I withered into nothingness.

Three hundred men stood in one group, many more in the other. The sippers were together in the smaller group, and those who'd cupped their hands to drink of me gathered in the larger assembly. The cupped-hand drinkers remained behind, and the three hundred sipping warriors departed, marching onto a dusty plain.

Next, I saw blood pouring from the golden snake before me, and I jerked my hands free. Instantly, I stood in front of the mirror, hands beet red, and the basin black as ink. As water dripped from my scalded hands, I could still see them, the three hundred men who'd marched into battle with swords and shields raised, blood flowing all about them. But it was not their blood that flowed before me. I had filled these men, somehow. In my wetness, through my insanity, I could see that because of me they were protected. Even sanctified. They all lived.

The image vanished as Andrea burst through the door, her sweet voice a haven of rest. "Kate! You're a mess. How can I help?"

My knees buckled, and I reached out for the edge of the granite countertop, sinking into a pile of ruined clothes on the bathroom floor. Andrea caught me as I flopped onto the stone tile, lowering my head, arms around my knees, hands red with water burns.

For the first time since I was seventeen, I really cried. One of those deep, soul-shuddering sobs that flood the core of your being, bringing the flotsam of life to the surface. I didn't care how many more crazy pictures washed over me. Andrea's hand on my shoulder, then her warmth near me as she sat on the floor, arm around my blackness, were like a giant valve turning inside me, opening up a lifetime of bottled pain.

I bawled. With every choke and sniffle, a water demon danced in my head. Pain drained out of me in heaving sobs as Andrea gently wiped my face; two decades of self-imposed pressure finally found release.

Draped in the black filth of copy toner, my mind nearly gone and my hands scalded, I curled up in her arms and wept.

CHAPTER FOURTEEN

"D O YOU LIKE coffee?" I typed late on Thursday evening, wondering at once if it sounded like a dumb question. I sat in a coffee shop—at ISIP—asking someone I'd never met about his personal preferences. He might think me a stalker.

He?

How do I even know the person I'm talking to is a guy? We've been corresponding for what? Less than a week? He—she—never said. Gender has virtually no meaning in the world of instant messaging. I like that about the net.

"I love the stuff. Why?" The reply came back immediately.

"I'm in a coffee shop."

"Where?"

"Just a coffee shop. And they have great wireless."

"If you're in Seattle, you must be at ISIP," came back the reply. It made my skin crawl. I knew more about the Internet than ninety-nine out of a hundred people, and I knew enough to be wary of meeting someone at random from the net.

"I'm not in Seattle." Lies came easier, it seemed, with my sanity on the fritz.

"OK. How did work go today?"

The confrontation with Xavier, the toner fiasco, and the horror at the sink today were all memories I'd just as soon forget.

"Let's talk about something else," I responded.

"And the visions?" came the immediate reply. "Any better?"

"I'm all washed up," I wrote, chuckling at the pun but not the pain. This person seemed to really understand me. But to go further meant I had to bare all.

They probably think I'm nuts.

"Have you seen a doctor?"

"Yes. I had a bad wreck on my motorcycle, and I've fainted a couple of times. I've been to the hospital twice."

"I meant, have you seen a psychiatrist?"

"I won't do that." I pounded out the words. Shrinks were for mental disease. I was determined that would not be me.

I stared at a blinking cursor for a long moment. "Why?" came the long-awaited reply.

"They prescribe antipsychotic chemicals," I wrote, banging the keys again. The wisdom of a hundred websites all pointed me to the same conclusion—toss in the towel and go for the drugs. "I'm not psychotic." I stared at my words for a long moment before I hit Enter, then added, "I just want to be free."

WRKRJC responded in an instant. "So, you plan to diagnose yourself?"

I pondered how honest I wanted to be with this person. Maybe this buddy was just a shrink in disguise. "There will always be time for psychologists if I can't figure this out on my own."

"I understand. But you don't have to do it alone. I'd like to help."

I understand. I'd like to help. I stared at those words, a warm glow replacing my frustration.

I dove in headfirst. No caution. I'd tell all. "I see things, vibrant colors, realistic animals, scenery, people, and action, like I'm actually living it. I become the water in nearly every scene."

"Tell me more. What causes the visions?"

I pondered that question a moment before I keyed in the response. It seemed too easy, even stupid. But I could think of nothing else to say. "Water. When I touch it, even when I cry and sometimes when I sweat, the visions come. The more the water, the more vivid the pictures. It's come to the point that I can't even wash my hands or take a shower without some kind of insane movie erupting in my head."

"Got it. Describe your last two experiences."

"You're sure about this?" I wrote. Reliving these scenes was painful.

"I know I can help. But I can't tell you why just yet. Tell me about your last vision."

So I did. I started with the copper bowls and the snakelike faucet, and the sensation that I had become some kind of stream or spring, with men wading into me and drinking. Then the part about blood, when I pulled my hands out of the scalding water. The water had run so hot that my reddened skin bordered on first-degree burns. I told my Internet buddy about the warriors and what seemed to be a one-sided battle between three hundred men and a large force of sweaty soldiers. From the spring to soldiers, from drinking to blood, I confessed it made no sense. I hit Enter, like pulling the handle on a slot machine, and waited. Perhaps I'd hit the jackpot and I'd get back a diagnosis that made some sense.

"Got it."

That's all?

"Keep walking backwards," WRKRJC wrote. "I think I have an idea what's going on. What vision came before that?"

"You're up to this?" I asked.

"I'm up to it. But I'd like to know more."

"How much more?"

"Tell me everything. I'm all ears."

"I just told you enough to prove I'm crazy." Caution pulled me back, a little voice that said to be careful with this anonymous surfer on the net.

"These visions might be more than an inconvenience, and you—we—should talk them through to see what the common thread is."

"Are you a medical professional?"

"I'm a licensed professional, but not in medicine."

"What's that mean?" I asked.

"It means I want to help. I have experience in this kind of thing. Call me a water professional, if you want."

"You might be an incantation-humming candle-burning voo-doo-worshipping axe murderer," I wrote, sorry the moment I hit Send.

"I'm not, but I don't blame you for wondering. I can help. I promise."

"Prove it," I responded. The challenge seemed fruitless as soon as I sent the message. I started to leave the laptop and grab another cup of Hiram's new blend when the next note appeared. My heart skipped a beat as I read it.

"In one of your early visions, you saw a rainbow."

My knees buckled and I sank back into the chair, my mind's eye replaying the brilliant colors spawned by the rain that fateful evening on the Ice Rocket. The night I should have been killed.

The laptop pinged again, and the next message stole my breath.

"In another vision you were drowning. Something really big came along and swallowed you."

✦ ✦ ✦

Candice wiped at the edges of my table, careful not to touch my laptop with her damp cotton rag. She stood beside me until I looked up from the screen, my heart pounding.

Despite her simple ways, Candice understood eye contact. Gramps used to say that your soul lived in your eyes and that those people who looked away had no soul. They had nothing left in them to view, transparent creatures whose inner being was devoid of color. Lost people.

Candice certainly was not lost; her blue eyes were ablaze with care. What birthed that spark in her that caused so many to brighten? Simplicity defined her. Life had to be more complex than she made it seem.

Or was it?

Captured by her childlike purity, I ignored the laptop, my eyes locked on hers. Candice cocked her head like a cat contemplating a mouse that won't run. Somehow, by not looking away, I'd broken her routine.

She rested her wadded cloth on the edge of my table and reached out with her other hand, touching my forearm. A huge grin spread across her unpretentious face, and her eyes misted. She spoke a message I'd heard dozens of times at ISIP, but this time her words were special, a pronouncement meant just for me. Her fingers, though damp, were warm where they rested on my skin.

"Jesus can make you clean, Miss Kate." She paused, her eyes full of love. "I promise."

CHAPTER FIFTEEN

"PULL THE blade along this line. And go slowly," I cautioned.
Liam's mother watched over his shoulder the next afternoon on the deck of the *St. Jude* as her son worked the short blade of his new pocketknife along a length of balsa wood. Mother might be scared for her son, but I could tell this boy had used a knife before, just as I had the first time Gramps put one in my hands. Liam smiled and whittled in silence. He lived in boy heaven at this moment, and it made me feel warm inside just to watch him.

"How deep do I cut?" he asked, pulling slowly along the line that defined one edge of a series of wooden links.

"About half an inch, Liam. We make two slices on each of the four sides. Then we'll mark off the links and carve out the centers. It goes fast."

I think Mrs. O'Malley—Gloria—was as fascinated with the carving as she was with her son. We made this a threesome. Warmed under a hot sun and clear skies, we laid out the project and whittled our way into a couple of sticks of balsa. By the end of the hour, Liam had a crude five-link chain joining two square blocks.

"This is a good place to take a break," I said. "We'll dive into the ball and cage next."

"Coffee?" Gloria offered. Much as I loved Hiram's imports, I hated to turn her down.

"Sure."

Liam marveled at the chain. "Your grandfather liked to fish?" he asked.

"He was the best. He worked the Grand Banks, then moved to New York. I grew up on the docks." Life repeated itself. I had been Liam once, many years ago.

"Did he ever get caught in a big storm?" the boy asked as he pared off some rough edges with the blade.

"Lots of 'em. Including some hurricanes that worked all the way up the east coast."

"Was he a line fisherman?" Liam talked as he worked, like Gramps used to do. I loved to watch him, his hands at one with the blade. The boy carved like a natural.

"Yes. Like your dad. He spent lots of time in the sun."

"And the rain!" Liam exclaimed. "I have my own slicker. It's yellow."

"I like the rain, too—at least, I used to."

Liam paused his whittling and looked up. "Not anymore?"

I shook my head, unable to speak. For a blessed hour, I'd not thought about the visions. I'd been a little girl again, in my grandfather's tugboat wheelhouse, curled up on the bench with a knife in hand and shavings all over the floor. Gramps sat there in his wheelhouse chair, a stained coffee mug in his hand and an old cap pulled back on his head, watching me. He could watch me for hours and be happy, sipping his coffee on a bobbing boat.

"It rains a lot here, doesn't it, Miss Pepper?" Liam's reminder doused my memory of Gramps. I became "Crazy Kate" again.

Wacko when wet.

+ + +

Liam's first carved ball and chain looked far better than my first one did twenty years ago. His initial attempt at the captured ball in a cage looked more like a jagged boulder pinned between four skinny trees, but it made for a good start. He twirled the loose chain and its captured ball as he ran the length of the boat to meet his dad at the gangway. It felt good to watch the boy, to be released from my mental baggage through him.

"Tom's back. We'll have dinner tonight about seven, if you want to stick around," Gloria said. "I know Liam would like it. And so would I." She pressed a hand against mine where we sat on two folding chairs on the boat's fantail.

Late afternoon sun lit the base of thick clouds to the west. Like a spotlight on an approaching bulldozer at night, it made it possible to see just what was headed our way. The sunny Friday Andrea had forecast had turned out to be just that. But rain would be here over the weekend. Maybe this evening. It sent chills down my spine.

"I'd love to, Gloria. Really would. But there's rain coming, and I need to get home."

She laughed. "You're not walking back, are you?"

"No." I hesitated. "I took a cab."

"Then stay. You won't melt if it rains a little. We'd love to have you join us for dinner tonight. To celebrate."

I couldn't take my eyes off the wall of wet anguish marching toward me from the west. The sun-drenched orange and red flames on the bases of the clouds dipped into the horizon somewhere beyond Seattle. In minutes, that sun would set, and darkness would obscure the approaching crazy water.

"Celebrate?" I asked, trying to fixate on Gloria, not my problem.

"Celebrate you! A new friend. Please stay, Kate."

Perhaps I could. Her touch, her warmth, and the joy Liam had brought me today all made this feel like home. No, not home. More like being with Gramps on the tugboat. "Home" meant lectures about proper dress and hours of Father's television, big loud gatherings of extended family, and an endless stream of acid chatty gossip.

This day had been private, nonjudgmental, and the best part—we'd spent our time on a boat.

Before I could say no, Gloria pulled me up from the chair and took me to meet her husband. Half an hour later we toured the bowels of the *St. Jude*, where I learned the business end of albacore fishing from the captain as I stood in a shiny silver freezer with Liam at my side. Embraced by this family, I felt every one of my concerns vanished. I was safe in the belly of *St. Jude*.

I didn't want to leave.

✦ ✦ ✦

Xavier's ringtone warbled in my purse, stopping my fork halfway to my mouth.

"Excuse me," I said, embarrassed to have interrupted the family's meal.

"Take the call; it's no big deal," Tom said, dismissing the interruption with a wave of his hand. "Use the galley." He pointed behind me to the tiny kitchen. We filled their micro–dining room, also used as a chart and tackle room. Until now.

I jerked the loud interruption out of my purse and tapped the Answer icon, pressing it to my ear as I pushed back from the table. "Xavier?"

"Where in the world are you, Kate?"

No "hello, how are you?" or "I miss you." Just the demand. Vintage Xavier. I rushed through the hatch into the privacy of the small cooking area.

"I'm at dinner. With friends. Why?"

"You left the office early."

"Yes. I had an appointment."

"I hope you're at a meeting with a client, because we're all still here at the office, and you're the only one who's not pulling with my team. I'm disappointed."

"It's nearly eight o'clock, X. Who's at work at eight on a Friday night?" I could almost see him glancing at his watch, ever vigilant of time.

"We all are. After you left for one of your afternoon siestas, we received the Request for Proposal from Riddle Corporation that we've been waiting on—for a big purchase. They dropped it off around five."

"On a Friday night?"

"On a work night, Kate. Revenue. Sales. Profit. That's what this is all about."

"I know what an RFP means, Xavier. What I meant was that it's Friday."

"And the Kate I remember would relish a chance to dive into a proposal. Why lose the weekend? The response is due next Friday. We're working tonight. 'We' means all of us. So get down here. Now."

"I'm at dinner, X."

"Then swallow and leave."

I held the phone away from my ear and stared at it, jerked back into the real world from an afternoon in Shangri-la. As Xavier continued to rant, I powered off the phone.

The family was chatting away as I returned to the galley, Liam with a left hand locked on his new wooden chain, and his right hand shoveling food. They stopped in unison when my long face entered the room.

"I have to go," I said. "Business. The team is working tonight on an important proposal."

"The fish are running," Tom said with a smile. "Wake up and put out a line." Liam laughed. He understood the metaphor.

Liam's chortle brought a smile to all three of us adults. These were working people, and they understood the dynamics of "do it now." That made me feel better.

"It's a big fish, and a great deal of money," I said, gathering up my things. "I'm sorry that I have to leave so suddenly. This afternoon has been a great vacation for me."

All three of the family stood up. Xavier never did that for me.

"Don't apologize, Kate. You made our day special. We hope you'll come back soon." Tom turned and smiled at his son.

Gloria led me to the gangway to say good-bye. I could smell the approaching storm, the air laden with the warm, wet feel of rain. It made my skin crawl, and I wanted to run. Her hand lingered on my arm a moment before she let me go, like she could read what was going through my mind. "Tom meant what he said back there. We hope you can come back. Often."

I nodded, in a hurry to get going. She didn't let go and pressed her point.

"If there's something we can help with, we're as close as a phone call." She handed me one of Tom's cards, her eyes locked on mine. "Don't be a stranger, okay?" She released her hold on my elbow, but I didn't leave right away. I stared in silence into her gaze. I felt like she understood the storm that roiled inside me, the worry that I might indeed be losing my mind.

Gloria smiled, as if she'd read that very thought. "Remember, Kate. You're not alone."

You're not alone. That's what Dr. Lin had said.

How could she possibly know?

✦ ✦ ✦

"You have to cooperate to graduate," Xavier said late that night as he leaned with one hand on the huge office copier while I fed originals into the yawning mouth of the tree killer.

Xavier picked the dumbest metaphors sometimes, and this was one of those occasions. Nevertheless, I understood his point. Gramps would call his comment a "warning shot across your bow." In a matter of days, I'd gone from being the boss's sweetheart and his winning Technology Commercialization Director to a woman desperate for change. Desperate for a new relationship, and desperate to get my mind back.

I pulled papers from the collator and tucked them into a bundle in my crossed arms like a 'sixties schoolgirl. I made brief eye contact with X but said nothing. I wouldn't give him the satisfaction of knowing that he'd hit home. He'd made it abundantly clear in that last comment. There was no way to keep my job, other than to yoke myself to him. The implications of staying with Xavier made me gag.

"Don't threaten me, X. And I do intend to 'graduate'," I said, pulling my shoulders back and making myself as tall as I dared. "The main question is, do I help *your* team win, or help someone else's?"

That return shot registered, and X stood speechless. I walked out of the copier room and headed for the proposal center, our hub for the production of this latest bid. I could hear X pounding down the hall about five heartbeats behind me. Something in me said this would be the defining moment of my career at Consolidated Aerodyne. The footsteps accelerated, and I smacked my stilettos even louder as I walked. The staccato fire of my heels in the corridors late on a Friday night was like a series of gunshots. Bullets aimed at my soon-to-be ex-lover.

"Kate." One word, the tone of which was certainly not a "can you help me?" or "over here!" message. My name had become a verb, a synonym for "stop." I kept walking, smacking heels all the louder. He demanded again, and I pounded my stilettos into the cherry floor so hard they surely made dimples in the wood. The proposal center lay a few strides away, and I wanted the protection of others around me. I'd heard his tone before. The tiger had been riled.

One stride short of the open door into our little proposal war room, Xavier grabbed me and tried to hold me back. I was moving too fast to stop, taken by surprise. While I balanced on those tiny

Fendi heels, his firm grip about my right elbow spun me like a top. His iron fingers shot darts of pain down my arm, and bent me in two as I cascaded to the floor. Then he let go—at the worst possible time. With my head lower than my waist, my back arched, and Justus and Andrea upside down in my vision, the back of my head hit the floor with a smack.

There wasn't any water this time, just the sharp blow to my head and stars in my eyes, followed by blackness.

Everything hurt.

✦ ✦ ✦

"She fainted again," Xavier said somewhere in the dim reaches of my consciousness. My eyes didn't work, but I could hear. I could smell Andrea's distinctive perfume and felt her gentle touch. It felt better, just knowing that she was there.

Fainted? Is that what he said?

I tried to mumble but it came out gibberish.

"I tried to grab her when she went down," Xavier said. "I raced to catch up with her, even yelled her name to get her attention, but I reached her too late."

I couldn't see him, but the voice towered over me. Typical.

I shook my head but Andrea gripped my forearm. I heard her whisper, "Shhh." Her breath warmed my ear. "Don't worry. We saw it."

I squeezed my eyes closed. If I put my mind to it, this nightmare would end. My boss and erstwhile boyfriend telling people he'd tried to help me.

But had he?

Maybe I did faint. I felt Andrea's hand slide under my back and I opened my eyes. Xavier stood silently above me, with not a word to say. Andrea put her lips close to my ear again as I got my bearings.

"He's a snake," she whispered. That sealed it. The fall was his fault.

"Here," Andrea said, moving in front of me. Before I knew what happened, she smothered my face with a damp cloth.

"This will make you feel better," she said as the cool rag touched me. For a brief interlude, the wetness was refreshing. But the cloth soon morphed into a suffocating veil, and I tried to turn to avoid the contact. Andrea daubed at my face with motherly intent, but her wet care sparked vivid explosions in my brain.

I lay in a well, deep in the ground, looking up. The shaft stretched out above me so far that only a tiny point of light shone above me. Yet, the tiny beam shone brilliantly, almost heavenly. It radiated a sense of peace, of caring. It was a strong light, almost like a rope that I could grab and hold to pull me up. But I had no hands. I rippled and dripped as a clay flask dropped into me and was filled. A thin cord pulled at the flask and jerked it out of me. I tried to hold on, but my watery liquid fingers dripped off the braided line as the flask disappeared into the heavenly light.

I could hear voices far at the upper end of this deep vertical tunnel. One Voice spoke strong, slow, and full of love. I wanted to see the face that declared words with such authority, but I could see nothing of it, my sight clouded again by another flask dropping into me, draining away more of me to fill the clay vessel. I tried in vain to hold on to the flask but dripped off as it ascended. Part of me went with the flask, but that part no longer claimed me once it left. My soul remained locked in the bottom of the well, wedded to an eternity deep in the earth. I yearned to rise up and be free. The Voice, though nearly a whisper so deep in the ground, rang clear in my fluid ears, calling me upward.

The Voice infused me, as though its hands had formed me long ago. I knew this Voice somehow, like I'd heard it many times before, calling to me, knocking at a door long unanswered. The words rang clear, and they spoke about me, a watery grave deep in the ground. "Everyone who drinks of this water will be thirsty again," the Voice said, the strong utterance of a patient man. "But whoever drinks of the water I give him will never thirst."

A flask fell into me a third time, and I leapt into it, brimming over the clay lip and screaming in tinkling tones to "take me." I wanted to be that special water he spoke of, to touch him, to be held by the Voice. He called me, pulled at me with a rope of love. I wanted to be with the source of that call, but the flask departed, and again I dripped away.

The Voice dimmed, and I lay wet and cold at the bottom of the shaft. No more flasks came to me, only the faint sound of a woman yelling to someone in the distance. "Come! See! A man who told me everything I ever did!"

I awoke. My eyes snapped open, but I shut them again, trying in vain to recapture that Voice, that warm, loving spirit I'd felt so keenly in the solitude of the deep and dark. I wanted it back. For the first time since my mind had led me down dark paths, I wanted to be back inside my head, not in the real world. My heart ached, the woman's words echoing inside me. Perhaps those were my words. Perhaps that was my voice echoing from the top of this deep well.

I became aware again. I was sitting up, with Andrea holding the cloth and her other hand on my shoulder. My heart felt like it would break, and I couldn't understand why until I looked up—into the dark eyes of Xavier, their blue no longer inviting. The words of the Voice reverberated inside me, radiating distant memories of that brief but glorious glimpse of peace.

I doubled over, breaking eye contact with a man I now despised, desperate to learn more about the One I'd just heard but could not see. A man who had once proclaimed that he loved me had now thrown me down, and the Other whom I craved to know better had just disappeared beyond my reach.

I lay broken, beyond hope.

CHAPTER SIXTEEN

MONDAY.

THE LETTER fell from my hands at the kitchen table. Its words screamed at me from where it landed on the floor. "Due to corporate downsizing and unfavorable results from our quarterly audit, we regret to inform you that your position has been eliminated effective immediately. Consolidated Aerodyne values its relationships with its loyal employees and regrets this sudden notification. In keeping with our long-standing policy of 'Employees first!' we wish to offer you a generous twelve-week severance package, less any debts outstanding on corporate accounts."

I looked at the form letter where it lay at my feet. The small print at the bottom, too tiny to read from so far away, had tattooed itself in my memory. "Please return your computer and retrieve personal effects at our security office during normal working hours. Your IT account has been disabled."

Fired.

How long had it been? Less than seventy-two hours since Xavier knocked me off my feet at the office Friday night, and now it's Monday afternoon and there's a letter waiting in my mailbox after I get home from work. It must have been mailed on Saturday, even Friday while I was at the office, to reach me so soon. No hints all weekend while we slaved on a critical proposal, no notice about what was about to transpire when we went to work today, as I helped him to win this new bid. This had the marks of Xavier all over it. Tossed out before I could blame Friday's fall on him, tossed out before I could jump ship for another company.

Tossed out before I could cause him any more grief.

What had he said that night, in his "shot over the bow"? "You have to cooperate to graduate, Kate." He had tested me then, giving me my graduation exam. In his mind, I'd failed.

But I didn't care.

My cell warbled, and I pulled it from my jacket pocket. If it had been anyone but my one-and-only girlfriend, I'd have never answered.

"Andrea?"

"Kate, I just got home. Guess what letter bomb waited for me in my mailbox?"

"It probably looks like mine," I said, my heart sinking for my friend. She didn't deserve this. "'We value our relationships with our loyal employees . . .' Something like that?" My spirits sank as I talked. My friend had gone down with me.

"The same. Gosh, I'm sorry, Kate. I didn't know they got you, too."

"I'm the reason we're gone, Andrea. You were swept along for the ride."

"Don't be too sure," she said. Andrea sounded confident, almost cocky. Not like her.

"There's more?" I asked.

"Lots more. It's dirt, and you won't like it."

"All ears," I said, my anger on the rise.

"Remember the Japanese deal that fell through? The guys who flew to town but you were unable to meet with them?"

How could I forget? After I'd collapsed with a vision, I lost track of time, all because of the stupid hallucinations. The water's fault. My fault. Losing my mind made me lose my job.

"Get this. Xavier managed to reel them back in. He contacted them without telling you and convinced them to return to the States the next week. Paid their way back first class with the corporate card, along with a boatload of gifts, which sparked the corporate audit. The same audit you were told had been poking into your corporate card expenditures. That was just a cover for the real problem."

She paused and I tried to get a word in, but she cut me off.

"All his money and talk won them over. They wrote a contract on the spot for a thousand airline seats. A five-airplane deal, with options on ten thousand more seats and fifty more airplanes. Very generous pricing for us, a big profit for Xavier, and non-negotiable terms. Among them? You had to go. It was Xavier's idea, by the way, not theirs."

"How'd you learn all this?" I asked, trying hard not to scream.

"Xavier's been 'sampling the candy' at the office, girlfriend. None of us knew until Friday. Justus ran some e-mail filters and caught a message he wasn't supposed to see. He approached the woman about it, and she talked to me at the proposal center after you went home Friday night." She paused again. "They've been seeing each other for a long time. Justus found out, and that exposure put us all on the street." Her voice cracked. "It's not fair."

Screams died in my throat, and I choked. No more anger, just pain. Deep bleeding rawness. How long had he been jumping beds? For days? Weeks? Months?

A tear formed at the corner of my eye. I could feel its wetness, a warm globule welling up, ready to roll. I held my head still, knowing what would surely come next. I moved the sleeve of my jacket to catch it, but it jumped as another tear replaced it. Dripping down my cheek, the liquid pain worked its illusion, and the first wild image danced in my mind.

Lakes and rivers, then gurgling brooks, rainstorms, and tossing white-capped waves. A mind full of water imagery.

I clawed at the tear on my cheek, ripping at it with the edge of my jacket sleeve. Damnable water, ripping out my sanity drop by drop. Water that had distracted me from the Japanese meeting. Water that felled me too many times in the past days, water that eroded the foundation of my career. Everything pointed back to water. Water in my mind that made me think for a moment that someone out there knew me, knew everything I'd ever done; a commanding Voice of authority who cared for me, even forgave. All of it just a hallucination.

I was no one, jobless . . . and crazy. An unemployed woman with nutty images dancing in her head every time she got wet.

I don't remember saying good-bye to Andrea. At some point, I simply pushed the Hang Up icon and turned the phone off. The world turned me off, so I returned the favor. No more world. No more water.

It was time for action, on my terms.

I would recapture my sanity by controlling my environment.

Control. The only path to success I'd ever known.

✦ ✦ ✦

Two months later.

"I refuse to wear sweatpants," I said to the screen of my laptop, a dingy old Dell I'd rescued from a thrift store; I didn't dare buy something exotic at this point in my life, in between jobs. I talked to my computer a lot these days. I lived alone at the condo, by choice. Life resembled a pit, and I stood smack dab in the middle of it. A tar pit.

Sweatpants were the cotton feel-good clothes for women who lounged around with nothing to do. I wouldn't let myself sink to that level of despair. Yet, how could I make a case for a life of anything but despair at this point? Of all the things that mattered to me, only my waist size had gotten better. The rest of my life, like my apartment, lay in a mess, and I hated messes. What little food I ate had to be eaten without cleaning. Paper plates and plastic forks worked tolerably well, but it hurt me to see such large trash bags go out of a household that had once recycled everything except toilet waste. Bottles of hand sanitizer sat everywhere, including one to the left of my computer. I squeezed out a dollop of the clear liquid, my only form of cleansing. I took spit-baths with the stuff. And, blessedly, I'd lived for eight weeks with no visions.

I looked across the room to where Shogun plied dark waters in his own dingy home. I'd not found a way to get water to clean or refill his tank without touching it, so I resigned myself to the decision that Shogun would make it on his own or perish along with me. Fatalism cast a broad net.

I'd become the expert on living without pure water, but that lifestyle was taking its toll. I never ventured outdoors if I couldn't see a clear sky. Even fog had an effect on me now, and I resolved to never encounter clouds in any form. Hand lotion, a battery powered razor and a sharp blade made shaving my legs and armpits tolerable, albeit infrequent. The one major drawback? Washing my hair. It turned into a grease trap without a good shampoo. I lusted for a good lathering and a long dunk under the caress of the steaming-hot jets of a showerhead. But I dared not get wet. I would win this battle, at any price.

I could drink anything liquid as long as pure water never crossed my lips, and coffee became my drink of choice. Cases of Diet Dr. Pepper and gallon jugs of orange juice were second and third on my list. I lived in a perpetual caffeine-and-sugar high, truly deep sleep a thing of the distant past. Sometimes I went days drinking only coffee, preferably the hard stuff at Hiram's ISIP when I could venture out for it safely. Hyper-caffeinated, I slept only when exhaustion overwhelmed me. Sleep would hold me in its nightmarish dream-crazed grip for a few hours, until another waking zombie state ensued. Then I waited for more exhaustion. Troubled dream-plagued sleep was only slightly worse than hallucinating from lack of sleep, but I preferred to fight my battle awake.

I peed all the time, loaded as I was with diuretics. But at least I lived hydrated. A doctor would condemn my diet, and no doubt, I would wreck my poor kidneys, but there had not been a vision in sixty days. That counted for something. The other part of using the bathroom involved a bit more complication. I loaded the bowl with a puffy ball of paper to prevent any splash-back, and I went through two rolls of paper a day. As long as we had a sewage treatment plant in Seattle where people needed jobs, I didn't care. I'd long cast off any pretense of saving the Earth. I intended to save Kate. Trees died every day to keep my butt dry and my head clear.

Andrea came over two weeks ago and left after only fifteen minutes. She said she couldn't stand the mess, but I didn't notice it anymore. Life is war, and this was a war zone. Try living like me for two months. I thought I did a good job of adapting. I'd become a Bedouin, living a nomadic waterless life in the Arabian desert of Seattle, a place where one underwent great pains to stay 100 percent dry.

My laptop became my solace. The recycled machine was a far cry from my old MacBook, a three-hundred-dollar foray into the digital world. I'd determined to stretch out my twelve-week severance package as long as it would last, and with my current approach, that might be as long as a year. I tried not to think about what state I'd be in after twelve months of self-imposed water exile. But I was sure of one thing as I typed away—I'd never sink to the ignominy of wearing sweatpants.

Where my laptop became my solace, WRKRJC served as my constant digital companion. Girl or guy? I cycled from certain to unsure on a weekly basis. *He* became my pronoun of choice for the chatterer's complicated screen name. Perhaps that was wishful thinking, that there could be a man who listened, a man who cared enough to keep showing up online to help me day after day with no hope of any "payback." A spiritual element ran through WRKRJC's writings the way a single gold thread courses through a bolt of white cloth. Yet, I never felt pushed to buy into something I didn't believe. And for some unexplainable reason, I never bothered to ask if my messenger friend was a guy.

It's funny how the most mundane things we talked about could lead to a serious discussion about the meaning of life. I lived as an instant-messenger addict now, waiting for every opportunity to talk to *them*. I hoped—no, I fantasized—that WRKRJC was a "he." A single man, an attractive trustworthy man who liked a dry woman with greasy hair, a woman who bathed with hand sanitizer and shaved with skin lotion.

My ISIP cup had been running on empty for too long. I needed another jolt. I checked the weather on the Dell, starting with local observations downtown and at the airport. Then I checked the extended two-hour and daily forecast, followed by a few peeks at webcams around town, and finally a trip to the window. The coast looked clear, no sign of rain. I speed-dialed the cab company. My brand new Ice Rocket was parked in a display at a local motorcycle shop. Many days I wished I'd not spent the insurance money on a new bike. I could use the cash right now, and I dared not ride again considering my struggles with rain. The cab would pull up to the front of my condo, and in a few minutes, I'd be safe in the embrace of Hiram's coffeehouse. I'd done it fifty times in the past two months.

ISIP. My nirvana.

◆ ◆ ◆

Three hours of coffee shop Internet chatting and countless instant messages later, I'd loaded up on two super-grande cups of Hiram's special blend and another of Hiram's brilliant grilled cheese sand-wiches. Life was more than tolerable today. It was good.

The phone warbled, one of my rare calls coming in. Since my days at Consolidated Aerodyne, I'd spoken less and less with Andrea. It had been almost a week since we talked last. No one else used my number, and I jumped when the phone rang. Coffee made me hyper. I stared at the number on the screen through two more rings, trying to place it. A 212 area code.

My parents.

"Kate?" It was my father. I'd answered the phone without so much as a greeting. "Are you there?" he asked after my long pause.

When had we last talked? A month ago? No. It had been much longer. I'd had a job the last time I had spoken with my father. I'd had a boyfriend, if you could call him that. I knew now that I'd simply been one of three women on his string, each of us convinced we were his one and only. And remarkably, all of us worked in the same office. When I had talked to my father the last time, fall knocked at Seattle's door. By now, Thanksgiving meals had long been digested and the Christmas countdown started days ago. It had been a long, long time since we had talked.

"Yes. It's me."

"Kate. We haven't heard from you in forever. Are you all right?"

I hated that sound of pain in his voice, as if he was feigning hurt or something like it. But I knew better. I'd been a source of distress for him as a daughter, and surely this pain was more of his contrived concern, putting on a show for Mother. My father never called. Not without provocation. Telephones interrupted his television, an unforgivable violation of Norman Pepper's media sanctum.

"I'm fine. Been busy, that's all." What else could I say?

"That's good. Real good. Mom's here and she wants to talk to you, but I thought I'd get on the line first. We've been worried. Real worried. Mom's having lots of messages about you."

No! Don't take me there.

"Dad, you know I don't—"

"I know, Kate. I know. But hear me out, okay? Mom's had some real visions this time. Strong ones, and they're all about you. We don't hear from you. Not even a letter—"

"Get e-mail," I replied. "Join the real world."

"Anyway. She's never had visions like these. Okay? So, talk to her. She's worried stiff about you, Missy."

"My name is Kate. It's been Kate for twenty-nine years. Not Missy."

"You'll always be Missy to me. Listen, here's your mom. And call us once in a while."

I could imagine life in the brownstone in Queens at this moment. Mother would walk in from the kitchen, set down her apron, and my father would hand her the phone. One of those old dial versions connected by a long cord to the wall. They'd never invested in a wireless device of any sort, not even a push-button phone. The concept of cellular telephones eluded them. And they didn't own a computer. My parents belonged on *Leave It to Beaver* or *The Ed Sullivan Show*.

"Kate?" Mother asked. As soon as I said yes, she launched into her crying spell. Bawling about how it had been weeks since she'd heard from me, how my aunts and uncles all asked about me and she had no idea. Stressing out about my cousins who all managed to live within two blocks of their own parents, and how they'd all had such a great time at Thanksgiving, but where was I? Her visions about me, predictions about something horrible happening, about some bad men in my life. At least she'd gotten that part right.

Mother never asked about me. Calls were always about her, about how I'd wronged her by living so far from home, hurt her by not calling, offended her by wearing stilettos, or sinned against God by not going to church.

"Come home for Christmas. Please?" she pleaded after ten minutes of a one-way conversation, then she was silent at last. Every call went like this. Rant, rant, rant . . . then wait.

"Mother, this is a very difficult time for me. I don't know if I can do that."

"I know it's difficult. I've seen that."

"How can you see anything? You're not here. You don't even know what I'm going through."

"But I do, Missy. I have these dreams. I sense that you're in some kind of horrible trouble at work, and you're with a bad man. That's all I know, but I know the vision is true. It always is."

I'd spent a lifetime listening to her imaginings, her wild and vivid hallucinations. Every morning at the table, long-winded recitations. More of it every evening at dinner, as though the rest of us did nothing with our lives. And at Sunday gatherings after church with a dozen Italian cousins, everyone looking like her, all conversation centered on her revelations—Mother, our family prophetess. Now, here I sat, in the midst of the worst grunge of my life, on the brink of becoming my mother.

No visions for me. Not a chance. I dared not get wet.

"Your father's calling me, Kate," she said after a short pause. "He says there's a really important show coming on, so I need to go. It was great to talk with you."

Talk with me? This was a transmission, not a conversation.

"Please, come home for Christmas, Kate. We miss you so much."

"And if I can't?" I asked, regretting the words as soon as I spoke them.

She didn't answer right away.

"I . . ." Mother stopped, speechless.

"I'm sorry. That didn't come out the way I wanted it to."

"No, you asked me a valid question. I . . ." She paused, and I could hear a long wheeze as she took a breath. "I want you to know that I love you, Kate. Whatever it is that's separated us these past twelve years, I hope you can forgive me. Forgive *us*. Let's not miss a chance to hug each other once more, before it's too late."

Too late?

"You think about it, okay? We'd love to see you."

"Mom . . ."

I'd never called her "mom" since I left home. It slipped out before I knew it. I could tell that the word stunned her as much as it did me.

"I need to go, Missy. I'm not feeling well these days. Please, come home soon." She wheezed again, and then the phone clicked off.

✦ ✦ ✦

"No!" I pounded the table with my fist, slopping a brimming new cup of brew onto the deeply etched "funt." Precious brown liquid ran into the pen-gouged grooves, and I reached for a napkin to mop up the mess.

Mother had done it again. She'd made the one-way call, laid the great guilt trip on me, and then run away before I could tell her anything about my life or learn anything substantive about hers. My father had placed the call, and then succumbed to the addiction of the television, unable to pull himself away for more than a minute. His attention span measured the duration of two advertisements. I'd seen it at home as a kid. If he had a call to make, it came during the commercials, and only during the ads he didn't like. He had a sixth sense for how long the ads would run. My father shut off many a conversation with me just in time to be reclined in front of the set as the show came back on. I'd served as his commercial break this afternoon.

Candice swept by my table making her rounds as I dabbed at the coffee mess. Before I could stop her, she whipped out her wet rag.

"No!" I yelled, pushing away from the table with both hands. The base of the cup went away from me, and its top tipped straight at me. Candice moved fast and grabbed the cup, but it sloshed a few sips on my jacket. My hands flew in the air, and Candice had the rag on me before I could stop her. I wore Gore-Tex neck to foot and rain pants, waterproof everywhere but my hands and face. Her dreaded rag had no effect.

I lowered my hands and smiled. For a moment, I forgot the call. I'd defeated water, my ultimate enemy.

I sat down, nodding with embarrassment to the other patrons who'd been startled by my outburst. Candice wiped the table, but tarried before she moved on to another wiping task.

"Jesus can make you clean," she repeated for perhaps the thousandth time that month. I once counted her recitations for four hours soon after I started coming to ISIP, and determined that she said it to the patrons at least thirty times a day.

"Thank you, Candice. I'm fine."

The pillar of blue stood like a statue, her rag tucked into her bosom, where she carried it against that dingy blue golf shirt. She stared at me for a long moment. Her eyes were not stark or beautiful. But they were wet. Candice hurt, and tears had welled up.

"You're not fine, Miss Kate. I can see that."

In all my days with her, I'd never heard her speak so clearly, so succinctly. She dropped one hand from her grip of the wet rag against her shirt and put it out to touch mine where it rested against the table. As she did, a tear rolled from her eye unchecked, trickling down her pudgy cheek.

Her hand was rough, cracked by too many hours clutching a damp rag. She took my hand in hers and squeezed it for a long moment as another tear broke free.

She held with a grip that was warm and strong.

Her hand was wet. New lights sparked in my eyes.

✦ ✦ ✦

"Go! Wash!" I heard. Someone lived in my head, commanding me. I could smell myself, the filth of years, not of days. My eyes were covered in mud and smelled like spit. Hands pulled at me, dragging me. My vision ceased to exist, my mind filled with black. I was blind.

A crowd jeered. People laughed at me. My knees bumped against rocky outcroppings as hard hands jerked me along and I stumbled.

Someone yelled, "Take him to the pool!" I could smell animals and cooking fires, and heard lambs bleating.

Moments later I felt the wash of water. A gentle hand took me from the grip of the rough ones that had led me to this place and carefully guided me to the edge of a pool. I could smell it, the sweet odor of dampness in a bone-dry place. The gentle hand placed mine into water, forming my hands into a cup and drawing them toward my face.

"Wash," the Voice said. That commanding, yet gentle timbre, once again. The Voice from the well. The Radiant One.

I splashed water on my face, wetting the dry scaled mud that covered my eyes. The water trickled into my mouth, slaking a thirst that seemed unquenchable. I cupped more water and splashed it again, drinking and washing at the same time. Feeling the edge of the pool, I bent over and put my face into water, scrubbing at the hard dirt on my eyes, now softened by cool liquid. Loosened mud fell from my eyes, and a brilliant light filled my mind as I stood.

Brightness consumed me. Colors, vibrant dancing hues that dazzled me, shapes I had felt for a lifetime but had never seen. And dozens of faces, heads with eyes that were like my own, yet every person about me different. After being locked in a dungeon of blackness for a lifetime, I could see at last.

I grabbed at the person closest to my left. The laughing and jeering had stopped; all were looking at me in stunned silence. I laughed, raising my hands to the sky as water dripped down my arms onto my filthy rags. I shouted out loud to all those near me.

"I was blind, but now I see!"

CHAPTER SEVENTEEN

TWO MONTHS LATER.

"How FAR can a person sink?" I wrote from the prison cell of my condo in the middle of the day. Somewhere out there my constant companion WRKRJC waited, ever ready with a wise answer and a listening heart. I could never meet him. I'd fallen too far, careening down a slope too steep to climb back up to my old life.

"Some people hit rock bottom. But they come back. With help from their friends. And help from above." His response came immediately, as though he'd waited all day to speak to me, carrying his laptop or his BlackBerry at the ready in his mysterious career as what he called a "water professional." I was convinced my digital pen pal was a "he." I wished it so.

"Help from above?" I wrote. "Don't see any need for that."

"Lots of people don't until they sink so low that they realize they need a helping hand."

"You weren't talking about a hand," I wrote back in hopes we could prolong this talk, one of his many forays into a gentle spiritual tongue-lashing. I wanted to talk, to communicate. Even if it was about issues that I had no interest in.

"Have you ever fallen and needed someone to lift you up?" he wrote.

"I *am* fallen," I wrote. "I've slid so far that there's no way back."

"Now you're the one who's speaking metaphorically. And you're right. We've all fallen. But I meant did you ever fall down as a kid and need someone to lift you up?"

"Sure. Everyone does."

"How did that make you feel?"

"Are you with the media?" I asked. Only TV reporters asked that stupid question.

"No. When that someone helped you up, did you appreciate it? Why?"

"Of course I appreciated it. It made me feel good that they cared. They were strong when I was weak."

"Good. That's what a hand from above can do for you. Physically, like you experienced. Metaphorically. And spiritually."

"Some big daddy in the sky's going to reach down and clean me up? Lift me out of this pit?" I chuckled aloud, imagining a godlike housekeeper who descended to shovel out the trash in my apartment. I looked around at the mess, a gradual accumulation since late November and my last trip out.

Candice's wet hand drove me to this. Wanting no more chance connections with water, I determined to dine in my own home whenever possible. But it was a living hell. I hadn't basked in sunshine, except through my bay window. No fresh air, except the breeze through my screens, in nearly four months. You start feeling sorry for yourself and the things that matter start to slide. Months ago I'd have vomited at the sight of an apartment like mine. Now I hardly noticed it.

The laptop dinged again.

"Yes, the 'Big Daddy' in the sky will reach down and lift you up, metaphorically. God won't lift you out of the grunge you say you live in, but He'll show you a way out of it. If you trust Him. He'll give you the inner strength to do the hard work yourself. He'll take the old you and make you into a new creature."

"Why are you capitalizing the word *He*?" I wrote back.

"I cap it because 'He' is Lord. The Big Guy deserves a little respect. The shift key's not too much trouble considering all He's done for me."

"You're drifting pretty deep into the spiritual world again, WRKRJC."

"And you don't like it, do you?"

"I like to talk to you, but no, I don't like it when you go yoga, incense, and confession booth on me."

"Yoga's not what I'm talking about. In fact, it's exactly the opposite of what I'm talking about. Don't get too wrapped up in the old church trappings from your childhood. You mentioned you were raised by a family that went to church, right?"

"Yes. We were—I mean, my parents are Catholic." I hated to think about it. More memories of Mother's control.

"I want you to think about spiritual things in the context of relationships, not church trappings, confession booths, incense, or even your parents' rules. God wants a relationship with you. He wants you to know Him, to trust Him. He loves you."

"Do you type that fast on a BlackBerry, or do you have a laptop strapped to your hip?" I wrote.

"You're changing the subject again."

"Answer the question."

"I will if you'll answer mine first."

"Be quick about it. Gotta go to the bathroom."

"God wants to help you out of your 'pit,' as you call it. The question is, do you want to change? How badly do you want to climb out of that hole?"

I really did have to go, and my body wasn't going to let me wait much longer. He deserved an answer so I spit it out, surprised as soon as I hit Send that I'd been so frank with him. "Want to change? Yes, I do." I paused, and then added, "I want out of this hole more than anything in my life."

I jumped up, clutching at my stomach, but hoping he'd answer quickly.

"I use a netbook and a Smartphone. Always wired."

That's what I thought. He had a laptop strapped to his hip like the Japanese. I typed a quick "b r b" and ran for the bathroom, about to explode.

It wouldn't be pretty.

+ + +

I hate fixing things. I particularly hate to fix things that should be simple but aren't. There's something insultingly straightforward about a clogged toilet that infuriates me. It's a nasty mess, and people like me can't seem to make the sewage go away. Yet, bring in one urban professional and *whoosh*, the clog is gone, for a hundred bucks. Using nothing but a piece of wire or a special plumber's tool. I'd plunged all I could stand; nothing went down. My life reminded me of this toilet bowl. A fetid swirling mess.

I dared not get closer to the bowl. Nasty, brown . . . and wet.

It was time to call for help.

Five pumps of the hand cleanser for this one. A dozen empty cleanser bottles choked the wastebasket to the right of my sink, and more flowed onto the floor. I'd taken the trash out four weeks ago, and more plastic spilled over in a nauseating stream of waste.

The mirror snagged me before I could escape the bathroom, insisting that I embrace truth. I faced the real me, not the one I imagined as I wiled my day away in front of a computer screen, hoping WRKRJC would write back every time I sent him a comment or question. I tarried at the reflection, wondering where the old Kate had gone.

Purple-black handbags hung below my eyeballs; ugly wrinkled things that waited to catch my pupils when they fell out. My skin was yellow. I used to think the funny coloration came from the constant application of baths of hand sanitizer, but I realized now that I suffered the jaundice of a rotten diet and no sun. I was killing myself, one day at a time. I looked back at the toilet. Water had ruined me and turned me into that mess.

Bushy eyebrows not plucked for three months resembled a fur coat, a reddish hairy line atop deep gaunt sockets. My oily head of hair was pulled back into a tight slimy ponytail. Pragmatism bested beauty at this point in my life. The top of my head shone like Xavier's old chrome, oily strands reflecting the bathroom light. Those bulbs that still burned, that is. I needed a handyman to fix this place. It had become a pigsty.

I tried hard not to notice the mess because my surroundings proved my failure. I'd determined to control and conquer, but to look at my habitat and survey my health, a visitor would conclude that "Kate gave up a long time ago."

One more glance at the toilet reminded me that I'd have to escape my condo to use another bathroom unless someone came and fixed my plumbing. The reckoning time had come. Another human would see this pit and laugh. I could smell the alternative; what waited in the bathroom would fester forever unless I got some help soon. I headed for my comfort, my friend who never talked back; the laptop and Google would lead me to a plumber.

I love the web. If I need something, it's out there. A quick Google and I'm in the domain of whatever world I desire. This time I searched a world I'd never before entered—the domain of pipes and tools and burly guys. I needed a plumber, and I had no plans to wade through a phone book when surely I'd find a tradesman who understood the net. It didn't take long.

"Virtual Plumber," I read out loud, chuckling at the thought of a wireless plunging job. That would be the ticket. Enter my debit card number, my drain would open magically, and the mess dissolve away into the Internet. I entered my information, checked the "clogged toilet" box, entered "please help!" in the comment box, and hit "submit."

It wasn't thirty seconds later that I got an e-mail response, a simple yet effective greeting.

"Plumber J is on the way!" From PLUMBRJ@VirtualPlumber .com.

I panicked. I'd done it. A man was headed to my home and I looked like crap. I scanned the mess around my condo; there was no way to fix this place or myself before he arrived. I assumed it was a "he" coming to help. I'd never met a lady plumber.

Considering what he might encounter soon in the bathroom, the rest of this disaster, including me, looked pretty good, so I returned to the laptop.

"I'm back," I wrote to WRKRJC. "Sorry it took so long. You still out there?"

No response.

♦ ♦ ♦

Not much to look at, an average sort of guy. Maybe a little on the heavy side, but he had a super smile. I didn't see his eyes wander a bit while he stood on my door stoop, half an hour after I'd summoned him on the web. He never seemed to notice the mess in the condo or my disastrous state of dress. And he didn't disrobe me with his eyes—a remarkable and pleasant change, considering my experiences with men. On the other hand, considering my state, who would give me more than a passing glance?

Too scared to talk, I didn't even introduce myself but ushered him directly to the bathroom and turned him loose. The less said the better. WRKRJC had answered my last instant message and I wanted to return to the net, addicted to his attention, and determined not bother the plumber.

"Where r u?" I typed. I hadn't heard from him in over ten minutes. That delay represented an eternity for my timely web friend.

A minute later, he wrote back. "Fixing stuff."

"What?" I asked, and again waited much too long for his return reply.

"Clogged toilet in a messy condo."

I froze, listening to the rattle of tools and the sound of metal against ceramic that came from the direction of the bathroom. My heart pounded as my fingers hovered over the laptop keys.

"How messy?" I stared at the two words for an eternity before I hit Send.

The sounds from the bathroom silenced a moment, then resumed as his answer hit my screen.

"Toilet's pretty rough but the lady's nice."

"You're a plumber?" I wrote back quickly. Again, the sounds in the bathroom silenced just before his answer appeared.

"That's one of the things I do. I help people fix stuff. I build, too."

More sounds of plunging and metal tools rattling in a bag were sounds of progress in the bathroom.

My heart raced. I hadn't needed my iPhone for days. But I knew right where to find it, buried under a pile of bills in the kitchen. I turned it on, grateful for a little residual battery power and a paid-up data plan. Typing with my thumbs as I walked, I returned to the den and approached the door to my bedroom.

"What's this lady look like?" I typed. As I hit the Send icon, I watched the back of the plumber through the bathroom door from a distance. There was little chance he'd hear me sneak up on him.

He dropped his tools and reached to a Smartphone on his hip, typing away quickly as he hunched over the raunchy bowl.

"She's really pretty but looks like she could use a friend."

I sucked in my breath as I read the response, with my hand to my mouth in surprise.

He heard me, stood up from his crouch over my toilet bowl, and turned. I stood there, red-faced I'm sure, my iPhone in one hand, the other hand covering my lips. The plumber—WRKRJC—smiled and stared at me for a long time in silence, then turned back to my toilet and continued plunging.

✦ ✦ ✦

When I was ten years old, my father took us all down to Rockefeller Plaza for a family outing. Something Mother said that day about his sloth set him off. They argued about who was harder to live with, and he compared Mother to her sister, a wild buxom Italian creature who'd flown the coop early and escaped the urban jungle. His comparisons weren't flattering, particularly to Aunt Isabella and her plunging necklines. Mother jumped on one of her favorite harangues: don't talk about someone, because you never know when they're listening.

Just as my father spit out some particularly derogatory term about my Italian aunt and her ample cleavage, I tugged on Mother's dress in desperation. Aunt Isabella ran toward us, arms outstretched and her chest bouncing under a tight blouse. Somehow, she'd come all the way from Jersey and tracked us down on our family day. No one paid attention to my warning, and Isabella collided with Mother and Father while they argued about my aunt. She'd heard my Father's last comment about "the tramp from Tuscany" as she ran up, and family nuclear warfare raged for half an hour on the sidewalk in front of a crowd of onlookers. It was the most embarrassing moment of my life.

Until now.

The only thing I could think to do was rearrange the oil slick on top of my head and put on some lip gloss. Everything I owned to get pretty was located in that bathroom, and I couldn't primp in front of him. What were the odds? A man who knew my deepest fears, deepest secrets, an anonymous ear on the web who'd walked me through the valley of despair for months, was now working in my condo where he could see the worst of me. I wanted to run, to avoid facing him. I'd heard the toilet flush a couple of times. Minutes, at most, separated us.

Yet, I desperately wanted to meet him, to talk, to share just as I'd done for months, to let him listen to what scared me, to ask him help me get a grip on this phobia—no, not a phobia, but a rational dread of water and what it had done to me. I'd descended into a grunge pit, given up on life. I wanted his assistance, to help me understand these pictures in my head, and to help me climb out of the pit.

He cared and he listened. I'd never known a man like that.

I stared into my reflection on the oven glass when he spoke. He might have been watching me for a long time. I'd lost track of how long I preened.

"That toilet would work better if you didn't flush the whole roll," he said.

As I spun about, he had a funny little smirk, like he was suppressing a larger smile. He wanted to laugh at me, at my toilet, my apartment, and my ugliness. My heart dove for the bottom of an endless abyss.

"Anything else I can do to help?" he asked as the smirk broke into a full-fledged smile. Not a laugh, but genuinely happy. Surely, he couldn't have enjoyed what he had just done. Or liked what he saw. The human mess and her urban sewer.

I fished for something professional to say but drew a blank. I just shook my head, words stuck in my mouth, red heat rushing to my cheeks. My yellow hollow cheeks probably turned orange as I blushed.

He extended his hand, and I jumped back, cutting off whatever he might say. A damp sheen showed on his fingers from where he'd washed. His hand represented a bomb in my mentally stable world of dry.

"How much?" I stammered, clutching the counter that blocked my retreat.

He shook his head, a broad toothy smile getting even larger. "My name's John. And no charge, okay? This one's on the house."

For the first time in months I smiled. I could feel an odd assortment of facial muscles work their magic; the sensation was tantalizing. Something warm, something funny, bubbled up inside me. It felt good to be amused.

"John?" I asked, nearly giggling. I couldn't stop myself, as though I'd sucked in a lungful of laughing gas.

"What's so funny?" he asked, his smile growing on me by the minute. "You're not going to make some kind of toilet joke about my name are you?"

He didn't seem the least bit bothered by my middle-school humor, and I cringed, even more embarrassed than when he'd walked into the room. My first response had been to insult him. I could feel the red in my cheeks deepen, and my face was hot.

"No. No, I—I'm sorry. No jokes." I paused, taking a deep breath. "John. It's a common name. It's nice."

"Common? That's funny. So is Kate."

I wanted to crawl inside that smile of his and wrap it all around me. A smile wide enough to paper a wall, to make a dress, or to sleep in. Something made this man happy, and he had it plastered all over him. Nothing about me seemed to put him off; it was like he could look past the dirt in my condo and past the filth I had become, yet see goodness in all of it. I wanted some of that.

His hair hung brown and straight—straight like mine used to be when I cared for it. A mop head, tousled like the hair of a boy who'd been on the run and cared nothing about a comb. His eyes squinted when he smiled, turning his whole face into joy. Brown eyes, brown hair, and a brown sweater against the January chill. But his color wasn't brown. He radiated brilliance, a bright and engaging man.

A tingle shot up my spine as I recognized something else in him. I couldn't place it at first, but I'd seen that smile many times, that same radiance. But where?

Candice!

He didn't look a thing like her, but I could sense something about him, see something in his smile, his demeanor, that reminded me of her. Why?

"How'd you know my name was Kate?" I stammered.

He tapped the Smartphone on his hip, and then shrugged. "Your online plumber request." He winked at me. "I've known you online as 'IceRocket'. But I don't see that name anywhere on your job order," he said, pointing at his Smartphone. He was a jokester, an easygoing humor mill.

"I'm Kate," I stammered. "Kate Pepper. My mother named me Katherine, but I hated it."

Why did I tell him that?

"It's a beautiful name. Not mediocre or common at all," he said with another wink.

"Mediocre?" I snapped. The warm fuzzies inside me ran for cover. Every time I heard that word, I saw my middling father, stuck in his stupid recliner.

"Katherine is a very pretty name. You should be proud of it." He offered his hand again, moving toward me. "I'm John. John Connor." He shrugged. "Or, 'Worker John Connor', as you know me online. WRKRJC."

He paused, looking at me like he could read my soul. I felt naked, stripped bare by his penetrating gaze. Yet, part of me wanted to be naked in front of him, to expose what hid inside and get it all out. To be clean.

"I've really enjoyed our talks online." His extended hand screamed "wet." I dared not touch it and recoiled a little more, trying to become one with the counter behind me.

"Maybe we can get together again? But not over a toilet?" he asked, the smile changing form but still defining his face. He lowered his hand, then bent to pick up the bag of tools he'd set on the kitchen floor. I could only nod, unable to form a word. We watched each other through a tense half-minute of silence.

He shrugged a second time. "Great to meet you at last, Kate Pepper. Guess I'll see you online." He turned and headed for the door, letting himself out. Before he closed it, he looked back at me with a long gaze.

Frozen in place, I waved.

+ + +

How could I have done that?

A man had just walked into my life, my dreary dirty miserable life, and smiled. He'd called me by name, had helped me, yet accepted nothing in return. Xavier would have never done that in a lifetime of attempts. When he'd done something nice for me, he expected payback, and it had usually involved sex. This man, the moral antithesis of Xavier, had just given all and accepted nothing.

What kind of man does that?

A tear formed at the corner of my eye, and I swiped it away before the liquid torment could turn on me. Please, no visions. Not now. I dashed for the dining table and my laptop, my only connection with John.

"I'm so sorry. I'm an awful host." They were stupid words but the start of a deeper apology for the way I'd acted. I had to talk to him, at least online. I craved that smile. If I could reel him back, rewind time, or pull my words out of the air and stuff them into the miserable gut they'd come from, I'd do it. I wanted him, his peace, his caring. I needed someone. And I wanted to be noticed. He saw me, but not the oily hair, the T-shirt, the sweatpants of surrender, and the trash. I could feel it.

He saw *me*.

If he didn't respond, I couldn't blame him. I'd been awful. I sat at the screen, wiping away tears as fast as they formed. I grabbed at a paper towel and kept one plastered to each tear duct using both hands, watching for any word from him. At last, something popped on the screen, but not what I'd hoped for or needed. He was putting me off, a delaying tactic to avoid seeing me. Something he'd never ever done before.

"b r b"

Be right back.

❖ ❖ ❖

Water visions filled my head as tears flowed unabated. I gave up trying; I couldn't daub the wet on my face fast enough. Micro-visions of wells, streams, buckets, and showerheads filled my head. Toilets, lakes, oceans, and clouds. I banged my forehead with a fistful of wet Kleenex, trying to pound the pictures out of me, and as I did, sobs crawled out of my chest, forcing more tears and more visions while I sat cross-legged in front of the door.

Please come back!

I'd waited half an hour and heard nothing from him. He hated me, I knew it. I'd scared off the only human contact I'd had—other than anonymous food delivery boys—since Thanksgiving. The one person in the world I desperately wanted to know was gone. My head swam in water imagery as I sank into a tear-filled well of pity.

The doorbell rang, deep-throated gongs of my door chimes announcing another food delivery. But I hadn't ordered anything. I peered through the bay window at the stoop.

John!

I jumped up, blowing my nose and wiping my face as I dashed for the door. I didn't care if my eyes were as red as beets, and I forgot to check for stuff running out of my nostrils. I was desperate to see him again, to apologize, to connect. I tossed the wad of sodden tissues in a corner with the rest of the junk and threw open the door.

My plumber stood there clutching a pair of Chinese takeout boxes in one hand and a drink cup in the other. "Hungry?" he asked with a big smile as he handed the food my direction.

My face felt hot again, and I could imagine what I must look like. Puffy cried-out eyes, tear stains, and a snotty nose—the crimson face of yet another embarrassment. Despite all that, he looked at me in a way that made me feel pretty, not the desperate ugly woman I'd become.

"You . . . you did this for me?" The aroma of hot pork and fried rice rose from the little boxes. I was famished.

"Yeah. You looked like you were busy around here and didn't have time to head out for food." I'd not yet accepted his gift and took the dinner from his hands. He nodded toward the meal. "I thought I'd bring you something."

Most men would have walked through the door the moment I opened it. All the men I'd ever known before him did, one eye on my bare legs, one on the bedroom door. But John just stood in the portal, not inviting himself in. He didn't act like he owned my flat or me. That was another first.

"I . . . I'm starved, to tell you the truth. Please. Please come in." I stepped aside so he could get past me. More smells of hot Chinese food filled the gap between us as John entered and I pushed the door shut with my foot. With the chilled cup in one hand, food buckets in the other, and balanced on one foot, I played ballerina in my condo, welcoming a man I'd hoped would forgive me and return.

The drink cup, ice cold and sweating in the damp Seattle air, sent tiny rivulets coursing onto my hand. My first connection with water in weeks.

As I pivoted on that one foot, my head suddenly filled with images of a raging sea, frothy waters, and a bobbing boat. Twelve men cried out for help, tossed on the waves, their wooden craft swollen with water and men bailing for their lives. One of them, a tall, burly man, stopped bailing and stepped out of the boat, his crazy departure raising more cries from his shipmates. He put his foot on the angry water—and walked.

I stumbled, the cup leaping from my hands, headed for a sure splash on the wooden floor of my den. As I heard it crash in a sickening *smack*, I saw another figure, a Man in brilliant white who approached from the distance, walking on the water toward the boat. The one who'd bravely stepped off into the waves had started to sink and called out to him. Like the sinking one, I went down, alternating between my world and this watery vision of men swallowed by a mad sea.

He caught me. In that instant, I saw the sinking man reach out and take the hands of the One in dazzling white who walked on the water. And in that instant I felt John's rigid arms encircle me, taking my weight as I sank in my own desperate wave.

He drew me closer to him, his smile no longer toothy and boyish but strong and warm. His gaze caught mine as the image of the sinking man vanished; the bulge of one of John's biceps wedged in my back, his other flexed under my right side. His hands gripped my forearms, and he pulled me tight into his chest.

It felt so good to be in the arms of another, to be touched.

To be lifted up.

To be saved.

CHAPTER EIGHTEEN

THREE DAYS LATER.

"LIFE IS GOOD." I once saw a T-shirt with that saying printed on it and thought it funny. Why would someone wear a shirt with such a ridiculous slogan?

At the time, it seemed readily apparent that life was wonderful. Who would see it otherwise? I never dreamed then that I'd find myself in the despair that had gripped me these past weeks. Finally, that T-shirt slogan held some promise for me, a hope of someplace I could reach again. With John's help.

Dental floss, toothpicks, and toothpaste without water were the latest weapons in the arsenal of the new Kate. No more trench mouth from lack of brushing for fear of water. I wanted to get close to John without wilting him. I tossed the used floss in a new trashcan, admiring the kitchen and the adjoining dining room of my renewed home. I'd cleaned it at last; all the trash was gone, the vacuuming completed, and all the surfaces wiped down with alcohol or vinegar cleansers. It felt good to be pristine.

"I want to be pretty," I said to the mirror near the front door, admiring my latest attempt at hygienic hair. I'd tried half a dozen recipes I found on the Internet. Quaker Oats was the weirdest; I rubbed a couple of cups into my scalp and my grease-laden locks. But it worked. I tried cornstarch, baking soda, even flour for a dry shampoo. But the best by far was baby powder. After a good scrubbing with dry oatmeal and brushing it out, I'd rubbed a few liberal douses of sweet-smelling powder into my hair and whisked it away. I smelled good, and the nasty sebum oil on my head disappeared. My hair had bounce! Half an hour of straightening, and I had my old hairdo back. I felt great.

Baby wipes became my new best friend. I shopped carefully for just the right kind. I called them the "nonvision wipes." Instead of lathering up with hand sanitizer, I could scrub with the little cloths. I bought dozens of packs at a time.

A beep from my laptop meant a new message, and I dashed across the room to see if it came from John. He insisted on continuing our messaging with his pseudonym for "Worker John Connor." However, a new message flashed on the screen from my physician at the "doc in a box" across town, a friendly elderly man I trusted. He gave quick and honest advice. "Test results," read the subject line.

"Kate, I wouldn't normally e-mail a patient, but you've been a good friend and I'm writing because I'm concerned about you and your health. The girls in the front office told me that your insurance claim bounced because you're no longer employed at Consolidated Aerodyne. Maybe you've changed jobs, but from your condition at your last visit and judging from these test results, I suspect there may be a serious problem on your end. I need you to call my office about the insurance issue, but I'm even more concerned that you call me about your health. We need to talk soon. Dr. Hunt."

Was it the liver test? The kidney stones? My mind raced as I thought through a million possibilities, always coming back to Dr. Hunt's impossible advice. "Hydrate, Kate. Drink more water. You're living on caffeine and juice, and that's building up nasty stones in your kidneys by the day."

He didn't understand. I saved my sanity by destroying my health. I heard once about a man who drank Coca-Cola as his only liquid for fourteen years. That might be me—a lifelong addict to Hiram's coffee blends and Tropicana with pulp. An addict loaded

with kidney stones and no medical insurance. I deleted the message.
I knew what he wanted, and what it required. I could afford cash for
my treatment, at least for now.

The future, however, was less certain.

✦ ✦ ✦

"Dinner tonight at my place?" I typed, desperate to see John again.
It had been three days since he had brought me the Chinese takeout
and saved me from a nasty fall. The vision from my contact with the
wet drink cup had an additional outcome. It confirmed my fears.
The visions were more intense than ever, triggered by less water. I
dared not get the least bit damp.

On the other hand, I was willing to suffer the unexplainable
mental imagery in order to spend time with John, however hard that
might be.

"What's for supper?" he wrote back. I imagined John at work on
some other poor soul's toilet or clogged drain, diverting his attention
from their pressing need to answer my message. He'd been doing
that for months, carrying on a lively conversation with me while
staying employed with his hands. A champion multitasker.

"Sushi," I responded. "Ever had it?"

"Raw fish?"

"You'll love it. Trust me."

"You're sure?"

"Absolutely."

"What about your visions? Don't you have to use water to prepare it?"

John thought about me, not the food. What a change. If he were
Xavier, he'd be leaning on me to buckle down and "suck it up."

"I'll manage. I promise not to poison you."

"You eat poison fish?"

"No. Just making a point. It will be a sanitary meal." Somehow. I trembled thinking about it, wiping the knife with the sanitizing cloth. I'd tried using rubber gloves once. That should work.

"You're on. What can I do to help?"

I'd never heard those words from Xavier. In fact, very few men I'd ever known had a mind that ran in that direction. I was quickly coming to the conclusion that my past problems with men were largely my fault. John had proved, in our short time together, that all men weren't self-centered bedroom creeps.

"I need some shopping done. Want to buy the fish?" It was the only ingredient I didn't have in the condo—and the most important.

"Sure. Can I get it at the local market?"

"No!" I wrote back, revolted by the thought of stale California rolls in the deli section. "I'll send you directions and call in the order. We'll have some ahi tuna, and if you don't like it raw, I can cook it all the way."

"I'll try anything once."

I sent John the directions and phoned in my request to a local fish supplier. I'd have sent him to Fisherman's Terminal and the *St. Jude* if we could have waited for the meat to thaw. It's funny how getting involved in some dinner planning suddenly changed my entire outlook. I found myself thinking about Liam again, about cooking and shopping. Thinking about a man. That slogan I'd seen a while ago wasn't so far off base after all.

Life *was* good.

◆ ◆ ◆

An hour later, I stared into a bottomless pit.

The deep stainless-steel sink in my kitchen resembled a silver cave without end. Water poured from the spout, coursing down the drain as though the metal had no cares. It directed the flow and sent the nasty stuff out of my condo. No screaming, no fainting. Just water. The sink wasn't bothered.

I saw the clear liquid as some horrible snake venom that sparked mind-bending visions. It wasn't just water. What spilled from my faucet represented the most intense form of mental agony.

I thought of John. I could weasel my way through this dinner without touching the poison that spewed from my tap, and dinner might even taste good. Or I could remain pure to my classical sushi training and do it the way it should be done. But to do that, I had to get wet.

Gramps told me once while we were plying the harbor on his tugboat that "everything has its price, Kate. The stuff you can touch, and the stuff you can't." He'd paused, staring out from his spot at the helm and added, "Sometimes you have to pay a steep price for something or someone you love." I'm sure he meant my grandmother, who'd died years earlier, but he might as well have been preparing me for today.

I shut off the tap and reached down slowly, rapping the side of the damp sink with bare knuckles. It made a solid *tink* when I tapped the damp sides, and immediately colors flashed in my mind's eye.

I saw a small pool of water amid a Roman bath-like structure. Two dozen sick men and women waited around it, anxious about something. The surface of the pool rippled suddenly and a mad dash ensued, every invalid desperate to be the first in the water.

I jerked my hand from the sink and wiped it on a towel before the vision consumed me. I'd found that, if I moved fast, I could stop the mental games by drying quickly. That strategy would have to work for dinner as well. Everything had its price.

The vision spurred by John's drink cup had been my first in two months. As powerful as it had seemed, like this latest micro-vision, I discovered that I could now manage in both worlds—the visionary and the real. I didn't have to crash through glass doors or get a concussion from a fall to the floor. I could weather the impact and even come through to the other side intact. With my hands on opposite rims of the sink bowl, I pondered my next step. I had to wash the knife.

I'd ordered two sets of rubber gloves from a chemistry laboratory, elbow-length heavy rubber that would deflect acid and deadly poison. I took my thousand-dollar slicing knife in one hand, gripping the edge of the sink with the other while I maneuvered the knife under the tap. Bit by bit I worked my way forward, knife slicing the stream of water in two.

Getting a tighter hold on the sink rim, I advanced my hand into the flow, the black rubber of my gloves barely touching the silver wetness, then fully immersed. I dropped the knife in the sink and shut my eyes, waiting for the inevitable. Nothing came.

Dry! Safe! And sane!

✦ ✦ ✦

For the next four hours, I cleaned house. I've never enjoyed cleaning like I did that day. From kitchen to bath, to den and bedroom. I picked up, swept up, vacuumed, and wiped. I started with food preparation materials and finished with the bathroom, arrayed in a second set of gloves meant just for toilets and cleanser. The thick gloves were hardly tactile, with big bulky fingers that held a rag well but would never allow me to slice a fish with precision. Nevertheless, it made me feel clean to have order in my home again. The second cleaning in as many days. John was my inspiration for change, my "tipping point."

At five o'clock he landed on the stoop, packages in hand. Punctual and, I'd bet, no excuses for what he didn't remember or had done wrong. John didn't strike me as an excuses kind of man. He was solid, a model of dependability.

"We're not going to eat this thing raw, are we?" he asked, holding a bag of fish toward me when I opened the door. "Seems kind'a crazy." His smile gave him away.

"Heat ruins the taste, John. You'll love it," I replied, reaching out to grab his arm and pull him in. My smile mirrored his. "Thank you for coming."

"I think I'll prefer cooked fish," he insisted, pretending to be stuck in the doorway to make me urge him inside. He had a sense of humor—another trait sorely lacking in the Kate Pepper stable of man-hunks.

We stopped in my living room, and I swept my arm about the space, waiting to see if he noticed. It was unfair to expect him to notice my work, but I hoped he'd see the difference.

John let out a long low whistle. "Merry Maids has been busy!"

That's all I needed—a recognition of something done well. It had been so long since I sold a million-dollar deal, launched a new web service, or even received a compliment. I'd been a hermit since last year. Slowly, I spread my wings. A clean apartment represented a major life change for me.

"Come on," I said, pulling him in the direction of the kitchen. "I'll show you something."

Somewhere between the doorbell and the kitchen counter, I lost touch with the present. I became the old Kate, the self-confident Kate, afraid of nothing and ready to take on the world. The Kate who worshipped wet weather, hard work, and fast motorcycles. In those few steps, basking in the smile of a man I'd spilled my heart out to over the past months, I found myself at peace with myself and with the world.

Life was good.

"I have an appetizer ready for you!" I said, beaming as I held up a platter of some of my best sushi rolls ever. I'd boiled the rice, cleaned the seaweed wrappers, rolled the vegetables and sticky rice, all free of any visions. Sanitized and scalded, those big rubber gloves had worked wonders. And I'd been a cook again. John looked at the wooden tray, his head cocked to one side.

"What is it?"

"A special roll. My secret recipe, just for you. It's delicious." I simply needed to slice it. The wasabi and the slivers of pickled ginger were ready on our platters. I offered him something to drink, bustling about the kitchen, oblivious to my last three months of torture.

John took a seat at the counter bar in the kitchen and talked as I worked. He shared stories about his day, about a particularly tough plumbing repair he'd done for an elderly lady in an apartment downtown. Stories about the trip to the fish market, and stories about me. We walked through months of instant messages and e-mails, sharing what he'd imagined I was like during the digital period of our "relationship," and telling me his impressions about the moment I'd discovered him—I.M. buddy and plumber, wrapped up in one. That day had been a huge surprise to us both.

I felt so at peace with him that life seemed to have flashed back to my old days, but with someone who had a real interest in me. He didn't mention the visions, and I forgot them. For a time.

At some point, as I was busy with the dinner preparations, it came time to slice fish. While I worked, John's voice took on a more serious tone. He hesitated, somehow treading on sensitive ground. "Remember when you said you were ready for help—for God's help—to climb out of your pit?"

He knew my typical reaction to his "spiritual discussions." But tonight, with him here in the kitchen, that resistance to his "God talk" melted away. I wanted to climb inside his head and understand him. Even more, I yearned for him to climb inside my crazy head and understand me.

"I remember," I said, answering his question. "And I am. I'm ready to climb out."

"Then remember this promise," he said, moving to my side. "He will show you the way. And He'll never test you beyond your ability to endure."

It all seemed sort of fuzzy, this talk about "the way." Like describing a map to someone without showing it. But at least, now, I knew there might be a map to lead me out of my despair. John's presence, and his assurance, was the most encouragement I'd had in months.

John shared more: his thoughts when we first made eye contact, his reaction when I stood like a statue after the plumbing job and let him leave without so much as a goodbye. I hung on his every word. While he talked, I followed old habits, preparing the meat for our dinner. I unwrapped the fish, tossed the wrapping paper in the trash, and turned to the sink. I caught his eye as I turned on the water. It was one of those moments where you see something coming but don't realize what you're about to do. I smiled at a comment he made about the mountains of empty sanitizer bottles he'd found in my bathroom, and then pushed the fish under the stream of water.

John yelled my name.

I saw the fish fall from my hands before I lost total connection with reality. I could hear it *clank* in the bottom of the sink and sensed, but could not see, John moving to my left. Something firm held me, and I was instantly transported into another world. No more dualities. I was gone, to a hot place. I became a dry wooden thing, floating on water.

"Haven't you any fish?" I could hear the Voice that asked the question but couldn't see the face of the person that uttered it, just the form of a Man clad in white robes standing on a shore far away. Though I could barely make him out in the brilliance of his white, I knew that Man from somewhere else. I felt like we'd met before but didn't know why, or where.

I was far out at sea, or perhaps a long way from some kind of lakeshore. Mountains in the distance told me we were near land, but the beach blended in with the water and he stood, a small figure, so far away. Yet I could see the Man vividly, his presence filling my mind.

How could I hear the Voice so clearly this far from shore? Men stood atop me as I bobbed in the water, large men rugged from long days of hard work. I smelled like fish and pitch, and I felt old. Parts of me creaked in the cool sun of an early morning. I felt like I'd been at sea for a very long time.

"Throw your net on the right side of the boat and you will find some." The Voice spoke strongly, yet the figure stood so very distant.

Men tossed big nets over my side, the coarse rope of their trade scraping at me. They didn't wait long. I felt the strain, the pull of a mysterious force in the water below me as it dragged me sideways and pulled me off balance. The men rushed to the opposite side of me to balance our load, yelling in unison, urging each other to pull harder on the ropes that linked them to the net below.

Ropes sliced into my sides as they hauled their load from the water. Nets clogged with fish crept up my rough brown hull, pulling me more off balance, precariously close to tipping. Yet, the nets held firm and I stayed afloat. Hundreds of fish, huge fish, poured out of the net into my hold. The men couldn't haul the net in completely, and the leader directed the others to set the sail. They would pull the net to shore. I complied, unfurling my cloth in the morning breeze, and moved with the wind toward the Voice in white.

We were not yet to the shore when one of the men, the leader, tore off his tunic and jumped into the water. Others yelled at him to hang on, that we would soon be ashore. He couldn't wait, yelling at the top of his lungs with the encouragement that made me pull harder in the wind to reach the One in white. I knew him. It was the Man from the well. The Voice at the pool. The Radiant One from the river. The fishermen joined in a chorus of shouts.

"It is the Lord!"

✦ ✦ ✦

When I awoke, I lay in John's arms, seated on the floor in the kitchen. His hand caressed my forehead, stroking hair out of my eyes. I could hear John before I saw him, and his voice remained subdued, as if he were speaking to someone else, or talking to himself. When I opened my eyes, he stopped the gentle speech. He cradled my head in the crook of his arm, kneeling at my side.

"Is it like this each time?" he asked. His voice soothed me. It had a strangely comforting tone, as if he were asking a question about which he already knew the answer and planned to tell me something I needed to know.

I nodded my head in his embrace, blinking.

Is this a dream?

"How long do you think you were out?" he asked.

I tried to connect with where I was standing when this all started. The memory remained fuzzy.

"You were washing the fish," he said. He could read my mind.

"I . . . I don't know. I was on a boat. No. I *was* a boat. Maybe half an hour?"

John chuckled and his smile broadened as he looked down at me. "Thirty seconds, Kate. At the most." He ran his hand along my forehead slowly, tracing the line of my hair and pushing back a few strands of my powdered bangs. His fingertips were calloused but his caress was gentle. I craved his touch and didn't want to move.

"What happened?" I asked. I knew too well, but his summary would be the best independent feedback I'd had about my fainting.

"You looked at me when you put the fish under the faucet. I yelled your name, and you got a surprised look on your face, then dropped the tuna in the sink. You remained standing, wobbling but standing, staring into the distance like you saw someone. I caught you just as you collapsed."

"I fainted."

"No. You didn't faint. You groaned and bent over like you were trying to carry a heavy load. You started leaning, then you went over like a tree falling." He paused. "What do you remember?"

The visions never faded, imprinted on me like metal engravings. But they were hard to put into words. If you'd been blind since birth and suddenly saw purple, how would you describe the experience?

"There was a boat. And a man on a shore, far away. I've seen him before. Always the same man dressed in a brilliant white."

"Like a recurring dream?"

"No," I said, shaking my head. I rolled toward him, putting out a hand and leaning into his arm as a pillow. I didn't want him to let me go. "Not like that. I've seen this man before, but he's always doing something different. He's a gentle man. This time he told some men where to fish. With a net."

John sucked in a breath like he'd heard something that really spooked him. His arm tensed, and the coursing finger on my brow stopped its motion. He stared at me for a long moment, and then spoke with deliberation.

"Did they catch any fish?"

"The net nearly pulled me over. I think I was the boat. And they caught hundreds."

"And that's when you fell."

"Maybe."

"Is that all?" he asked, his question more clinical, as though he were quizzing me in a police station or on the witness stand.

"That's most of it. We sailed back to shore."

His finger began its track across my face, his gaze meeting mine in silence. No words were needed. He spoke again at last, tears in his eyes, and his voice cracking as though he spoke about a dear friend.

"After you caught the fish, did a man jump overboard and swim to shore?"

My face—or my gasp—gave away the answer. He nodded and put his finger to my lips, his cheeks now wet with tears, his chin quivering.

John pulled me closer and rocked me, his strong arms tight around my neck and shoulder. He held me for a very long time, whispering words to someone else, not to me, words I could barely make out.

Tearful words of thanks.

✦ ✦ ✦

John listens. He uses his ears at least twice as much as he uses his mouth. He wants to know about me, wants to know what I think, what motivates me, and what hurts. He wants to know about my visions, every step in my journey from normal to "crazy when wet." And even though I object sometimes when he starts to talk about God, he doesn't judge me. I could open every dark recess of my heart to this man and he'd accept me just as I am. It's refreshing to be in the company of a person who's not consumed with "all about me!"

He liked the sushi, too. After our "interruption," I taught him some fundamentals of slicing fish and then laughed as he butchered his first tuna. Raw fish did not qualify as his favorite, but I loved his half-inch-thick wedges—no, his *hunks* of fresh meat. With a little oil and some spices, his tuna had found its way into the pan before the night ended. In truth, he liked it cooked much better than raw. But I didn't mind. He had come, he listened, and he cared.

It took us until nine p.m. to make it to the dessert stage. He dined on my stories, my tale of woe at the doctor and the kidney stones, and my Hobson's choice about the lack of proper hydration. He learned all about Consolidated Aerodyne and my fall from grace, about Candice and Hiram and my favorite coffee. Even about the new friend I wanted to reconnect with—little Liam, the chain-carving son of a sailor.

"This dessert isn't in the sushi theme," I said, lighting a tiny torch that I used to melt sugar. "But I love crème brûlée." I whisked the torch over sugar atop the yellow dish of my special concoction. "The British called it burnt pudding."

He laughed. "Cold raw fish and burnt pudding. What a strange combination."

I waved the torch in John's direction in mock threat as the phone rang. I ignored the number on my iPhone and answered, cradling it precariously on my shoulder while I put a dollop of whipped cream and slice of mint on his miniature bowl.

"Kate?" the voice asked. It was a strange pained voice and not one I recognized at first. "This is your father." I heard other voices in the background, the distant wailing of women as though they were crying uncontrollably.

"Yes?" My hand fell to the counter, my own whipped cream splattering on the granite top.

"Your mother. She's—she's been very sick."

"What's wrong?" My knees were like rubber, and I steadied myself against the granite counter top. John moved toward me, no doubt concerned I might be slipping into another of my trances. I waved him off and plopped onto a counter stool.

"Your mother passed away tonight, Kate. We're at the hospital. She's gone on. I'm—I'm sorry. It happened so fast we couldn't call. She was fine this afternoon—"

"Mother died?" I blurted out. Instantly I could see myself at ISIP, taking his last call, and her desperate request for me to come home for Christmas. A holiday that I'd spent wallowing in self-pity in my dank condo. My heart took a dive for the bottom of the pit, and I landed back in my dark cave of despair. Mother had reached out to me, and I hadn't responded when she needed me most.

"Yes, Missy. You mother passed away a few minutes ago. Just after midnight."

I could hear Aunt Isabella, the family drama queen, bawling in the background. Others were crowding around my father, asking him when I would be home. He choked on sobs and could barely talk.

"Come home, Kate. I need you." He hung up.

I set the phone down slowly, and John's eyes met mine when I looked up. He reached across the granite and took my hand.

Words stuck inside me, a storm of emotions blowing them away before they could escape out my mouth. So much that I wanted to say, but nothing emerged. Even tears were bottled up, the shock so sudden, so severe.

I'd known that this day would come. Maybe I had even fantasized about it twelve years ago when I left home, ripped apart on the inside and with no way to go back. I dreamt of a life on my own, away from control, free of my mother and father, free to be who I wanted. Free of the dreadful memory of what died in New York in my seventeenth year.

Battles raged deep inside me, and I hoped none of that showed as John caressed my hand. There were secrets, deep pains that had never gone away, deep regrets I couldn't make over. I had estranged myself from my mother, by my own doing. She'd never known how deeply she hurt me, nor did I ever give her a chance to find out or give her an opportunity to make it right. Now it was too late.

"There's a lot—a lot you don't know about me, John." I chose my words carefully for fear that if I didn't maintain a lock on my mouth, I might spill it all, a confession for the ages to the only man who'd ever listened. The story of my frustrated youth under the thumb of parents who put church and television ahead of me, of my first boyfriend and a Valentine date that led to a pregnancy. Dreaded memories of a child carved out of me for convenience, leaving a black hole of regret that I'd never filled with any amount of stuff or success or speed. I feared I'd confess my past proclivity for hot men with big muscles and tiny brains, men who loved themselves and their careers more than they loved sacrifice or loved me. I might spill the beans about my vices, my past addictions to money, to massages and hot bikes, to expensive coffee and fast company. In the few months that we'd known each other by web, and in the few days I'd known him in person, one thing was sure. John embodied none of the things through which I'd tried to gain pleasure in the past. Yet, he had become the greatest source of pleasure I'd ever known. I'd been chasing all the wrong priorities.

He squeezed my hand, massaging it with that same care he'd shown as he stroked my forehead. He chose his words carefully, and then spoke up, his eyes locked with mine.

"You don't have to share secrets, Kate. They're yours. But I'll be here for you when you need to talk."

"Will you go with me?" I said, tears finally starting to form. I knew I had to get my words out quickly before the water imagery hit me. This was one flood I wouldn't be able to stem. "Go to New York?"

He clutched my fingers with one hand and lifted the other to wipe away my tears. His calloused fingertip sucked the pool from the corner of my eye like a sponge. John nodded, then took my hands in both of his as he spoke.

"Yes, to New York. When do we leave?"

CHAPTER NINETEEN

TWO DAYS LATER.

I THINK THAT the guy I read about in *USA Today*—the one who only drank Cokes for fourteen years—must have been nuts. I've been at this "water avoidance" thing for what? Four months? And it was killing me. If getting wet didn't spawn such nightmares, I'd drink a swimming pool. As much as I love coffee and juice, there's a point at which only water will slake a thirst. Denying that fact simply made me want water more.

My insides were killing me. The pain was intense deep in my lower back. Dr. Hunt said to "drink a gallon a day, half of it at night, to pass that kidney stone." Try doing that with orange juice. You turn into a walking acid drum. And with coffee? You can't sleep for a week. I needed water. But I refused to drink it. Walking hurt, but sitting was worse, and I'd been seated in an airplane or a cab for the past eight hours. The only good thing about this day, as I headed to my parents' house in Queens, was being with John. Having him with me made it all tolerable.

"You okay?" John asked as he helped me out of the cab in front of our old brownstone in Queens. The pain in my back made me grimace, but that hurt less than this sudden return to a place I used to call "home." Twelve years ago I'd vowed to never come back. I left here on a tearful July day as a post-abortive seventeen-year-old girl determined to strike out on her own. That muggy summer morning seemed so very long ago. I nodded at John and let him give me a tug,

219

glad to be free of the old Yellow Cab. It reeked of cigarette smoke and cheap people.

We stood together in silence on the sidewalk, and I pointed out the house—115-53 122nd Street in Ozone Park. Nothing fancy. Two bedrooms. Two baths. Brick. Over sixty years old. A little over a thousand square feet, half the floor plan I had in Seattle. A depressing place, and unchanged since I'd left.

"Can we just stand here for a minute?" I asked John as he paid the cabby and returned to my side.

"Long as you want," he replied, infinitely patient.

"Isabella or someone else will eventually see us out here and come running. Before we get caught in that weepy crowd of old gossips, I wanted to tell you something."

He took my hand where we stood side by side on the old cracked concrete sidewalk. Despite January's brutal cold, John didn't flinch. Muddy lawns between the street curb and sidewalk were worn down to dirt. Neighbor's yards overflowed with the stuff of kids. Plastic trucks and bikes, plastic slides and dollhouses. Old cars jammed the curb and left no place to park. Nothing had changed; it was just different trash in the yards and mounds of unmelted dirty snow.

I struggled with the words, unable to form them easily. I feared that if I didn't get this out now, someone would tell him my story when we went inside. Perhaps it would be Isabella, the family mouth. Or one of her children who'd grown up just like her. I wanted John to know my dark past on my terms, and I'd procrastinated through an entire flight across the United States without telling him, on the threshold of the big family event. I hoped beyond hope that my revelation—an emotional cancer that I carried inside me—wouldn't scare him off.

"I made a terrible mistake many years ago." There. I had said it. At least the start of it.

He squeezed my hand again and moved to face me. "Kate, I told you before that you don't have to share any secrets. I like the Kate you are. I'm not here to judge the Kate you were."

"Either way, it's Kate."

"We've all made mistakes. We've all fallen short."

"I fell a long way, John."

"As did I."

"I got pregnant, John. And scared. I took what I thought might be an easy way out, and I've lived with that memory for twelve years—a nightmare that comes without the water. I can't ever forget it. Coming back here"—I waved my hand at the old brick homes— "Coming back here drags it all back up for me." I pointed down the block. "He lived over there."

"Kate. Do you understand what forgiveness is?"

I looked at him. What did he mean by that? Was it an opening to one of his spiritual lectures? Yet, part of me craved just that, words of wisdom that poured refreshment on a dry soul. I nodded. I understood forgiveness, at least in my head.

"I forgive you. And He does too," he said, pointing into the sky. "If you'll ask Him."

I shook my head. We'd already had this conversation more than once. It made no sense to me that someone I couldn't see would forgive me for something I deliberately chose to do and could have avoided. It seemed too easy a path out of perdition—the ultimate cop-out.

His words finally registered. "You forgive *me?*" I asked. "I don't understand."

"You're sharing something with me that I have no right to know. The fact that you're telling me shows there's something about your past that you hope to make clean. I want you to know that, if there's something I need to forgive, then it's done."

I took a deep breath and watched his expressive face. Not the boyish smile but the serious one, the "I'm on your side in this battle" look that I'd seen him wear more than once on this trip. Like when I snapped at a waitress after she tilted a cup of water in my direction.

"It's that easy for you? *Poof*, and my past is past? Slate wiped clean?"

He nodded.

"You don't think less of me for what I did?"

"No."

I shook my head. "I never thought the day would come when I'd meet someone who could say that." Deadly tears began to form, in part due to the blowing wind, but mostly because he'd just lifted the tar-like burden that I'd carried for twelve years. Since my abortion, I'd dreaded the day I'd be forced to face my past with a man I cared for. I never thought it could be done. Yet, confronting my ghosts at the front lawn of my old home, I'd found a man who accepted me for who I was and forgave me my past with no strings attached. What manner of man does that kind of thing? John must be a saint. That's what Mother would say.

Mother.

I looked up at the house, squeezing John's hand and pulling him toward my old home. "It's time to find my father. You'll like him. His name is Norm." I thought about it, then added as an afterthought, "And he's probably watching television."

✦ ✦ ✦

My parents' house looked a wreck. Not dirty but jammed. Filled to the brim with relatives, neighbors, and about a dozen men from the paint shop at subway maintenance where my father worked for the city. Food had been set everywhere, in a combination of an Irish wake and an Italian wedding. Isabella saw me first; her wail would have earned her a job at the firehouse.

"Kaaaate-uh!" she said with a feigned Italian accent. She was all Jersey but put on the Italian airs when she came to the city. The old family way.

I waved sheepishly as the entire mass of Irish-Italian humanity went silent and turned to face me. I felt like I'd pulled the emergency stop cord on the commuter train. My father rushed out of the crowd to embrace me.

John shoved a handkerchief into my hand as my father reached me, closing my fingers on the cloth with rough warm hands. John knew what I faced. If I cried, I'd immediately lose contact with reality. But this would be a cry fest for the next three days. I had to hold back my tears, which made no sense. Until I had fallen into this water problem, I never cried. Now that I needed to, even wanted to show emotion, I dared not. Nothing made sense anymore.

We hugged. My father felt bonier than I'd remembered as I pulled him close. He gave me a long bear hug, and then pushed me back to take a good look. Not until he'd held me at arm's distance did the hens start clucking. Every aunt on both sides of the family commented. "She's skinny!" "Look at those legs!" "Have you ever seen clothes like that?" "How long did she intend to wait before she came home?" "It's about time." My father didn't seem to notice. Maybe he didn't because he'd listened to it for so many years. Or perhaps it didn't bother him. Either way, the stream of whispers infuriated me.

"You're so grown up, Kate," he said. "You're—you're beautiful!"

My father had never said those words in seventeen years of parenting. My heart melted and the first tear ran. I daubed it away.

"Your mother would be so proud of you," he continued. "It happened so fast, you know? A little wheeze one day, a cough the next, and then—then she's gone." He choked and his own tears ran. "She never suffered, Missy. Strong to the end."

That was Mother. A stoic's stoic. No complaints, no pain; even if she'd suffered some problems in her life, she'd never tell my father.

She had her own way of maintaining control. Pain meant weakness, and she never showed either, a perspective I'd inherited from her.

I couldn't look at him crying, so I pulled my father closer. I never remembered hugging him like this; it's impossible to hug a man in a recliner. But it felt good and he needed me. We connected.

At last, he separated and turned to John. "Who's this, Kate?" My father's smile looked worn and weak, but it rivaled John's in size. For some strange reason, he seemed genuinely glad to meet my friend.

"John Connor, sir," he said, extending a hand to my father. "I'm Kate's friend. And her plumber." They shook hands.

"Hey! Good grip there, John. A tradesman. My kind of guy," my father said. "Thank you for coming with her."

I could hear more clucking, one Italian hen whispering to another. "Are they going to sleep in the same bedroom? Surely Norm wouldn't allow that."

"Shhh," hushed another hen. "She might hear you. You know why she left all those years ago, don't you? Pregnant. The shame of it."

In that instant, I hated coming back here. I looked at John, who rolled his eyes in the direction of the clucking hens. He'd heard it, too. His eyes and smile calmed me as if to say, "Ignore them." I tried and failed. My ears burned in the vitriol of low voices.

"John and I met on the Internet," I said, loud enough for the gossips to pick up on. Murmurs ran throughout the room, and I decided to make this a little bit of fun. "I asked him to my condo, and we met for the first time in my bathroom." The murmurs instantly grew louder, and I could see people bending to whisper in each other's ears. My father looked confused.

"I have a plumbing business, Mr. Pepper," John said with a chuckle. "She found my address on the Internet and called me to fix a clogged toilet." They shook hands again. A sure sign of approval from Norman Pepper, the son and grandson of working men, Irish immigrants who built New York City. John and my father bonded, leaving me, for the time, to deal with the clucking hens.

Gossip rippled through the room as I made my way through the hugs of crying women whose tears dried up the moment I left them. In the eyes of my inbred family, I personified a mail-order East European bride, and John a mafia boss masquerading as a tradesman intending to take advantage of twenty-nine-year-old girls who didn't have the brains to find a husband.

As much as I regretted not seeing my mother in her last days, I was glad I had a home far away from this place.

And, I thought looking back at John as he laughed and talked with my father, *perhaps I've found the right someone to share a home with.*

❖ ❖ ❖

I pulled my jacket tighter as we walked away from the brownstone. Despite the cold, I jumped at the chance to escape that stifling henhouse. I could still hear Aunt Isabella's last bombshell, the one that pushed me out the door. "Is she sleeping with him?"

I tasted acid in my throat as we passed "the house," the site of my boyfriend's dreaded bedroom on a February evening long ago. The place that my slide from grace began. I stiffened, trying to divert my gaze. I felt John's glove slide past my wrist and envelope my hand. My heart skipped and I turned to face him. John smiled and pulled me along, his accepting silence a soothing balm.

We walked for blocks, my hand in his. He waited on me to speak, as if he knew I needed the time. Playgrounds, intersections, corner stores—each held dozens of memories, ragged fragments of the past given new life now that I'd slipped back into their presence. Mental rubble that I'd buried, jumbled images of a life I'd left a dozen years ago layered under the dust of a life newly made. A life far from here. I couldn't help but be reminded of the visions that plagued me in Seattle. Were these sights more of the same? This town was my nightmare.

We passed Saint Michaels, my parents' lifelong parish. I tugged at John, anxious to escape the condemning stares of smog-stained stone gargoyles that leered at me from above the front door. I wanted to move on.

John had walked in silence for blocks, demanding nothing. I needed to hear him, to converse and connect with the present. The past clawed at me with every step.

"So. I have a question." I squeezed his hand and stopped, pulling him around to face me. I needed to see John, to grab some of that smile, that life that sprang from him with every step.

"Question?" he asked with that infectious grin. How could he be so childlike, so happy? It wasn't normal. He paused, then added "Should my answer be 'I do?'"

His last words astounded me. He wouldn't joke about something that important. I tingled with anticipation that there might indeed be a hope for us, a future together. Yet, I dared not voice that hope, knowing what waited for us tomorrow at the funeral, and after. John might run when he discovered the dysfunction that sank its claws deep in my family tree. My relatives had started the windup to the big day. The past two hours were no more than a feeble practice session for the nuclear conflict we'd encounter tomorrow at Mother's wake.

"Okaaaay," I replied, trying to not focus on the dream that he might eventually pop the big question. I turned and pulled him along while I talked. "When we were still chatting over the Internet, before we met in person, you mentioned something that's been really bugging me."

"Yes?"

"In one of your e-mails you said something about my visions, where they might come from."

"I remember."

"That there might be an alternate source—other than being nuts or sick."

"That's true."

"Are you going to talk to me in two-word sentences all evening?" I asked, glancing at him as we stepped off a curb. A cabby honked at us, aggravated at having to wait until we crossed. I threw the driver an Ice Slice and we kept walking.

"I might," he said, smiling.

I shook my head and plowed on. "So, if I'm not nuts or sick, what's your diagnosis?"

"I'm not a doctor, Kate."

"I'm serious!" I protested, squeezing his hand hard enough to make him wince.

"I am too. But I might have an answer you won't like."

"Why?" I asked, looking at him as we strolled past my old elementary school. More memories, but most of the recollections of this place were good ones.

"You don't like it when I get 'preachy.' But you do need to hear this."

I sucked in a deep breath, bracing for a sermon. "I won't run."

"Your visions. It's possible someone's trying to get your attention. The question is, who?"

Again, John had voiced the words of that crackpot at the acupuncture clinic, and Dr. Lin at the hospital. I held my tongue, pulling him back before we reached the next street crossing. I used to be a guard at this light as a fifth-grader. I wanted to linger here. To remember. Colors in the fall, new classes. School supplies. Growing up. The old maple on this corner had grown gnarled but persevered in the shackles of a cracked sidewalk.

"Okay. So I told you before I wasn't interested in that theory," I replied, breathing deep. "But I am now." I stood by the friendly old tree, my hand stroking ancient bark that had watched so very many children pass by. "Who would want to get my attention? And why?"

He nodded, at first biting his lip, and then spoke. "Some images come from God, Kate. It might sound strange, but it's true. He can find lots of ways to reach us. Does that surprise you?"

"No." I'd asked for this, although part of me didn't want it. Not now. I flaked a bit of bark off the tree, like shedding scales to expose the raw part of me. Something inside craved to hear more.

He continued. "And some images are not from God."

"From where, then?"

"For some people, that mental imagery comes from the enemy."

"The Devil? There you go again." I pulled away from the old maple, stepping into the intersection and walking away fast.

"You asked the question," he called out as he followed a few steps behind. "I warned you."

"Is that who's sending these pictures I'm seeing?" I asked, scared to turn and hear the answer—or see it in his face. "Is that who's responsible?"

"I'm not inside your head, Kate," he said with the patient endurance that always drew me back. "But no. It's not the Devil, based on everything you've told me."

I stopped on the next curb and waited on him. "How can I know for sure?"

John moved in front of me, his hands shoved deep in his coat against the cold. He smiled, an assurance I desperately needed to see. "You have to ask God. Ask Him to reveal Himself. I promise you, He will."

I followed his stare. Long shadows growing toward us as the sun dipped behind the tall stone steeple of Saint Michael's.

For the first time ever, John's smile vanished, replaced by a deep sadness in his eyes I'd never seen, a part of him I'd never touched before. It scared me. He looked back at me for a long moment, his brown eyes strangely misty.

"So how will I know when He answers?" I asked.

His voice grew tight and broken as he shuffled closer to me on the sidewalk, moving out of the way of children brushing by. "God reaches people in different ways, Kate. If all this imagery truly is from Him, then maybe you've been missing all His earlier attempts to reach you."

A cold shiver ran down my spine. "And if it's not? Not from God?" I hadn't spoken that name in years. It felt strange, yet good. Like uttering the name of a friend I'd not spoken to in far too long.

For a moment, the light went out of John's eyes. "You can't know it's from God unless you *know* the Word of God, Kate. To test the spirit of these visions." He bit his lip again. "And that's one of my biggest fears."

❖ ❖ ❖

John led me through the cemetery the next morning, headed to the graveside service. I'd been so pummeled by aunts and other relatives that my emotions were shot. I wondered at times whether all of Mother's sisters realized how they murdered others through their verbal assassinations. I felt like I'd been run through a gossip gauntlet since we landed on the front porch at 122nd Street.

"It's going to snow, Kate. Can you hang in there?" John asked.

He gripped my forearm tightly, helping me across some icy patches of sidewalk. I looked up at the gray clouds, a sure sign that flurries threatened.

"I'll survive. I have to."

"I brought extra napkins. We'll keep you dry, I promise."

That little show of support meant a lot. I forgot my aunts, and the cold disappeared. I had John.

We stood at Mother's grave five minutes later, my father on my left and John on my right, at the head of the casket. Mother's coffin sat on a pedestal draped with something that looked like fake grass, its green in stark contrast to this dark day. The morning hung gray, the turf was brown, and the people were all dressed in black. Green was a garish contrast. I wondered at all the other funerals that had stained that grass-colored drape around its edges where it rested on fresh dirt. How many other mothers had it planted in this soil?

I felt like a tiny cog in a giant *mortis machina*, mother's corpse yet another in a long line of dying people. I looked around and realized that's exactly what this was, another cycle of the burial season in a never-ending trek through this frozen plot of ground in Queens. We have a little time on earth to enjoy life, and then we're gone. Funerals baseline your thinking very fast.

Flecks of snow drifted down when the priest started his eulogy. Mother had known him since he was an altar boy at our church; he joined the priesthood serving the same parish that had birthed him. He looked older than me, but not by much. I tried to listen to his words, but my eyes were locked on the sifting white of frozen rain, dreaded wet stuff. I pulled my coat collar higher around my neck and adjusted a broad-brimmed black hat, donated by Aunt Isabella. I feared blowing snow the most. I couldn't protect against that.

I remembered the psalm that the priest read, from another service like this one, but long ago. "Yea, though I walk through the valley of the shadow of death, I will fear no evil: For thou art with me; Thy rod and thy staff they comfort me."

Memories of Gramps came flowing back, of another wintry funeral, but with more tears than today. My best friend had died, and hardly anyone came to see him off. Just a few of our family, not even all Mother's sisters, his very children. I'd tarried so long at the graveside on that day that the burial crew had covered up the site before someone realized I'd been left behind.

For a long moment, I might have been laboring in another of my micro-visions brought on by a snowflake. In those precious memories, I crewed on the tugboat with Gramps, chugging around the harbor, moving freight or pushing a big vessel. I was on the water, Gramps's favorite place to be. I thought it ironic that, after all those days getting wet as a kid, and as an adult reveling in the rain in Seattle, I now feared anything the least bit damp. I clung even tighter to John's arm. The priest ended his eulogy and I realized that, other than the psalm, I never heard a word.

Ten minutes later, the graveside service broke up, my aunts saying nice things about Mother and false niceties about me. Thank goodness for this bitter weather, too cold for them to tarry and whisper; they'd wait and do that at the house tonight. Someone would say, "I shouldn't share this, but . . ."

I called it the "deadly 'but.'" The word always bound the opening phrase "I shouldn't tell you this . . ." with some hurtful story destined to slice hearts and destroy reputations. Gossip was my aunts' favorite pastime. Their excuse? "Well, it's the truth!" they'd exclaim with a shrug, justifying their verbal savagery.

As the family filed away, I pulled John toward me and laid my head on his shoulder. I wanted to stay here with him, to remain outside, to be normal again. I needed him. I'd depended on myself for so many years that I'd forgotten how good it felt to be part of life with another. He pulled me close.

The wind blew, a low whistle in bare trees, and silence wrapped its arms about us as we stood at Mother's side. Sighs of wind in the branches above and distant sounds of the city beyond the cemetery walls drifted to us, muffled by falling snow. Yet, I heard another voice, a tiny whisper, gentle words. Words of supplication, asking for someone or for something.

The words came from John. I clung to his side, my ears pricked, listening. He rocked gently as he whispered, talking to himself or to the wind, but not to me. It was comforting, his habit of speaking peace in times of trial, as he had when he had caught me in his arms days ago at my sink.

I watched flurries gather and settle on Mother's casket, white, the polar opposite of the world of black that consumed her. Tiny crystal flakes melted quickly and formed a gentle wet sheen on the polished lacquer of her final resting place. Mother lay there—wet—and she'd spoken her last vision. My mother's daughter, I took my place as the next in a line of Italian-bred women who saw things. For a moment, I started the slide back into my despair, until I caught more snatches of John's whispering. At that moment, I realized what kind of man he was.

John prayed. For me.

Not since I'd been a pregnant teenager in a confession booth with this priest's predecessor, old Father Murphy, had I uttered a prayer. Prayers were acts of desperation, words invented to get you out of a jam, to unmake a terrible deed, or for weekly atonement at confession. I'd never heard a word uttered in thanks on my behalf. But his words printed themselves in my mind. I'd heard them clearly, and they melted away the coldest recesses of my dark past.

"Thank you, Jesus, for Kate, for what she's shown me, for what she's done. Heal her, Lord. She needs you." He took a long breath. "And I need her."

❖ ❖ ❖

"I don't understand you," my father said at the cemetery curbside, where he waited with a hired limousine. "You never cried at your own mother's funeral." He wiped his eyes, red and puffy from many hours of tears.

"I can't," I said, hoping to avoid the entire issue of visions and tears. "It hurts too much."

My father nodded as if that explanation covered it, then put his arms about me. He hugged me for a long time, then released me and moved to the door of the limo. "We need to go. Your aunts are wait-ing for us."

John walked me to the other side of the limo and opened the door. He held my hand, ever the gentleman, while I bent over and sat down. I looked up to say "thank you," and as I did, I saw disas-ter looming. Above John an icicle had formed, dripping down from the stonework of an overpass that crossed the perimeter road of the cemetery, and under which the driver had parked to keep the family out of the wet. When I looked up, a deadly drop let loose from that spear of ice and fell, hitting me directly in the eye. As if a flashbulb had gone off in my face, I went blind. Moments later, when the flash faded, I saw my mother's face.

I was a small child, completely immersed in water, staring up through soapsuds that stung my eyes. Walls of pink and black sur-rounded me, the 1950s-era alternating porcelain tiles that framed our tub in the little brick house in Queens. Mother kneeled by the edge of the tub, massaging my hair under the water, washing it free of soap, and singing.

I could feel the warm water embrace me; I was a water sprite, always ready to shed my dresses and head for the bath. I loved to swim in the tub, to run the water and hold my face under the hot stream, to blow bubbles, and make suds with lemon-sized balls of soap. My hair grew down past my shoulders, to the middle of my back. I especially loved it when my mother would massage the long tresses free of tangles after each washing, rubbing my scalp and sing-ing to me. A memory I'd lost many years ago.

I could hear her singing, hear her through the water that filled my ears. Like it had been yesterday, her words came back, her tune woven into the fabric of my heart, a Catholic melody she'd sing every night we entered that pink-and-black bathroom for my favorite part of the day.

Soul of my Savior sanctify my breast,
Body of Christ, be thou my saving guest;
Blood of my Savior, Bathe me in thy tide,
Wash me with waters gushing from thy side.

I blinked and woke from the hallucination, John daubing water from my cheek.

"You okay now?" he asked.

"Yes." But I'd lied. As he scooted in next to me, wedging me in between himself and my father, something troubling grabbed at me. The vision struck a chord from long ago. Her words were familiar, not because I'd heard them so many times, but for the passion and her love for what she sang. I'd heard it, that same love, someplace else that I'd been recently.

I couldn't escape the sense that her song and my visions were now connected. A common theme was emerging, and it hounded me as we drove to meet the family for yet another gossiping meal. Mother—and something I'd done—were linked inextricably, but for a reason I couldn't yet decipher.

Truly, I *had* become my mother. But for some strange reason, I no longer considered that a curse.

✦ ✦ ✦

"My father gave me this journal. It belonged to Mother." I placed the thick book in front of John on his airline tray the next afternoon as we watched the city disappear below us.

John took the journal and gently paged through it, not reading her private words but looking at the inserts. Church bulletins, a dried flower, a funeral announcement, a yellowed obituary for my grandfather. As he reached the front of the book, a little lock of hair fell onto the plastic table. Tied with a pink bow, the red curly lock lay stark on the white surface. John looked at the entry.

"Your birthday," he said. "This is yours, Kate." He held the lock up against my hair. I had lots more red in those days, and my hair had been much longer.

He held the book open where the clipping had fallen out, and I saw a verse written in Mother's handwriting with some music notes above each word. She'd captured the tune from my vision—in her journal.

"*Anime Christi,*" John said. "Soul of My Savior. It's an old Gregorian chant."

"Can I see?" I reached for the journal. I could almost hear her sing as I connected with the book. Her words made me shiver, yesterday's vision revisited me in a way I'd never experienced. I saw in my sane state what I'd experienced in my crazy time. This could not be happening. The words jumped off the page; the song played in my head as though Mother were washing me in the tub that very moment.

Soul of my Savior sanctify my breast,
Body of Christ, be thou my saving guest;
Blood of my Savior, Bathe me in thy tide,
Wash me with waters gushing from thy side.

"How did you know the name for this?" I asked John, my hand shaking.

"I studied church music," he said, shrugging his shoulders. How many men could rattle off something as obscure as the name of a Gregorian chant, including its Latin name?

"When?"

"In college. And after college. I have a couple of degrees." He winked. "It's not really important."

"It might be. You're a mystery, John Connor."

"Yep. Might just keep it that way."

I slid the lock of hair back into the pages and replaced the journal in my bag. It spoke too many memories that I preferred remain silent.

"You sang all those hymns at the service like you knew them by heart."

John snickered. "I do."

"What's so funny?"

"Nothing. I'd never thought about it. Songs are as natural for me as sushi is for you, I guess."

"Church songs?"

"Yeah, mostly. I like the old stuff, like that chant your mom wrote down. It's still used for communion and offertory."

"Mother sang it to me every night at bath time." I watched him, the clouds beyond our airplane wing reflecting in his deep brown eyes. Eyes that stared out the window at something I couldn't see. John had a mysterious unknown about him that remained to be explored.

"What did you and my father talk about this morning?" I asked, anxious to change the direction of the conversation. The two of them had spent a long time together in the television room before we left. Remarkably, my father's attention had been diverted from his shows.

"He wanted to know if I go to church."

"Well, do you?"

"No."

I let out a sigh, relieved to have the answer to that nagging question. All of his spiritually leaning answers had led me to wonder if I was courting some sort of a church nut.

After a moment, he spoke up again. "I mean, how could I? I don't have a church yet."

"Yet?" My heart started to sink. Revelations spilled forth every day in our growing relationship. My revelations—and his.

"I'm a missionary, Kate. I moved to Seattle to plant a church."

"I thought you were a plumber."

He reached across the airline table and laid a hand on mine. "Being a plumber seemed like a great way to help and connect with people. I'm really glad I met you, for instance."

I pulled my hand away and turned to the window. I felt betrayed.

I could see it now. His quiet whispers were prayers. He knew Gregorian chants. A man at home in any church setting. Visiting unsuspecting women to fix toilets and spread his vision of goodness to anyone who was willing to buy it.

But he'd never pushed anything on me. In fact, while I sat there stewing, John waited. He was the textbook definition of patient.

"So. You're a Christian, then?" I snapped. "If so, I have a question."

"Hold on, Kate," he said, holding up his hands. "'Christian' is a term that's got lots of baggage attached. Sounds like you're carrying some of that weight yourself."

"What do you mean?"

"Some terrorists and abortion clinic bombers call themselves 'Christians,' too and feel justified doing so. That's not me."

"So what are you?" I asked, puzzled. My question was burning a hole in my cheek, a hot coal I had to spit out.

"Do I have to be 'something?'" he asked. He had that sad look, like he'd had on the street near Saint Michael's.

"No. I'm not trying to force a label on you. It's just that—"

"It's okay, Kate. I didn't mean to make you uncomfortable, but I also don't like labels. They separate people. They build walls. I want to tear walls down, to get people together." His eyes brightened with his next words. "I tell people I'm a 'Christ follower.'" He nudged me with his knee. "So. You had a question?" he asked with a grin.

I hesitated, teetering on the edge of a spiritual discussion that I wasn't sure I wanted to have. Yet, the question plagued me. I took a deep breath and then blurted it out. "What about Mother? Where is she?"

John put his hand to his chin in thought. A long silence invaded the space between us.

"It depends. From what you've told me about your childhood, and about your mom, I believe she's with God now."

"But how? She was so controlling."

"Your mom could have been saved, but just as confused and imperfect as the rest of us. Being a Christ follower doesn't make us perfect. Don't judge all 'Christians' by your mother's faults—or by mine, for that matter."

"Your faults?" I said, forcing a laugh. But I really wanted to know.

"I have a past, too. I struggle with things every day. The Bible calls that 'sin,' and it's something we all struggle with, whether we want to admit it or not."

My fingers cramped from my vise grip on the hand rest. *Sin.* Mother used that word all the time—the guilt word—her sword to slay me whenever I did something that went against her rules or her definition of 'proper.' I hated it.

"Is it a 'sin' to be a control freak? To ruin your daughter's life?"

"It depends. I wasn't there." He paused, looking at me like he understood the turmoil that raged behind my mental veil. "I'm not pointing any fingers at you or your mom, Kate. We've all fallen short of God's goal for us, and we're all a work in progress. Your mom, too. For all her faults, at least she admitted them." John shifted in the seat to face me dead-on. "And God understands."

John's words tore through me, and I turned away. I had a thousand prepared speeches about my mother's hypocrisy, but something about his simple acceptance quenched my fires.

"Water?" a voice asked behind me.

Before I could get a grip on my tongue, I spun about and snapped at the flight attendant. "No!"

John put a hand up between us and plastered on another of those ice-melting smiles. "Maybe not for her, but I'd love some. Thanks."

The flight attendant served him, then threw me her own version of the Ice Slice as she moved on down the aisle.

"Keep it away. Please," I said, then laughed. "Sorry. I went over the top with that."

"True. This is the stuff of dreams, Ms. Pepper," he said in jest, holding the glass my direction. "Want a sip?"

"No thanks." I moved back as close to the window as I could get. John downed the glass in a single gulp. Perhaps he did it to save me any grief.

"So. What else did you and my father talk about?"

He didn't answer right away, and then he looked me in the eye. "He asked me what my intentions were."

"Your intentions?"

"About you."

"Why would he ask that?"

"Why indeed? A strange man travels with you all the way from Seattle to New York and doesn't let go of your hand the entire time you're within reach of your wild tongue-lashing relatives. That might mean something," he said with a chuckle.

"It might."

"Kate, your dad loves you. He doesn't present your image of success, like a business executive might, but he's a good man. He's always done his best to give you the most he could. I'm afraid that if you don't resolve the differences with your dad, you'll lose him, and then it will be too late."

What did John know about this? He lectured me again, like in our early days on I.M.

"He loves you. People show love in lots of different ways. You might not recognize that love at first, but if you look for it, you'll find it."

"My father said that? I mean, talked about the love part?"

"He did. You should visit with him more often. I think you'd find you have more in common than you realize."

"Are you lecturing me?"

"No. I'm sharing with you. I've become a middleman between you and your father, from the sound of things."

"So. Just what are your intentions, Mr. Connor?" I asked with a girlish lilt.

John didn't respond, but smiled his impish-boy grin again. I didn't understand him well enough to read it. I poked him gently in the side to get a verbal response. "John. What did you tell my dad?"

"Now that's a start."

"What?"

"That's the first time since I've known you that you called him 'dad.' That's a good start. 'Father' is a little too formal for my blood."

I poked him again, but harder this time. "You're avoiding my question."

"I am," John said, moving his hand close to mine on the table again. "I love you, Kate. I told him I want you to be happy, whatever it takes."

He paused, wiping at the tears that sprang from my eyes. John, my caregiver.

"I told him that I want to care for you. For you to be content."

CHAPTER TWENTY

I LOVE THE outdoors. Today promised a safe haven, a clear blue cold sky and not a cloud in sight. I could spend all the time I wanted in the open and not fear getting wet. I headed out for a long walk across town to the Fisherman's Memorial, to stroll along the piers and listen to the call of gulls on a cold winter morning. This was balm for my soul after yesterday's return from New York. Although I wanted to see Liam and his family, I craved solitude even more. I walked alone, at home in the harbor.

"Kate, sometimes we have to make hard choices."

I could hear Gramps now, uttering those words as he stood with me on the boat alongside my dying seal. That one memory would never pass away. Metaphorically speaking, I stood on that same boat again. I had a difficult decision to make, a choice of one lifestyle over another, and each had significant negatives. There was no middle ground.

I thought back to the drip of water that had fallen from the icicle suspended over John's head when I sat in the limo after Mother's funeral. That little drop sparked a feature-length movie in my head. Less and less water was required for ever greater mental punches. It would come to the point, I feared, that a single droplet of fog would send me over the crazy cliff. Could I take that chance?

"Hard choices," Gramps had said, as though he'd known all along that I would catch that seal when I let out a net so close to shore. He'd let me make that mistake, even at the cost of the seal's life. Perhaps to teach me an important lesson about living.

I could be my mother, a woman consumed with visions, every day a new revelation, with new imagery and graphic depictions of things that might have some importance. I'd not made that connection with my visions yet. They were images, dreams—that's all. They meant nothing, though I sensed there could be some message in them. John had shown me that. There were some common elements in nearly every vision. That Man in white, for one.

Then again, what if, as John suggested, these visions were actually evil? John said that I had to test them, that I needed to "test the spirit." The thought chilled me. I remembered enough from my Catholic upbringing to know what he meant.

I thought back to old Father Murphy and years of attending mass with Mother. My memory drifted to the scripture readings at our family dinner table, thousands of them over the years, Mother insistent that we not miss our daily Bible feeding. Could I test this spirit like John said? Something warm inside me spoke hope, a sense so strong you could almost touch it in my memory of the Man in white. I knew enough about the Devil to know that hope was not his language. Perhaps that was the acid proof. Hope, and the Man in white.

When you stripped away all the possible meanings, including the religious ones, the fact was I might be going nuts in Technicolor. Bottom line: If I chose to be Mother, I could be clean. I could bathe, wash my hair, and stand in long showers while craziness danced in my head. I'd eventually learn to control the punch of the vision, and at least be sanitary again. I could have a man; I could be clean, even though I was crazy.

On the other hand, I could be my father. I could choose to be a slob, dirty despite the bottles of hand sanitizer and mounds of used baby wipes. No one would have me, particularly not a husband. I'd have my mind but no mate. Who would want to live with a woman who never bathed? The good side to that was I'd at least be able to enjoy a clear head. But was it worth it?

These were hard choices. Be my father, a sloth on two legs? Or be my mother? In the end, it all came down to that. I tried hard to ignore the nagging third option, John's option. "Perhaps God is calling you, Kate," he'd said. "These visions might be a letter, not a life."

Then there was the matter of my health. Dr. Hunt had two messages waiting for me when we landed. The results of the medical tests had come back and they weren't good. My kidney function bordered on "poor," the kidney stones were growing, and I hadn't paid the clinic's bills. If I kept up my self-imposed hermit lifestyle, I might never work again. I might die. The odds were stacking up against the option of choosing to be my father.

I imagined holding that old ball-peen hammer in my hand, raised above the head of one of these choices, prepared to strike and kill. In a perverse way, I had to murder the father option or the mother. Not murder my parents, but make my choice to put one lifestyle ahead of the other.

One of them—one lifestyle—had to die.

I stared out across a line of boats tied to their piers, bobbing in the light chop of a windy February day. A gull dove and grabbed a morsel in the water below me as I stood at a railing, nabbing it out of the harbor and winging away in one smooth motion. I wanted that. I was desperate to dive into the water and grab something tasty, to grab hold of life and move on. As I watched the gull climb and join her friends on the wing above me, I realized that, watching her, I had no idea what ran through the bird's mind. That tiny seagull brain of hers might be overcome right now with some crazy imagery of hot, dry lands and cool rivers. But I'd never know.

I whacked my hand into the other palm, pretending to practice my hammer strike. One of those options had to die. There could be only one choice.

I chose to be my mother.

She certainly wasn't perfect. But she did seem happy, even *content*. I'd so hated that word—until the visions, and until I met John.

I had to be her if I wanted to be a complete woman, and a wife.

Maybe Mother had been right all along.

✦ ✦ ✦

"Miss Pepper?" a voice asked behind me. A familiar voice.

"Liam?" I turned from the rail at the wharf, my place of solitude watching seagulls diving for fish. Liam stood beside a small bicycle, his helmeted head cocked to one side.

"Are you okay?"

I nodded. "Yes. I'm glad you're here." I patted my back pocket and motioned toward him. "How's your whittling?"

Liam flashed thumbs up and reached into the back pocket of his jeans for the knife I had given him months ago, and then fished a freshly cut ball and chain out of the liner of his jacket. His smile stretched from ear to ear as he dangled his new creation before me. "Do you like it?"

I took the carving in my hands and sat lotus style at the base of the railing, motioning to Liam to join me. I ran the links through my hand, just like I had decades ago at Gramps' feet on the tug, in wonder that wood could flow like liquid the way this chain rippled through my fingers. "It's your best yet, Mr. Fisherman." I extended a palm and he handed over the knife. "Let me show you something, right here."

Together we tuned up his carving, paring away the last of some wood on the inside curves of his links, and I handed the chain back to him. "I'm proud of you."

"Know what?" he asked as he stowed the treasure back in his jacket pocket.

"All ears," I responded.

"I prayed for you." He said it without any flair, no bragging. Just a simple statement of fact, like he said this to everyone.

I felt my face go flush. "Prayed for me?" I stammered. "Thanks, I mean . . ."

"I prayed that I'd meet you here. And you came."

"Today?"

"Uh-huh. Thanks for coming."

"You really expected me? Just ask, and *poof*, here I come?"

"You're here aren't you?"

"Excuse me?"

"I prayed that I'd meet someone who could teach me to whittle a ball and chain, and you left yours at the monument, remember? Then you came to our boat to show me how." He shrugged. "And I prayed that I'd get to see you again. I asked every day."

"For me?"

He nodded. "Every day." He jumped up, grabbing his bike. "Mom and Dad prayed for you, too. Come on," Liam said, mounting the saddle. "They told me to bring you home when I found you."

✦ ✦ ✦

One week later.

I needed John so badly. It had been three long days with no calls, and no sign of my dearest friend. Perched on a tall chair at ISIP, I scanned my email inbox yet again.

Where is he?

My ancient laptop knew John by name, and my fingers could type his I.M. address while I slept. I dreamed about him—not the wild visions brought on by water immersion, but real dreams. I imagined him in my life, wondered about him in his job. I imagined him with me in my condo at dinner, or riding a motorcycle together, on a bike more suited for a couple than my new Ice Rocket. I daydreamed about him when I plowed through my spider script at ISIP, and I imagined him returning to my apartment to sweep me off my feet. I felt like I was seventeen again, hanging on every call, every word, to learn more about the man I loved.

"More?" Candice asked, working her way past my table. I'd found a little spot off in a private corner today, a rare part of Hiram's shop that remained quiet. My spider script search had begun to narrow in on some key indicators of my horrible condition. I didn't have a complete diagnosis yet, but one thing was sure: John's guess had been right. I wasn't alone. The good news? Other people all over the world, some of them in Seattle, walked my path. The bad news came upon discovering in my search that none of them claimed to have defeated this debilitating disorder.

"Yes, one more cup please," I said to Candice and slid my empty mug in her direction. I watched her hands and that ubiquitous wet rag, keeping a safe distance. Water was a weapon in her grip.

The laptop beeped. Word from John! He'd been out of town since a few days after we returned from New York, off at a retreat in nearby Maple Falls. I always thought *retreat* to be a dumb word for a group of people going off-site to work out a way to advance their particular business agenda. Why not call it a "forward" instead? But that's where he was, retreating from Seattle and much too far from me.

This "forward" of his had something to do with church planting. I had a mental image of him with a microminiature white wooden church and its steeple, digging a hole in the ground and watering it patiently. After a time, he would have a big building sprouting up with lots of people. It made me laugh, and I'd not done that for months. Not until I met John.

His I.M. read so beautifully, no doubt prepared while he waited for a break in the action at their remote location. He loved to write, I'd learned. I loved poetry; the new Kate, the seventeen-all-over-again

Kate, also adored verse. I'd pretended to hate creative writing after I left home, but he'd brought it all back into my life. I opened the latest file he'd attached, a poem he'd entitled *I Can Wait Forever*. His message said he wrote this today, just for me.

Tears bubbled up the moment I finished reading it. I didn't wipe them away. I wanted to cry, to be normal, to be a woman and feel emotion—not to run from it. I wanted be touched by him, to be noticed by him. The tears grew and fell from their launching platform, sparking images of ice and snow, gurgling brooks and still lakes, as I read through his poetic imagery many times over. His words spoke about him. And yet, somehow, they were about me. A poem with two faces, the two of us joined as one in his words.

> *Winds are blowing,*
> *Flowing, growing;*
> *Feathering about me*
> *From the sprouting wisps.*
> *Rocking gently,*
> *Bowing saintly,*
> *I relax encapsuled*
> *From their wetting hiss.*
> *Longing, pensive,*
> *Inking missives,*
> *I pray to know His truth*
> *And feel her calling kiss.*

✦ ✦ ✦

"I've got something for you, Kate," a voice said. I heard, but the voice didn't move me. My eyes were glued to the poetry on my laptop, reading every line over and over, finding new meaning about me and about John in every word.

"Kate?" the voice repeated.

I looked up. Hiram had a furry brown smile plastered from bearded ear to bearded ear.

"From John?" I asked, my heart skipping.

"Who?" Hiram looked puzzled.

"Sorry. Never mind," I said, feeling my cheeks warm up in a sudden blush. I wiped away the wetness from my eyes, and the last of the image of a waterspout disappeared. Somehow, I'd found a way to coexist with these teary movies.

"Your spider script. It produced interesting results."

"It did?" I exclaimed, jumping up. Hiram had my full attention. "You ran it when I went to New York?"

"Yeah. You asked me to. Remember? You even paid me in advance." He handed over a single sheet of paper.

"What's this?" I asked as I scanned the report.

"Oh, sorry." He took it back, moving a finger down lines of code. "That spider script of yours is genius, by the way. I admit you came up with a super idea. I'd like to use it—maybe to provide a special search service here at ISIP—if you don't mind." His finger rested at a point in the middle of the page, but his eyes honed in on me. "Is that okay?"

"Fine by me. But I plan to sell it, Hiram, so don't scoop me. What did you find?"

"This." He held the paper out of reach. "I ran the script the day you left, and when I realized what it would do, I started tinkering with it. Actually, I spent a week working on the code. You needed a few key enhancements to really make this baby sing. Maybe we could share the intellectual property when you sell the rights?" He smiled again, holding the sheet above his head as I reached up for it.

"Deal. Partners. Fifty-fifty," I insisted, stretching as high as I could.

Hiram laughed. "Here you go, Miss Pepper."

The printout displayed several fields, and near the bottom, he'd composed a kind of handwritten summary. It showed how many websites, and how many related searches and collaborative fields he'd found. I couldn't believe it. Hiram's report looked like a Google directory. The script, with his additions, had run hundreds of millions of searches, and one sentence stood out from the others at the bottom, highlighted in yellow.

"Does it mean anything to you?" he asked, looking over my shoulder after I sat down. "Apparently this is some kind of common denominator with most of the people who describe your symptoms. This search went all over the world, Kate. There are people like you from pole to pole. It's like it's some kind of new disease."

Mental illness? I wondered.

I could be crazy or chemically imbalanced, the ugly conclusions I'd run into at every phase of my research—yet something in me said "no." John's encouragement, and Dr. Lin's words when I contacted him after the trip to New York . . . even Hiram's enthusiasm . . . drew me to a different conclusion. Perhaps they were right. Maybe it *was* a message. Somehow, that Voice from all my visions seemed to be calling me from deep inside, urging me in a different direction with my life. But that's as much as I had to go on. Nothing more concrete.

I looked up at Hiram, then back at the paper.

"Yeah, some new disease," I replied as I read. "Maybe all the people who see things are drinking coffee from Rwanda."

He laughed. "Smart people then." Hiram took off, headed for the coffee bar. Someone waited on a fresh cup of joe.

I read his summary three times, puzzling over the "common denominator" he'd highlighted at the bottom of the sheet, a mystical statement that supposedly captured the essence of all these people's problems. People plagued by water. People like me. It made sense, yet it made no sense. Sort of like John's poetry, I imagined there was some double meaning in it. I folded the paper at the bottom line and placed it on the table, looking down at it as I stood and stretched.

I needed John. I needed him to be with me to help sort this out. I picked up the paper again, studying its cryptic conclusion. Ten words that somehow encapsulated the common elements of visions and struggles of thousands of people just like me. Who could have dreamed that my symptoms would be so common? I wished again that I'd pressed Dr. Lin harder at the hospital months ago, and that I'd not been so hardheaded and resistant to advice in the months since. I read the words aloud that Hiram had highlighted in yellow, sure that if I did, their meaning would suddenly jump out at me.

"Water is eternal, and it has a tale to tell."

✦ ✦ ✦

I placed Hiram's search summary in my bag and pulled out Mother's journal, laying it on the "funt." Since I'd returned, I carried her words everywhere I went. One moment I'd be prepared to read it, the next I was packing it away, petrified. I imagined that I'd find some evidence that she had my symptoms, that our visions were tied back to our mutual DNA. An article I'd read said that mother and daughter shared the same mitochondria or something like that. Though I'd become more open to the prospect of a lifetime of pictures dancing in my head, I couldn't bear the idea that Mother and I were destined to be exactly alike.

I paged through the book, seated far from the other customers. Just as John had on the airplane, my fingers found their way to the lock of hair. It fell out, red curls bound with a pink bow. The book seemed to open naturally to that spot, as if Mother had gone there often, perhaps fingering the memento and rereading her words. She'd written a quote from the Bible, along with the chapter reference. I hesitated, unsure what to do next. I wanted to read it, but hadn't consumed a word of the Bible since I attended high school.

I'd avoided the Bible, to be honest. But her words pulled me to them, and I leaned over the journal, soaking them in. Something about the quote seemed to speak to me now, calling to me in a way that sounded so familiar. I could almost hear a voice speaking, a familiar voice.

If I wash thee not, thou hast no part with me.

Wasn't it Mother who'd read that to me once? Not likely. Perhaps the words came from our old family priest, before I put my foot down and quit going to Mass. I couldn't remember that far back with much clarity. I had quit church at a young age, much to the chagrin of my parents.

Had I heard these words at the funeral? Maybe I'd read them? They sank their tendrils into me, pulling at me from deep inside. It was like seeing someone you knew well a long time ago, but suddenly forgetting her name. I racked my brain for the connection. These words held some special meaning, and it was right under my nose. On the tip of my tongue. I could taste it.

Candice's rag caught my attention, and before she could damage me again, I dodged her swipe at my table with the wet white cloth.

"Happy Valentine's Day, Miss Kate," she said with a lilt in her voice.

"What?"

"Happy Valentine's Day, Miss Kate," she repeated, standing in front of me, her white cloth tucked into her bosom, dampening the dingy blue polo.

"Valentine's Day?" I looked down at my watch. February 14. Candice nodded, a smile plastered across her face. She pushed thick glasses up on her nose and wiped my table again. I dodged the wet bullet a second time.

Today made thirteen years. Thirteen years ago, one mistake, one evening of passion gone awry, one tryst with a boy I had loved, and it had changed the course of my life. A Valentine's Day date that ended up in his bedroom down the block at 122nd Street. A bedroom that led to a pregnancy and later to a doctor's visit, one that ripped the hole in my body that launched me out of New York. I sat here, in Seattle, because thirteen years later, I was on the run from that dreaded Valentine's night and one mistake that I could never bury deep enough to forget.

I looked up. Candice's smile faded into a quizzical look. Suddenly I had that same feeling again, sure that I knew exactly where or from whom I'd heard that verse in my mother's journal. The answer teased me, so very close.

I studied Candice, desperate for clues.

She reached down slowly, her thick, clumsy fingers touching the journal, at first caressing a page. Her gaze riveted on the pink bow. With her wiping-cloth hand, she set the rag down on the table, her mind focused on only one thing. The wet hand found its way to her head. As she touched the bow with her right hand, picking up the bound curls with a reverence, she stroked her hair, reconnecting with some memory of her own. Her eyes turned wet, blue irises awash in pools that threatened to spill over. She pulled the curls and bow to her cheek, rubbing the memento slowly across her skin, her eyes closed. Candice floated far from here, perhaps a child again in the hands of her own mother or someone else she'd loved.

At that moment, I wanted to be in her vision, to know what she knew. I could feel the déjà vu, that incredible sense that I'd been here, that I knew why the verse was so important, that in fact I'd heard this message spoken many times before. My inner being screamed at me to make this connection. I felt like I was leaning into a finish-line tape while running in slow motion, just inches from a win, but frozen in time.

"What?" I blurted out, a desperate cry in response to my search for some answer. That word jolted Candice back into the present. She looked at me, smiled as she replaced the lock of hair gently in

Mother's journal, and picked up her rag. She bent at the waist and wiped a third time about my laptop and the old book, then looked up at me. As she tucked her rag in place in the middle of her breast, she whispered in her simple voice to the famished yearning of my soul.

"Jesus *will* make you clean."

I remembered that Voice! It leapt off the page again as she walked away, headed to another table. I saw the words on the page, but felt Candice's warmth, felt John's warmth, felt Liam's warmth and that of his mom, as the words reverberated in my head, echoing in the same clear Voice I'd heard so many times before. It was the Voice of the man in the river. The One at the well. The Man at the pool. The Man who was walking on the lake. The Radiant One who told us where to fish. It was the voice of the Man in brilliant white, the One whom I'd seen so many times.

I drank in Mother's penned words again, desperate to understand them, and to see his face again more clearly.

If I wash thee not, thou hast no part with me.

CHAPTER TWENTY-ONE

W*ASH ME!*
    I jumped up from the chair, yelling at Candice as I dashed out of ISIP. "I'll be back!"

My laptop and rucksack, my purse, and all my spider script search results sat neatly arranged on Candice's favorite table in the corner of the coffee shop. For the first time I could remember, leaving valuable stuff behind didn't bother me. I ran for home.

Yes! Wash me!

I repeated the words in my heart, somehow aware that I didn't have to sing them out, or yell them as I ran. My words were heard when I spoke them in my heart.

I sprinted the blocks to my condo, reliving fresh memories of approaching storms that wet me on other days. Memories of dark days when I'd wandered so long in mental hinterlands, searching for an answer. I felt foolish as I jumped curbs and rounded the corner for my place. Dear Candice. She'd been there from the beginning, pointing me along the way. But I was too prim, too good, too professional or rich or brilliant or good-looking to listen to her, to really hear those precious words repeated so often. It took a mental pounding, a gut-wrenching depression, the death of my mother—and a gentle plumber—to get my attention. I dashed in the door.

"One hundred five!" I yelled with glee, ripping at my Gore-Tex jacket and pulling it off my head while I ran through the den. "No! One hundred ten!" I could hear the water click on in my voice-activated shower as the condo locked shut. I kicked off my sneakers and pulled at the zipper on the legs of my running pants, leaving a trail of waterproof clothing as I hobbled and skipped toward the bathroom door. Steam billowed from my unused shower stall as I hit the bath, dressed in my running shorts and a singlet. I didn't care. I dove in.

Ecstasy!

The first deliberate splash of water in months fell on my head, hot water soaking into shampoo-starved hair. I reveled in it, repeating over and over the words that had consumed me when I ran.

Wash me!

I could feel it coming. The vision. It took its time, as though the Author of these images knew I'd expected a vision, even wanted it. I craved the culmination that lay just around the corner, something glorious headed my way. Wet joy about to overtake me, I stood, face into the stream of liquid silk that coursed over me, eyes squeezed shut.

Show me!

No words left my lips. I knew words weren't needed; John had proven this by his example. I stood straight, sure He would hold me up. I wouldn't fight it this time—and I wouldn't faint. I wanted this moment more than anything I'd ever wanted in my whole life.

The onset of the joy struck me with bright, brilliant hues, a rainbow splashing over me and drenching me in deep colors. I could taste them. From the depths of the rainbow came a point of light, a brilliance that outshone all the Crayola shades. I lifted my hands in the direction of the light, anxious to pull it closer and to hold on to it, to never let it go.

My hands touched wood; the rough surface of a thick hewn timber rising before me. Light shone with a blinding radiance, and I stared up into it, desperate to plumb its depths. I leaned into the treelike pole, searching. Then I felt a gush of water, tasted its saltiness when it doused me from above. The light faded and I saw its source. The Man hung from a crossbeam, arms outstretched, and a wound pierced His side where the water flowed from Him to me.

I heard His voice.

"You do not realize now what I am doing, but later you will understand."

The timber disappeared; my hands clasped stone, a rugged rock near a hole in a cliff. A tomb. The Radiant One emerged, a towel in one hand, a basin in the other. I felt dry, dirty, scaly in His presence. Kate Pepper, unfit to be seen, and desperate to be clean.

Someone behind me spoke up, in a voice I'd heard before. It was the voice of the man who sank in the water, the man who jumped overboard to swim to shore. "You shall never wash *my* feet," he said. I wanted to find this voice, to ask why he refused the offer of the One.

The Radiant One spoke with a voice that made me weep, tears streaming as I stood immersed in the soaking warmth of my shower. Somehow, I lived in both worlds, vitally aware of each.

"Unless I wash you," He said, "you shall have no part with me."

I couldn't wait. I ran toward Him, falling to my knees at His feet, wiping at my tears with the dirty sleeve of a soiled torn cloak that hung like rags about me.

"Wash *me*," I cried. I wrapped my hands around His tunic, clutching at His ankles. I craved His water and His touch. "*Wash* me!" I buried my wet face in the wounds on His feet, sobbing softly. "Please forgive me. Make me clean."

"You are forgiven," He said, a gentle hand settling on my head. "Go, and sin no more."

Then the Radiant One knelt down and took me by the arm, lifting me up. Just as John had said He would. In silence, He brought His hand to my face, dampening His cloth and wiping at my eyes. Suddenly I could see Him much more clearly. His brilliance was like a star, yet He was also human. He knelt at my feet and washed them in the basin, then dried them. I touched the sleeve of His garment and felt His power surge through me. I wanted so much to be one with Him.

At last, the Radiant One refilled the basin and lifted it up, His eyes to the sky as He spoke a blessing upon the water, and then poured it over my head. Water coursed over me, drenching me, washing me free of crusty layers of filth—my sin. I could feel His water penetrate me, diving through me, blasting out charred flesh and smoothing horrid scars. It soaked me and lifted away a blackness I'd hidden deep from anyone's view, dirt I knew had been there for many years. I was scrubbed, gently, thoroughly, and I became a new creature.

He took my hands in His, facing me as I dried in His presence.

"Do you understand what I have done for you?"

Yes! I was clean at last. He had washed me. As though He'd become part of me, I felt the answer to His question without hearing it.

"Now, wash one another." He spoke to my soul. He was sending *me*.

The Radiant One handed me a cloth, and another basin filled with fresh water, then pointed me toward a dark area of my vision, a place where there were no colors, where no light shone. One hand on my shoulder, He walked with me, speaking in a soft voice, words of encouragement that gave me hope and strength. He promised to perfect me in my trials. I headed into an unknown, but now that I knew Him, I went with confidence that He would guard my path.

We arrived at a door, a portal beyond which I could see others, many of them people whom I knew. They were sad people, busy people. Xavier, Andrea, and Justus. They were all running, no one resting, their eyes covered with thick plates that reminded me of fish scales. He opened the door to the darkness and beckoned me through.

"Now that you know these things," He said, "you will be blessed if you do them." He withdrew from me, but I could feel His presence even as He moved away. As if the Radiant One lived inside me, part of me in a way that could never be separated. I was now one with Him.

His voice urged me as I headed into the blackness, encouraging me to extend a hand to the first desperate person I met.

"I tell you the truth," He said. "Whoever accepts anyone I send accepts me, and whoever accepts me accepts the One who has sent me."

I opened my eyes in the stream of the shower, its warm embrace stripping away tears of joy. I let the water pour into my mouth, drinking in its goodness. I had become a new creature, a restored woman. I raised my hands toward the top of the stall and cried aloud, gurgling as the water filled me, but sure He could understand.

"Yes, Jesus. Make me clean."

✦ ✦ ✦

I heard ringing. A distant bell, one I knew had called me often. Embracing the One, sharing His news with others in the dark, I sensed a need to leave, to head back to my world and the chime that rang my name.

Face in the hot stream, I heard it again. My iPhone! Warbling on the floor of the bathroom, where I'd dropped it when I raced for the cleansing of my inner self. I let it ring, drinking in the goodness under the showerhead, wet love pouring over me. He had been there for me all along, waiting for me to embrace Him. Stubborn and determined to control my life, I'd layered dirt upon dirt, until at last I saw Him in the faces, actions and words of the people He'd sent my way.

The phone started to ring again, the caller determined to find me, to get through no matter what. For how long had that caller been trying to reach me?

Leaving the water running, I threw open the new shower door, not used since I crashed through the previous one months ago. Slipping on tiles not wetted for as many days, I stumbled over my clothes, fumbling for the iPhone in a pocket of my running pants.

My feet went out from under me, and I landed on my bottom in a lotus squat, facing the wall, phone in hand.

"Hello?" I exclaimed, clutching the wet device upside down, laughing.

"Kate?"

I knew this voice. It was the patient and forgiving man who'd found me, listened to me and loved me. A man who spoke the same love expressed by the Radiant One, yet he was only a dim shadow of the Voice who'd called me, washed my feet, and sent me to others to do the same.

He spoke again. "Kate, are you there?"

I righted the phone, staring for a moment at his picture on the device, a simple man who worked wonders with his hands, a man who made things right with water. A man who loved me unconditionally, despite my dirt and my faults. A man who forgave my deepest sin.

I pulled the phone to my ear, tears coursing down wet cheeks, reminiscent of the salty flow that had drenched me moments ago. I could barely speak, but coughed up the words I wanted him to hear, to let him know that I'd found the peace he'd promised. I'd found release.

"I'm clean!" I blurted out. "He washed me and I'm clean!" I sobbed with joy, unable to say more, holding the slick phone to my ear, desperate to hear him speak, sure he could hear my tears of freedom and understand their source. His entire adult life, he'd followed the same Light I'd just embraced.

"Kate?" the voice repeated. "Did you ask Him?"

"Yes." I could manage only one word, but it spoke eternity.

I heard weeping. "I love you, Kate! I'm coming home."

I held the iPhone at arm's length, staring for a long moment at the picture in my hands, cradling my future and my protector.

My best friend.

John.

SUMMER

JOHN EXTENDED his hand as I stepped out of the entrance of the Water Tower at Volunteer Park, warm air embracing us both as we emerged from the cool of the century-old stone structure. All around us, Seattle lay sweltering under the overcast sky of a windless summer day. Views in every direction from the top of the tower were one of the highlights of our day in the park.

The other highlight? The smile on Liam's face at the fundraiser for St. Jude's Children's Hospital, and a hundred kids just like him, reveling in the attention of this day. I chuckled, stepping out of the Water Tower, at how Liam still carried his latest ball and chain carving wherever he went. Funny, I thought, how I'd hauled my own ball and chain around, albeit of a different sort, for so many years.

"Clouds are moving in," John said with a reassuring squeeze of my hand. "It's a few blocks to my car."

"I'll be fine," I answered, with more bravado than I felt. Sure as I was in my newfound cleanliness, I still preferred to control when I got wet, and how. John supported me, of course, but encouraged me every day to let go and enjoy God's wet refreshment.

A few steps later, as I emerged from the park on East Prospect Street, an old voice jolted me out of my joy.

"So that's the guy?"

I froze, holding John in place, squeezing even harder on his hand for strength—and my rock in the storm that was sure to come. I turned, facing the traffic, and Xavier's Mercedes Roadster, windows down. Stopped on the side of the street, holding up the traffic behind him, he leered. I cast a quick look at John, just to make sure that the hand in mine was the pillar of support I'd remembered, then looked back at X. He shook his head, frowning.

I felt a cool rush of wind, that just-before-a-shower blow of wet chill that precedes an approaching cold front. The weather had threatened all day on this fabulous outdoor fundraiser for the hospital. Until now, the rain had stayed away, blessing thousands who turned out to help Liam and his little friends. But that cool heralded rain. Soon. A chill ran down my back as I was haunted by my past parked at the street curb and a certain drenching so far from John's car.

"This is my friend John," I squeaked, gathering my voice. "John Connor." I pointed toward the Roadster. "John, this is Xavier. He was my boss at Consolidated Aerodyne."

John stepped toward the curb, pulling me with him. I wasn't about to lose this grip on my protector. He extended a hand, but Xavier, his arm bent at the elbow and resting on the open window of his door, waived a dismissive hand and shook his head as if to say "don't bother." John stopped with me at the curb as more cool wind blew in hard. Something wet was on the way.

"I saw you at the gala," he said, no words for John. "Your sushi was good."

"You tried it?" I asked, breathless.

Xavier smiled. That was a rarity.

"Yeah," he said with a nod. "Sounds funny, I guess. But some things about me have changed, Kate. Most of them for the better." He bit his lip, then extended his arm out of the car while he threw a scowling glance back at the honking driver behind him. He stuck his arm straight out of the car toward John, who took the grip in a long handshake. "I'm Xavier Morton," he said. "Glad to meet you." He paused, nodding my direction, and added, "You're a lucky guy. She's one classy woman."

"I know," John said when Xavier released the grip. The driver behind X laid on his horn again, this time with more gusto.

Xavier pulled his arm back in the car just as the first drop of rain, one of those big crocodile tears from heaven, fell on my forehead. The drip scampered down the bridge of my nose. Lights flashed.

✦ ✦ ✦

I stood on a road, surrounded by dry. The bone-dust parched landscape of desert rose up from a blue sea to a brilliant high place in distant mountains. Yet, for all the water behind me on the salty horizon, I stood in the grip of a thirsty desiccated place.

Ahead of me, along the side of the dusty road, sat a wagon. No, it was more like a chariot, shiny black and sleek, large enough to carry two people and drawn by two horses. In the shade of a rock outcropping, a muscular bald-headed man sat with a scroll in his hand, reading.

The Voice prodded me. "Go up and join this chariot."

When I drew close, moved again by the Spirit, I asked, "Do you understand what you are reading?"

"Well, how could I, unless someone guides me?" he replied. The traveler was dressed in fine clothes, so much finer than mine. But he implored me to join him, and I sat by his side, my gaze drawn to his scroll. Guided by the Spirit, I recited the entirety of that Scripture to him and explained all that he had read. After a time, we rode together in the chariot along the road, headed toward a jeweled city in the distance. We discussed the meaning of the scroll, climbing into the foothills of distant mountains as we drove. As we talked, he opened his heart to the One, and—like mine—his understanding grew.

More drops pelted me, little flashes of light popping behind my eyes as they hit. I felt a tug at my hand, but hung on to the chariot and the bald-headed man. We drove a long way, progressing up the road toward a brilliant city on a hill. Spying water at a curve in the dusty highway, he stopped the chariot and guided me to a nearby spring.

"Look!" he exclaimed. "What prevents me from being baptized?"

We left the chariot and descended together into the water. Again, guided by the Spirit, I dipped my hands into the cool spring, cupping them to gather the wetness, and poured it over the man's smooth head. Water coursed over a dusty scalp, washing away layers of grime thick from years of ignorance and sin.

As the man looked up, he instantly vanished from my sight. As if I'd suddenly been whisked away from that place, plucked out of that marvelous spring in the midst of a barren desert, I stood on the street with John, his hand wrapped about mine.

I saw him, my protector, smiling as rain pelted about us. The traffic moved past us at a good clip. Xavier's black Roadster had disappeared.

"I need to get you inside, Kate," John said, pulling on me again.

"No." I shook my head, lifting my face into the rain, my smile a gully for more drips that coursed over my cheeks. "Let's just stand here and enjoy this."

John moved behind me on the sidewalk and wrapped his arms about my waist. He steadied me as the clouds burst above us.

I looked up into raindrops, sky juice pelting my forehead with spiritual flashbulbs, each one a picture of the Radiant One, beckoning me on.

Face to the heavens, eyes closed to focus only on Him, I drank in a goodness that I'd run from for far too long.

ACKNOWLEDGEMENTS

AUSTIN BOYD

In 2008, my good friend, Brannon Hollingsworth, posed an idea while we escaped the office for a Value Meal dining experience at Wendy's. "We should write a novel together," he suggested over chili and a side salad.

"Coauthoring a book can really test a friendship," I said. "But we could make it work. So, what's the story?"

Never intimidated by a challenge, Brannon shared his brainstorm with enthusiasm. He described an edgy new idea: exposure to water sparks uncontrollable visions, imagery sent by God to draw His people to Him. "How long," Brannon wondered aloud, "could you go without a drink of water or a bath, if you were resisting God's attempts to get your attention?"

The next week Brannon and I ate lunch at a sushi restaurant, and Kate Pepper came to life as we watched the chef sanitize his knife to prepare sashimi and California rolls. Exactly three years later, we wrote these acknowledgements at the end of the editorial process. Ours is a strong friendship, and the coauthoring was a special experience that taught us more about writing, and about our Lord.

Special thanks go to Rick Steele and Dale Anderson at AMG Publishers for their "vision" to bring this novel to print. Many thanks also to our freelance editors and to the AMG staff who critiqued this manuscript and supported the marketing, especially Linda

Nathan, Mary DeMuth, Susanne Lakin, Rick Steele, John Fallahee, and Trevor Overcash. A host of supporting readers provided critical input for early manuscript revisions; we thank you all for your time, your wise comments, and your inspiration. I offer a special "thank you" to our agent and my dear friend, Les Stobbe, for his tireless efforts to find a home for this novel. We wrote the manuscript first, and then went looking for the right publishing house. Les never gave up on us, and taught us much in the process.

God places people and events in our lives to draw us to Him. He put Brannon Hollingsworth, and this unique novel, in my path so that I might understand Scripture in a new and vibrant way. For Kate Pepper, that person was her Instant Messenger friend John Connor, and the event was her unexplained visions when she touched water. Who is it—or what is it—that God has sent to draw you to Himself? Remember, Jesus will never give up on you, no matter how far you think you've drifted away.

BRANNON HOLLINGSWORTH

I would first like to acknowledge my Lord and Savior, Jesus Christ, for who He is and what He has done for me, for this book idea, and for the creativity that all comes from Him. This is YOUR BOOK, Jesus. Congratulations! Second, I want to acknowledge my bride, Heather, who walked faithfully beside me through every step of the amazing and unexpected H_2O journey. "Blue eyes," you complete me! Third, I would like to thank my dear friend, mentor, and coauthor Austin Boyd, for the opportunity to write this book together. It's been an amazing and invaluable experience. And thanks so much to AMG Publishers for having faith in our idea and taking the steps to bring it to market. I am honored to be partnered with a group of folks who are so passionate about spreading the Gospel.

To God be the glory!